JACK HIGGINS

Jack Higgins lived in Belfast till the age of twelve. Leaving school at fifteen, he spent three years with the Royal Horse Guards, serving on the East German border during the Cold War. His subsequent employment included occupations as diverse as circus roustabout, truck driver, clerk and, after taking an honours degree in sociology and social psychology, teacher and university lecturer.

The Eagle Has Landed turned him into an international bestselling author, and his novels have since sold over 250 million copies and have been translated into sixty languages. In addition to *The Eagle Has Landed*, ten of them have been made into successful films. His recent bestselling novels include *Without Mercy, The Killing Ground, Rough Justice, A Darker Place, The Wolf at the Door* and *The Judas Gate*.

In 1995 Jack Higgins was awarded an honorary doctorate by Leeds Metropolitan University. He is a fellow of the Royal Society of Arts and an expert scuba diver and marksman. He lives on Jersey.

Also by Jack Higgins

JACK HIGGINS

Eye of the Storm

HARPER

Harper
An imprint of
HarperCollins*Publishers*
77–85 Fulham Palace Road,
Hammersmith, London W6 8JB

www.harpercollins.co.uk

This paperback edition 2012
1

First published in Great Britain by Chapmans 1992

Copyright © Jack Higgins 1992

Jack Higgins asserts the moral right to
be identified as the author of this work

A catalogue record for this book is
available from the British Library

ISBN: 978-0-00-793784-4

Set in Sabon LT Std by Palimpsest Book Production Limited,
Falkirk, Stirlingshire

Printed and bound in Great Britain by
Clays Ltd, St Ives plc

MIX
Paper from
responsible sources
FSC
www.fsc.org
FSC C007454

FSC™ is a non-profit international organisation established to promote
the responsible management of the world's forests. Products carrying the
FSC label are independently certified to assure consumers that they come
from forests that are managed to meet the social, economic and
ecological needs of present and future generations,
and other controlled sources.

Find out more about HarperCollins and the environment at
www.harpercollins.co.uk/green

In memory of my grandfather
Robert Bell, M M
Gallant Soldier

The winds of heaven are blowing.
Implement all that is on the table.
May God be with you.

Coded message, Iraq Radio, Baghdad
January 1991

The mortar attack on Number Ten Downing Street when the War Cabinet was meeting at 10.00 a.m. on Thursday, 7 February 1991, is now a matter of history. It has never been satisfactorily explained. Perhaps it went something like this . . .

1

It was just before dark as Dillon emerged from the alley and paused on the corner. Rain drifted across the Seine in a flurry of snow, sleet mixed with it, and it was cold, even for January in Paris. He wore a reefer coat, peaked cap, jeans and boots, just another sailor off one of the barges working the river, which he very definitely was not.

He lit a cigarette in cupped hands and stayed there for a moment in the shadows, looking across the cobbled square at the lights of the small café on the other side. After a while he dropped the cigarette, thrust his hands deep in his pockets and started across.

In the darkness of the entrance two men waited, watching his progress. One of them whispered, 'That must be him.'

He made a move. The other held him back. 'No, wait till he's inside.'

Dillon, his senses sharpened by years of entirely the wrong kind of living, was aware of them, but gave no sign. He paused at the entrance, slipped his left hand under the reefer coat to check that the Walther PPK was securely tucked into the waistband of his jeans against the small of his back, then he opened the door and went in.

It was typical of the sort of place to be found on that part of the river: half a dozen tables with chairs, a zinc-topped bar, bottles lined against a cracked mirror behind it. The entrance to the rear was masked by a bead curtain.

The barman, a very old man with a grey moustache, wore an alpaca coat, the sleeves frayed at the cuffs, and there was no collar to his shirt. He put down the magazine he was reading and got up from the stool.

'Monsieur?'

Dillon unbuttoned his reefer coat and put his cap on the bar, a small man, no more than five feet five, with fair hair and eyes that seemed to the barman to be of no particular colour at all except for the fact that they were the coldest the old man had ever looked into. He shivered, unaccountably afraid, and then Dillon smiled. The change was astonishing, suddenly nothing but warmth there and immense charm. His French, when he spoke, was perfect.

'Would there be such a thing as half a bottle of champagne in the house?'

The old man stared at him in astonishment. 'Champagne? You must be joking, monsieur. I have two kinds of wine only. One is red and the other white.'

He placed a bottle of each on the bar. It was stuff of such poor quality that the bottles had screw tops instead of corks.

'All right,' Dillon said. 'The white it is. Give me a glass.'

He put his cap back on, went and sat at a table against the wall from where he could see both the entrance and the

2

curtained doorway. He got the bottle open, poured some of the wine into the glass and tried it.

He said to the barman, 'And what vintage would this be, last week's?'

'Monsieur?' The old man looked bewildered.

'Never mind.' Dillon lit another cigarette, sat back and waited.

The man who stood closest to the curtain, peering through, was in his mid-fifties, of medium height with a slightly decadent look to his face, the fur collar of his dark overcoat turned up against the cold. He looked like a prosperous businessman right down to the gold Rolex on his left wrist, which in a way he was as a senior commercial attaché at the Soviet Embassy in Paris. He was also a colonel in the KGB, one Josef Makeev.

The younger, dark-haired man in the expensive vicuna overcoat who peered over his shoulder was called Michael Aroun. He whispered in French, 'This is ridiculous. He can't be our man. He looks like nothing.'

'A serious mistake many people have made, Michael,' Makeev said. 'Now wait and see.'

The bell tinkled as the outer door swung open, rain blowing in and the two men entered who had been waiting in the doorway as Dillon crossed the square. One of them was over six feet tall, bearded, an ugly scar running into the right eye. The other was much smaller and they were dressed in reefer coats and denims. They looked exactly what they were, trouble.

They stood at the bar and the old man looked worried. 'No trouble,' the younger one said. 'We only want a drink.'

The big man turned and looked at Dillon. 'It seems as

if we've got one right here.' He crossed to the table, picked up Dillon's glass and drank from it. 'Our friend doesn't mind, do you?'

Without getting out of his chair Dillon raised his left foot and stamped downwards against the bearded man's kneecap. The man went down with a choked cry, grabbing at the table and Dillon stood. The bearded man tried to pull himself up and sank into one of the chairs. His friend took a hand from his pocket, springing the blade of a gutting knife and Dillon's left hand came up holding the Walther PPK.

'On the bar. Christ, you never learn, people like you, do you? Now get this piece of dung on his feet and out of here while I'm still in a good mood. You'll need the casualty department of the nearest hospital, by the way. I seem to have dislodged his kneecap.'

The small man went to his friend and struggled to get him on his feet. They stood there for a moment, the bearded man's face twisted in agony. Dillon went and opened the door, the rain pouring relentlessly down outside.

As they lurched past him, he said, 'Have a good night,' and closed the door.

Still holding the Walther in his left hand, he lit a cigarette using a match from the stand on the bar and smiled at the old barman who looked terrified. 'Don't worry, Dad, not your problem.' Then he leaned against the bar and called in English, 'All right, Makeev, I know you're there so let's be having you.'

The curtain parted and Makeev and Aroun stepped through.

'My dear Sean, it's good to see you again.'

'And aren't you the wonder of the world?' Dillon said,

just the trace of an Ulster accent in his voice. 'One minute trying to stitch me up, the next all sweetness and light.'

'It was necessary, Sean,' Makeev said. 'I needed to make a point to my friend here. Let me introduce you.'

'No need,' Dillon told him. 'I've seen his picture often enough. If it's not on the financial pages it's usually in the society magazines. Michael Aroun, isn't it? The man with all the money in the world.'

'Not quite all, Mr Dillon.' Aroun put a hand out.

Dillon ignored it. 'We'll skip the courtesies, my old son, while you tell whoever is standing on the other side of that curtain to come out.'

'Rashid, do as he says,' Aroun called, and said to Dillon, 'It's only my aide.'

The young man who stepped through had a dark, watchful face and wore a leather car coat, the collar turned up, his hands thrust deep in the pockets.

Dillon knew a professional when he saw one. 'Plain view.' He motioned with the Walther. Rashid actually smiled and took his hands from his pockets. 'Good,' Dillon said. 'I'll be on my way then.'

He turned and got the door open. Makeev said, 'Sean, be reasonable. We only want to talk. A job, Sean.'

'Sorry, Makeev, but I don't like the way you do business.'

'Not even for a million, Mr Dillon?' Michael Aroun said.

Dillon paused and turned to look at him calmly, then smiled, again with enormous charm. 'Would that be in pounds or dollars, Mr Aroun?' he asked and walked out into the rain.

As the door banged Aroun said, 'We've lost him.'

'Not at all,' Makeev said. 'A strange one this, believe me.' He turned to Rashid. 'You have your portable phone?'

'Yes, Colonel.'

'Good. Get after him. Stick to him like glue. When he settles, phone me. We'll be at the Avenue Victor Hugo.'

Rashid didn't say a word, simply went. Aroun took out his wallet and extracted a thousand-franc note which he placed on the bar. He said to the barman who was looking totally bewildered, 'We're very grateful,' then turned and followed Makeev out.

As he slid behind the wheel of the black Mercedes saloon, he said to the Russian, 'He never even hesitated back there.'

'A remarkable man, Sean Dillon,' Makeev said as they drove away. 'He first picked up a gun for the IRA in nineteen seventy-one. Twenty years, Michael, twenty years and he hasn't seen the inside of a cell once. He was involved in the Mountbatten business. Then he became too hot for his own people to handle so he moved to Europe. As I told you, he's worked for everyone. The PLO, the Red Brigade in Germany in the old days. The Basque national movement, ETA. He killed a Spanish general for them.'

'And the KGB?'

'But of course. He's worked for us on many occasions. We always use the best and Sean Dillon is exactly that. He speaks English and Irish, not that that bothers you, fluent French and German, reasonable Arabic, Italian and Russian.'

'And no one has ever caught him in twenty years. How could anyone be that lucky?'

'Because he has the most extraordinary gift for acting, my friend. A genius, you might say. As a young boy his father took him from Belfast to London to live, where he was awarded a scholarship to the Royal Academy of Dramatic Art. He even worked for the National Theatre when he was nineteen or twenty. I have never known anyone who can change personality and appearance so much just by body language. Make-up seldom enters into it, although I admit that it helps when he wants. He's a legend that the security services of most countries keep quiet about because they can't put a face to him so they don't know what they're looking for.'

'What about the British? After all, they must be the experts where the IRA are concerned.'

'No, not even the British. As I said, he's never been arrested, not once, and unlike many of his IRA friends, he never courted media publicity. I doubt if there's a photo of him anywhere except for the odd boyhood snap.'

'What about when he was an actor?'

'Perhaps, but that was twenty years ago, Michael.'

'And you think he might undertake this business if I offer him enough money?'

'No, money alone has never been enough for this man. It always has to be the job itself where Dillon is concerned. How can I put it? How interesting it is. This is a man to whom acting was everything. What we are offering him is a new part. The theatre of the street perhaps, but still acting.' He smiled as the Mercedes joined the traffic moving around the Arc de Triomphe. 'Let's wait and see. Wait until we hear from Rashid.'

At that moment, Captain Ali Rashid was by the Seine at the end of a small pier jutting out into the river. The rain was falling very heavily, still plenty of sleet in it. The floodlights were on at Notre Dame and the effect was of something seen partially through a net curtain. He watched Dillon turn along the narrow pier to the building on stilts at the far end, waited until he went in and followed him.

The place was quite old and built of wood, barges and boats of various kinds moored all around. The sign over the door said *Le Chat Noir*. He peered through the window cautiously. There was a bar and several tables just like the other place. The only difference was that people were eating. There was even a man sitting on a stool against the wall playing an accordion. All very Parisian. Dillon was standing at the bar speaking to a young woman.

Rashid moved back, walked to the end of the pier, paused by the rail in the shelter of a small terrace and dialled the number of Aroun's house in the Avenue Victor Hugo on his portable phone.

There was a slight click as the Walther was cocked and Dillon rammed the muzzle rather painfully into his right ear. 'Now then, son, a few answers,' he demanded. 'Who are you?'

'My name is Rashid,' the young man said. 'Ali Rashid.'

'What are you then? PLO?'

'No, Mr Dillon. I'm a captain in the Iraqi Army, assigned to protect Mr Aroun.'

'And Makeev and the KGB?'

'Let's just say he's on our side.'

'The way things are going in the Gulf you need somebody on your side, my old son.' There was the faint sound of a voice from the portable phone. 'Go on, answer him.'

Makeev said, 'Rashid, where is he?'

'Right here, outside a café on the river near Notre Dame,' Rashid told him. 'With the muzzle of his Walther well into my ear.'

'Put him on,' Makeev ordered.

Rashid handed the phone to Dillon who said, 'Now then, you old sod.'

'A million, Sean. Pounds if you prefer that currency.'

'And what would I have to be doing for all that money?'

'The job of a lifetime. Let Rashid bring you round here and we'll discuss it.'

'I don't think so,' Dillon said. 'I think what I'd really like is for you to get your arse into gear and come and pick us up yourself.'

'Of course,' Makeev said. 'Where are you?'

'The Left Bank opposite Notre Dame. A little pub on a pier called *Le Chat Noir*. We'll be waiting.'

He slipped the Walther into his pocket and handed the phone to Rashid who said, 'He's coming then?'

'Of course he is.' Dillon smiled. 'Now let's you and me go inside and have ourselves a drink in comfort.'

In the sitting room on the first floor of the house in the Avenue Victor Hugo overlooking the Bois de Boulogne, Josef Makeev put down the phone and moved to the couch where his overcoat was.

'Was that Rashid?' Aroun demanded.

'Yes. He's with Dillon now at a place on the river. I'm going to get them.'

'I'll come with you.'

Makeev pulled on his coat. 'No need, Michael. You hold the fort. We won't be long.'

He went out. Aroun took a cigarette from a silver box

and lit it, then he turned on the television. He was halfway into the news. There was direct coverage from Baghdad, Tornado fighter bombers of the British Royal Air Force attacking at low level. It made him bitterly angry. He switched off, poured himself a brandy and went and sat by the window.

Michael Aroun was forty years of age and a remarkable man by any standards. Born in Baghdad of a French mother and an Iraqi father who was an army officer, he'd had a maternal grandmother who was American. Through her, his mother had inherited ten million dollars and a number of oil leases in Texas.

She had died the year Aroun had graduated from Harvard Law School leaving everything to her son because his father, retired as a general from the Iraqi Army, was happy to spend his later years at the old family house in Baghdad with his books.

Like most great businessmen, Aroun had no academic training in the field. He knew nothing of financial planning or business administration. His favourite saying, one much quoted, was: When I need a new accountant, I buy a new accountant.

His friendship with Saddam Hussein had been a natural development from the fact that the Iraqi President had been greatly supported in his early days in politics by Aroun's father, who was also an important member of the Baath Party. It had placed Aroun in a privileged position as regards the development of his country's oilfields, brought him riches beyond calculation.

After the first billion you stopped counting, another favourite saying. And now he was faced with disaster. Not only the promised riches of the Kuwait oilfields snatched from him, but that portion of his wealth which stemmed from Iraq dried up, finished as a result of the Coalition's massive airstrikes which had devastated his country since 17 January.

He was no fool. He knew that the game was over; should probably have never started, and that Saddam Hussein's dream was already finished. As a businessman he played the percentages and that didn't offer Iraq too much of a chance in the ground war that must eventually come.

He was far from ruined in personal terms. He had oil interests still in the USA and the fact that he was a French as well as an Iraqi citizen gave Washington a problem. Then there was his shipping empire and vast quantities of real estate in various capital cities around the world. But that wasn't the point. He was angry when he switched on the television and saw what was happening in Baghdad each night for, surprising in one so self-centred, he was a patriot. There was also the fact, infinitely more important, that his father had been killed in a bombing raid on the third night of the air war.

And there was a great secret in his life, for in August, shortly after the invasion of Kuwait by Iraqi forces, Aroun had been sent for by Saddam Hussein himself. Sitting here by the French window, a glass of brandy in one hand, rain slanting across the terrace, he gazed out across the Bois de Boulogne in the evening light and remembered that meeting.

There was an air-raid practice in progress as he was driven in an army Land Rover through the streets of Baghdad, darkness everywhere. The driver was a young intelligence captain named Rashid who he had met before, one of the new breed, trained by the British at Sandhurst. Aroun gave him an English cigarette and took one himself.

'What do you think, will they make some sort of move?'

'The Americans and Brits?' Rashid was being careful. 'Who knows? They're certainly reacting. President Bush seems to be taking a hard line.'

'No, you're mistaken,' Aroun said. 'I've met the man face to face twice now at White House functions. He's what our American friends call a nice guy. There's no steel there at all.'

Rashid shrugged. 'I'm a simple man, Mr Aroun, a soldier, and perhaps I see things simply. Here is a man, a navy combat pilot at twenty, who saw a great deal of active service, who was shot down over the Sea of Japan and survived to be awarded the Distinguished Flying Cross. I would not underestimate such a man.'

Aroun frowned. 'Come on, my friend, the Americans aren't going to come halfway round the world with an army to protect one little Arab state.'

'Isn't that exactly what the British did in the Falklands War?' Rashid reminded him. 'They never expected such a reaction in Argentina. Of course they had Thatcher's determination behind them, the Brits, I mean.'

'Damned woman,' Aroun said and leaned back as they went in through the gate of the presidential palace, feeling suddenly depressed.

He followed Rashid along corridors of marble splendour, the young officer leading the way, a torch in one hand. It was a strange, rather eerie experience, following that small pool of light on the floor, their footfalls echoing. There was a sentry on each side of the ornate door they finally halted before. Rashid opened it and they went in.

Saddam Hussein was alone, sitting in uniform at a large desk, the only light a shaded lamp. He was writing, slowly and carefully, looked up and smiled, putting down his pen.

'Michael.' He came round the desk and embraced Aroun like a brother. 'Your father? He is well?'

'In excellent health, my President.'

'Give him my respects. You look well, Michael. Paris suits you.' He smiled again. 'Smoke if you want. I know you like to. The doctors have unfortunately had to tell me to cut it out or else.'

He sat down behind the desk again and Aroun sat opposite, aware of Rashid against the wall in the darkness. 'Paris was fine, but my place is here now in these difficult times.'

Saddam Hussein shook his head. 'Not true, Michael. I have soldiers in plenty, but few men such as you. You are rich, famous, accepted at the highest levels of society and government anywhere in the world. More than that, because of your beloved mother of blessed memory, you are not just an Iraqi, but also a French citizen. No, Michael, I want you in Paris.'

'But why, my President?' Aroun asked.

'Because one day I may require you to do a service for me and for your country that only you could perform.'

Aroun said, 'You can rely on me totally, you know that.'

Saddam Hussein got up and paced to the nearest window, opened the shutters and stepped onto the terrace. The all clear sounded mournfully across the city and lights began to appear here and there.

'I still hope our friends in America and Britain stay in their own backyard, but if not . . .' He shrugged. 'Then we may have to fight them in *their* own backyard. Remember, Michael, as the Prophet instructs us in the Koran, there is more truth in one sword than ten thousand words.' He paused and then carried on, still looking out across the city. 'One sniper in the darkness, Michael, British SAS or Israeli, it doesn't really matter, but what a coup – the death of Saddam Hussein.'

'God forbid it,' Michael Aroun said.

Saddam turned to him. 'As God wills, Michael, in all things, but you see my point? The same would apply to Bush or the Thatcher woman. The proof that my arm reaches everywhere. The ultimate coup.' He turned. 'Would you be capable of arranging such a thing, if necessary?'

Aroun had never felt so excited in his life. 'I think so, my President. All things are possible, especially when sufficient money is involved. It would be my gift to you.'

'Good.' Saddam nodded. 'You will return to Paris immediately. Captain Rashid will accompany you. He will have details of certain codes we will be using in radio broadcasts, that sort of thing. The day may never come, Michael, but if it does . . .' He shrugged. 'We have friends in the right places.' He turned to Rashid. 'That KGB colonel at the Soviet Embassy in Paris?'

'Colonel Josef Makeev, my President.'

'Yes,' Saddam Hussein said to Aroun. 'Like many of his kind, not happy with the changes now taking place in Moscow. He will assist in any way he can. He's already expressed his willingness.' He embraced Aroun, again like a brother. 'Now go. I have work to do.'

The lights had still not come on in the palace and Aroun

had stumbled out into the darkness of the corridor, following the beam of Rashid's torch.

Since his return to Paris he had got to know Makeev well, keeping their acquaintance, by design, purely on a social level, meeting mainly at various Embassy functions. And Saddam Hussein had been right. The Russian was very definitely on their side, only too willing to do anything that would cause problems for the United States or Great Britain.

The news from home, of course, had been bad. The build-up of such a gigantic army. Who could have expected it? And then in the early hours of 17 January the air war had begun. One bad thing after another and the ground attack still to come.

He poured himself another brandy, remembering his despairing rage at the news of his father's death. He'd never been religious by inclination, but he'd found a mosque in a Paris side street to pray in. Not that it had done any good. The feeling of impotence was like a living thing inside him and then came the morning when Ali Rashid had rushed into the great ornate sitting room, a notepad in one hand, his face pale and excited.

'It's come, Mr Aroun. The signal we've been waiting for. I just heard it on the radio transmitter from Baghdad.'

The winds of heaven are blowing. Implement all that is on the table. May God be with you.

Aroun had gazed at it in wonder, his hand trembling as he held the notepad, and his voice was hoarse when he said, 'The President was right. The day has come.'

'Exactly,' Rashid said. *'Implement all that is on the table.* We're in business. I'll get in touch with Makeev and arrange a meeting as soon as possible.'

Dillon stood at the French windows and peered out across the Avenue Victor Hugo to the Bois de Boulogne. He was whistling softly to himself, a strange eerie little tune.

'Now this must be what the house agents call a favoured location.'

'May I offer you a drink, Mr Dillon?'

'A glass of champagne wouldn't come amiss.'

'Have you a preference?' Aroun asked.

'Ah, the man who has everything,' Dillon said. 'All right, Krug would be fine, but non-vintage. I prefer the grape mix.'

'A man of taste, I see.' Aroun nodded to Rashid who opened a side door and went out.

Dillon, unbuttoning his reefer coat, took out a cigarette and lit it. 'So, you need my services this old fox tells me.' He nodded at Makeev who lounged against the fireplace warming himself. 'The job of a lifetime, he said and for a million pounds. Now what would I have to do for all that?'

Rashid entered quickly with the Krug in a bucket, three glasses on a tray. He put them on the table and started to open the bottle.

Aroun said, 'I'm not sure, but it would have to be something very special. Something to show the world that Saddam Hussein can strike anywhere.'

'He needs something, the poor old sod,' Dillon said cheerfully. 'Things aren't going too well.' As Rashid finished filling three glasses the Irishman added, 'And what's your trouble, son? Aren't you joining us?'

Rashid smiled and Aroun said, 'In spite of Winchester and Sandhurst, Mr Dillon, Captain Rashid remains a very Muslim Muslim. He does not touch alcohol.'

'Well, here's to you.' Dillon raised his glass. 'I respect a man with principles.'

'This would need to be big, Sean, no point in anything small. We're not talking blowing up five British Army paratroopers in Belfast,' Makeev said.

'Oh, it's Bush you want, is it?' Dillon smiled. 'The President of the United States flat on his back with a bullet in him?'

'Would that be so crazy?' Aroun demanded.

'It would be this time, son,' Dillon told him. 'George Bush has not just taken on Saddam Hussein, he's taken on the Arabs as a people. Oh, that's total rubbish of course, but it's the way a lot of Arab fanatics see it. Groups like Hizbollah, the PLO or the wild cards like the Wrath of Allah people. The sort who would happily strap a bomb to their waist and detonate it while the President reached out to shake just another hand in the crowd. I know these people. I know how their minds tick. I've helped train Hizbollah people in Beirut. I've worked for the PLO.'

'What you are saying is nobody can get near Bush at the moment?'

'Read your papers. Anybody who looks even slightly Arab is keeping off the streets these days in New York and Washington.'

'But you, Mr Dillon, do not look Arab to the slightest degree,' Aroun said. 'For one thing you have fair hair.'

'So did Lawrence of Arabia and he used to pass himself off as an Arab.' Dillon shook his head. 'President Bush has the finest security in the world, believe me. A ring of steel and in present circumstances he's going to stay home while this whole Gulf thing works through, mark my words.'

'What about their Secretary of State, James Baker?' Aroun said. 'He's been indulging in shuttle diplomacy throughout Europe.'

'Yes, but knowing when, that's the problem. You'll know he's been in London or Paris when he's already left and they show him on television. No, you can forget the Americans on this one.'

There was silence and Aroun looked glum. Makeev was the first to speak. 'Give me then the benefit of your professional expertise, Sean. Where does one find the weakest security, as regards national leaders?'

Dillon laughed out loud. 'Oh, I think your man here can answer that, Winchester and Sandhurst.'

Rashid smiled. 'He's right. The British are probably the best in the world at covert operations. The success of their Special Air Service Regiment speaks for itself, but in other areas . . .' He shook his head.

'Their first problem is bureaucracy,' Dillon told them. 'The British Security Service operates in two main sections. What most people still call MI5 and MI6. MI5, or DI5 to be pedantic, specialises in counter-espionage in Great Britain. The other lot operates abroad. Then you have Special Branch at Scotland Yard who have to be brought into the act to make any actual arrests. The Yard also has an anti-terrorist squad. Then there's army intelligence units galore. All life is there and they're all at each other's throats and that, gentlemen, is when mistakes begin to creep in.'

Rashid poured some more champagne into his glass. 'And you are saying that makes for bad security with their leaders? The Queen, for example?'

'Come on,' Dillon said. 'It's not all that many years ago that the Queen woke up in Buckingham Palace and found an intruder sitting on the bed. How long ago, six years, since the IRA almost got Margaret Thatcher and the entire British Cabinet at a Brighton hotel during the Tory Party Conference?' He put down his glass and lit another cigarette. 'The Brits are very old-fashioned. They like a policeman to wear a uniform so they know who he is and they don't like being told what to do and that applies to Cabinet Ministers who think nothing of strolling through the streets from their houses in Westminster to Parliament.'

'Fortunate for the rest of us,' Makeev said.

'Exactly,' Dillon said. 'They even have to go softly-softly on terrorists, up to a degree anyway, not like French intelligence. Jesus, if the lads in Action Service got their hands on me they'd have me spread out and my bollocks wired up for electricity before I knew what was happening. Mind you, even they are prone to the occasional error.'

'What do you mean?' Makeev demanded.

'Have you got a copy of the evening paper handy?'

'Certainly, I've been reading it,' Aroun said. 'Ali, on my desk.'

Rashid returned with a copy of *Paris Soir*. Dillon said, 'Page two. Read it out. You'll find it interesting.'

He helped himself to more champagne while Rashid read the item aloud. *'Mrs Margaret Thatcher, until recently Prime Minister of Britain, is staying overnight at Choisy as a guest of President Mitterrand. They are to have further talks in the morning. She leaves at two o'clock for an air force emergency field at Valenton where an RAF plane returns her to England.* Incredible, isn't it, that they could have allowed such a press release, but I guarantee the main London newspapers will carry that story also.'

There was a heavy silence and then Aroun said, 'You're not suggesting . . . ?'

Dillon said to Rashid, 'You must have some road maps handy. Get them.'

Rashid went out quickly. Makeev said, 'Good God, Sean, not even you . . .'

'Why not?' Dillon asked calmly and turned to Aroun. 'I mean, you want something big, a major coup? Would Margaret Thatcher do or are we just playing games here?'

Before Aroun could reply, Rashid came back with two or three road maps. He opened one out on the table and they looked at it, all except Makeev who stayed by the fire.

'There we are, Choisy,' Rashid said. 'Thirty miles from Paris and here is the air force field at Valenton only seven miles away.'

'Have you got a map of larger scale?'

'Yes.' Rashid unfolded one of the others.

'Good,' Dillon said. 'It's perfectly clear that only one country road links Choisy to Valenton and here, about three miles before the airfield, there's a railway crossing. Perfect.'

'For what?' Aroun demanded.

'An ambush. Look, I know how these things operate. There'll be one car, two at the most, and an escort. Maybe half a dozen CRS police on motorbikes.'

'My God!' Aroun whispered.

'Yes, well. He's got very little to do with it. It could work. Fast, very simple. What the Brits call a piece of cake.'

Aroun turned in appeal to Makeev who shrugged. 'He means it, Michael. You said this was what you wanted so make up your mind.'

Aroun took a deep breath and turned back to Dillon. 'All right.'

'Good,' Dillon said calmly. He reached for a pad and pencil on the table and wrote on it quickly. 'Those are the details of my numbered bank account in Zurich. You'll transfer one million pounds to it first thing in the morning.'

'In advance?' Rashid said. 'Isn't that expecting rather a lot?'

'No, my old son, it's you people who are expecting rather a lot and the rules have changed. On successful completion, I'll expect a further million.'

'Now look here,' Rashid started, but Aroun held up a hand.

'Fine, Mr Dillon, and cheap at the price. Now what can we do for you?'

'I need operating money. I presume a man like you keeps large supplies of the filthy stuff around the house?'

'Very large,' Aroun smiled. 'How much?'

'Can you manage dollars? Say twenty thousand?'

'Of course.' Aroun nodded to Rashid who went to the far end of the room, swung a large oil painting to one side disclosing a wall safe which he started to open.

Makeev said, 'And what can I do?'

'The old warehouse in rue de Helier, the one we've used before. You've still got a key?'

'Of course.'

'Good. I've got most things I need stored there, but for this job I'd like a light machine gun. A tripod job. A Heckler & Koch or an M60. Anything like that will do.'

21

He looked at his watch. 'Eight o'clock. I'd like it there by ten. All right?'

'Of course,' Makeev said again.

Rashid came back with a small briefcase. 'Twenty thousand. Hundred-dollar bills, I'm afraid.'

'Is there any way they could be traced?' Dillon asked.

'Impossible,' Aroun told him.

'Good. And I'll take the maps.'

He walked to the door, opened it and started down the curving staircase to the hall. Aroun, Rashid and Makeev followed him.

'But is this all, Mr Dillon?' Aroun said. 'Is there nothing more we can do for you? Won't you need help?'

'When I do, it comes from the criminal classes,' Dillon said. 'Honest crooks who do things for cash are usually more reliable than politically motivated zealots. Not always, but most of the time. Don't worry, you'll hear from me, one way or another. I'll be on my way then.'

Rashid got the door open. Rain and sleet drifted in and Dillon pulled on his cap. 'A dirty old night for it.'

'One thing, Mr Dillon,' Rashid said. 'What happens if things go wrong? I mean, you'll have your million in advance and we'll –'

'Have nothing? Don't give it a thought, me old son. I'll provide an alternative target. There's always the new British Prime Minister, this John Major. I presume his head on a plate would serve your boss back in Baghdad just as well.'

He smiled once, then stepped out into the rain and pulled the door shut behind him.

2

Dillon paused outside *Le Chat Noir* on the end of the small pier for the second time that night. It was almost deserted, a young man and woman at a corner table holding hands, a bottle of wine between them. The accordion was playing softly and the musician talked to the man behind the bar at the same time. They were the Jobert brothers, gangsters of the second rank in the Paris underworld. Their activities had been severely curtailed since Pierre, the one behind the bar, had lost his left leg in a car crash after an armed robbery three years previously.

As the door opened and Dillon entered, the other brother, Gaston, stopped playing. 'Ah, Monsieur Rocard, back already.'

'Gaston.' Dillon shook hands and turned to the barman. 'Pierre.'

'See, I still remember that little tune of yours, the Irish one.' Gaston played a few notes on the accordion.

'Good,' Dillon said. 'A true artist.'

Behind them the young couple got up and left. Pierre produced half a bottle of champagne from the bar fridge.

'Champagne as usual I presume, my friend? Nothing special, but we are poor men here.'

'You'll have me crying all over the bar,' Dillon said.

'And what may we do for you?' Pierre enquired.

'Oh, I just want to put a little business your way.' Dillon nodded at the door. 'It might be an idea if you closed.'

Gaston put his accordion on the bar, went and bolted the door and pulled down the blind. He returned and sat on his stool. 'Well, my friend?'

'This could be a big pay day for you boys.' Dillon opened the briefcase, took out one of the road maps and disclosed the stacks of hundred-dollar bills. 'Twenty thousand American. Ten now and ten on successful completion.'

'My God!' Gaston said in awe, but Pierre looked grim. 'And what would be expected for all this money?'

Dillon had always found it paid to stick as close to the truth as possible and he spread the road map out across the bar.

'I've been hired by the Union Corse,' he said, naming the most feared criminal organisation in France, 'to take care of a little problem. A matter of what you might term business rivalry.'

'Ah, I see,' Pierre said. 'And you are to eliminate the problem?'

'Exactly. The men concerned will be passing along this road here towards Valenton shortly after two o'clock tomorrow. I intend to take them out here at the railway crossing.'

'And how will this be accomplished?' Gaston asked.

'A very simple ambush. You two are still in the transport business, aren't you? Stolen cars, trucks?'

'You should know. You've bought from us on enough occasions,' Pierre told him.

'A couple of vans, that's not too much to expect, is it?'

'And then what?'

'We'll take a drive down to this place tonight.' He glanced at his watch. 'Eleven o'clock from here. It'll only take an hour.'

Pierre shook his head. 'Look, this could be heavy. I'm getting too old for gunplay.'

'Wonderful,' Dillon said. 'How many did you kill when you were with the OAS?'

'I was younger then.'

'Well, it comes to us all, I suppose. No gunplay. You two will be in and out so quickly you won't know what's happening. A piece of cake.' He took several stacks of hundred-dollar bills from the briefcase and put them on the bar counter. 'Ten thousand. Do we deal?'

And greed, as usual, won the day as Pierre ran his hands over the money. 'Yes, my friend, I think we do.'

'Good. I'll be back at eleven then.' Dillon closed his briefcase, Gaston went and unlocked the door for him and the Irishman left.

Gaston closed the door and turned. 'What do you think?'

Pierre poured two cognacs. 'I think our friend Rocard is a very big liar.'

'But also a very dangerous man,' Gaston said. 'So what do we do?'

'Wait and see.' Pierre raised his glass. '*Salut.*'

Dillon walked all the way to the warehouse in rue de Helier, twisting from one street to another, melting into the darkness occasionally to check that he wasn't being followed. He had learned a long time ago that the problem with all revolutionary political groups was that they were riddled with factions and informers, a great truth where the IRA was concerned. Because of that, as he had indicated to Aroun, he preferred to use professional criminals whenever possible when help was needed. Honest crooks who did things for cash, that was the phrase he'd used. Unfortunately it didn't always hold true and there had been something in big Pierre's manner.

There was a small Judas gate set in the larger double doors of the warehouse. He unlocked it and stepped inside. There were two cars, a Renault saloon and a Ford Escort, and a police BMW motorcycle covered with a sheet. He checked that it was all right, then moved up the wooden stairs to the flat in the loft above. It was not his only home. He also had a barge on the river, but it was useful on occasions.

On the table in the small living room there was a canvas holdall with a note on top that simply said, *As ordered*. He smiled and unzipped it. Inside was a Kalashnikov PK machine gun, the latest model. Its tripod was folded, the barrel off for easy handling and there was a large box of belt cartridges, a similar box beside it. He opened a drawer in the sideboard, took out a folded sheet and put it in the holdall. He zipped it up again, checked the Walther in his waistband and went down the stairs, the holdall in one hand.

He locked the Judas and went along the street, excitement taking control as it always did. It was the best feeling in the world when the game was in play. He turned into the main street and a few minutes later, hailed a cab and told the driver to take him to *Le Chat Noir*.

* * *

They drove out of Paris in Renault vans, exactly the same except for the fact that one was black and the other white. Gaston led the way, Dillon beside him in the passenger seat, and Pierre followed. It was very cold, snow still mixed with the rain, although it wasn't lying. They talked very little, Dillon lying back in the seat eyes closed so that the Frenchman thought he was asleep.

Not far from Choisy, the van skidded and Gaston said, 'Christ almighty,' and wrestled with the wheel.

Dillon said, 'Easy, the wrong time to go in a ditch. Where are we?'

'Just past the turning to Choisy. Not long now.' Dillon sat up. The snow was covering the hedgerows but not the road. Gaston said, 'It's a pig of a night. Just look at it.'

'Think of all those lovely dollar bills,' Dillon told him. 'That should get you through.'

It stopped snowing, the sky cleared showing a half-moon, and below them at the bottom of the hill was the red light of the railway crossing. There was an old disused building of some sort at one side, its windows boarded up, a stretch of cobbles in front of it lightly powdered with snow.

'Pull in here,' Dillon said.

Gaston did as he was told and braked to a halt switching off the motor. Pierre came up in the white Renault, got down from behind the wheel awkwardly because of the false leg and joined them.

Dillon stood looking at the crossing a few yards away and nodded. 'Perfect. Give me the keys.'

Gaston did as he was told. The Irishman unlocked the rear door, disclosing the holdall. He unzipped it as they watched, took out the Kalashnikov, put the barrel in place expertly, then positioned it so that it pointed to the rear. He filled the ammunition box, threading the cartridge belt in place.

'That looks a real bastard,' Pierre said.

'Seven point two millimetre cartridges mixed with tracer and armour piercing,' Dillon said. 'It's a killer all right. Kalashnikov. I've seen one of these take a Land Rover full of British paratroopers to pieces.'

'Really,' Pierre said and as Gaston was about to speak, he put a warning hand on his arm. 'What's in the other box?'

'More ammunition.'

Dillon took out the sheet from the holdall, covered the machine gun, then locked the door. He got behind the driving wheel, started the engine and moved the van a few yards, positioned it so that the tail pointed at an angle towards the crossing. He got out and locked the door and clouds scudded across the moon and the rain started again, more snow in it now.

'So, you leave this here?' Pierre said. 'What if someone checks it?'

'What if they do?' Dillon knelt down at the offside rear tyre, took a knife from his pocket, sprang the blade and poked at the rim of the wheel. There was a hiss of air and the tyre went down rapidly.

Gaston nodded. 'Clever. Anyone gets curious, they'll just think a breakdown.'

'But what about us?' Pierre demanded. 'What do you expect?'

'Simple. Gaston turns up with the white Renault just after two this afternoon. You block the road at the crossing, not the railway track, just the road, get out, lock the door and leave it. Then get the hell out of there.' He turned to Pierre. 'You follow in a car, pick him up and straight back to Paris.'

'But what about you?' the big man demanded.

'I'll be already here, waiting in the van. I'll make my own way. Back to Paris now. You can drop me at *Le Chat Noir* and that's an end of it. You won't see me again.'

'And the rest of the money?' Pierre demanded as he got behind the Renault's wheel and Gaston and Dillon joined him.

'You'll get it, don't worry,' Dillon said. 'I always keep my word just as I expect others to keep theirs. A matter of honour, my friend. Now let's get moving.'

He closed his eyes again, leaned back. Pierre glanced at his brother, switched on the engine and drove away.

It was just on half-past one when they reached *Le Chat Noir*. There was a lock-up garage opposite the pub. Gaston opened the doors and Pierre drove in.

'I'll be off then,' Dillon said.

'You're not coming in?' the big man asked. 'Then Gaston can run you home.'

Dillon smiled. 'No one's ever taken me home in my life.'

He walked away, turning into a side street and Pierre said to his brother, 'After him and don't lose him.'

'But why?' Gaston demanded.

'Because I want to know where he's staying, that's why. It stinks, this thing, Gaston, like bad fish stinks, so get moving.'

Dillon moved rapidly from street to street, following his usual pattern, but Gaston, a thief since childhood and an expert in such matters, managed to stay on his trail, never too close. Dillon had intended returning to the warehouse in rue de Helier, but pausing on the corner of an alley to light a cigarette, he glanced back and could have sworn he saw a movement. He was right, for it was Gaston ducking into a doorway out of sight.

For Dillon, even the suspicion was enough. He'd had a feeling about Pierre all night, a bad feeling. He turned left, worked his way back to the river and walked along the pavement and past a row of trucks, their windscreens covered with snow. He came to a small hotel, the cheapest sort of place, the kind used by prostitutes or truckers stopping overnight, and went in.

The desk clerk was very old and wore an overcoat and scarf against the cold. His eyes were wet. He put down his book and rubbed them. 'Monsieur?'

'I brought a load in from Dijon a couple of hours ago. Intended to drive back tonight, but the damn truck's giving trouble. I need a bed.'

'Thirty francs, monsieur.'

'You're kidding,' Dillon said. 'I'll be out of here at the crack of dawn.'

The old man shrugged. 'All right, you can have number eighteen on the second landing for twenty, but the bed hasn't been changed.'

'When does that happen, once a month?' Dillon took the key, gave him his twenty francs and went upstairs.

The room was as disgusting as he expected even in the diffused light from the landing. He closed the door, moved carefully through the darkness and looked out cautiously. There was a movement under a tree on the river side of the road. Gaston Jobert stepped out and hurried away along the pavement.

'Oh dear,' Dillon whispered, then lit a cigarette and went and lay on the bed and thought about it, staring up at the ceiling.

Pierre, sitting at the bar of *Le Chat Noir* waiting for his brother's return, was leafing through *Paris Soir* for want of something better to do when he noticed the item on Margaret Thatcher's meeting with Mitterrand. His stomach churned and he read the item again with horror. It was at that moment the door opened and Gaston hurried in.

'What a night. I'm frozen to the bone. Give me a cognac.'

'Here.' Pierre poured some into a glass. 'And you can read this interesting titbit in *Paris Soir* while you're drinking.'

Gaston did as he was told and suddenly choked on the cognac. 'My God, she's staying at Choisy.'

'And leaves from that old air force field at Valenton. Leaves Choisy at two o'clock. How long to get to that railway crossing? Ten minutes?'

'Oh, God, no,' Gaston said. 'We're done for. This is out of our league, Pierre. If this takes place, we'll have every cop in France on the streets.'

'But it isn't going to. I knew that bastard was bad news. Always something funny about him. You managed to follow him?'

'Yes, he doubled around the streets for a while, then ended up at that fleapit old François runs just along the river. I saw him through the window booking in.' He shivered. 'But what are we going to do?' He was almost sobbing. 'This is the end, Pierre. They'll lock us up and throw away the key.'

'No they won't,' Pierre told him. 'Not if we shop him,

they won't. They'll be too grateful. Who knows, there might even be a reward in it. Now what's Inspector Savary's home number?'

'He'll be in bed.'

'Of course he will, you idiot, nicely tucked up with his old lady where all good detectives should be. We'll just have to wake him up.'

Inspector Jules Savary came awake cursing as the phone rang at his bedside. He was on his own, for his wife was spending a week in Lyon at her mother's. He'd had a long night. Two armed robberies and a sexual assault on a woman. He'd only just managed to get to sleep.

He picked up the phone. 'Savary here.'

'It's me, Inspector, Pierre Jobert.'

Savary glanced at the bedside clock. 'For Christ's sake, Jobert, it's two-thirty in the morning.'

'I know, Inspector, but I've got something special for you.'

'You always have, so it can wait till the morning.'

'I don't think so, Inspector. I'm offering to make you the most famous cop in France. The pinch of a lifetime.'

'Pull the other one,' Savary said.

'Margaret Thatcher. She's staying at Choisy tonight, leaves for Valenton at two? I can tell you all about the man who's going to see she never gets there.'

Jules Savary had never come awake so fast. 'Where are you, *Le Chat Noir*?'

'Yes,' Jobert told him.

'Half an hour.' Savary slammed down the phone, leapt out of bed and started to dress.

*   *   *

32

It was at exactly the same moment that Dillon decided to move on. The fact that Gaston had followed him didn't necessarily mean anything more than the fact that the brothers were anxious to know more about him. On the other hand . . .

He left, locking the door, found the backstairs and descended cautiously. There was a door at the bottom which opened easily enough and gave access to a yard at the rear. An alley brought him to the main road. He crossed, walked along a line of parked trucks, chose one about fifty yards from the hotel, but giving him a good view. He got his knife out, worked away at the top of the passenger window. After a while it gave so that he could get his fingers in and exert pressure. A minute later he was inside. Better not to smoke so he sat back, collar up, hands in pockets and waited. It was half-past three when the four unmarked cars eased up to the hotel. Eight men got out, none in uniform, which was interesting.

'Action Service, or I miss my guess,' Dillon said softly.

Gaston Jobert got out of the rear car and stood talking to them for a moment then they all moved into the hotel. Dillon wasn't angry, just pleased that he'd got it right. He left the truck, crossed the road to the shelter of the nearest alley and started to walk to the warehouse in rue de Helier.

The French secret service, notorious for years as the SDECE has had its name changed to Direction Générale de la Sécurité Extérieure, DGSE, under the Mitterrand government in an attempt to improve the image of a shady and ruthless organisation with a reputation for stopping at nothing. Having said that, measured by results, few intelligence organisations in the world are so efficient.

The service, as in the old days, was still divided into five sections and many departments, the most famous, or infamous depending on your point of view, being Section Five, more commonly known as Action Service, the department responsible for the smashing of the OAS.

Colonel Max Hernu had been involved in all that, had hunted the OAS down as ruthlessly as anyone in spite of having served as a paratrooper in both Indo-China and Algeria. He was sixty-one years of age, an elegant, white-haired man who now sat at his desk in the office on the first floor of DGSE's headquarters on the Boulevard Mortier. It was just before five o'clock and Hernu, wearing horn-rimmed reading glasses, studied the report in front of him. He had been staying the night at his country cottage forty miles out of Paris and had only just arrived. Inspector Savary watched respectfully.

Hernu removed his glasses. 'I loathe this time of the morning. Takes me back to Dien Bien Phu and the waiting for the end. Pour me another coffee, will you?'

Savary took his cup, went to the electric pot on the stand and poured the coffee, strong and black. 'What do you think, sir?'

'These Jobert brothers, you believe they're telling us everything?'

'Absolutely, sir, I've known them for years. Big Pierre was OAS which he thinks gives him class, but they're second-rate hoods really. They do well in stolen cars.'

'So this would be out of their league?'

'Very definitely. They've admitted to me that they've sold this man Rocard cars in the past.'

'Of the hot variety?'

'Yes, sir.'

'Of course they are telling the truth. The ten thousand dollars speak for them there. But this man Rocard, you're an experienced copper, Inspector. How many years on the street?'

'Fifteen, sir.'

'Give me your opinion.'

'His physical description is interesting because according to the Jobert boys, there isn't one. He's small, no more than one sixty-five. No discernible colour to the eyes, fair hair. Gaston says the first time they met him he thought he was a nothing and then he apparently half-killed some guy twice his size in the bar in about five seconds flat.'

'Go on.' Hernu lit a cigarette.

'Pierre says his French is too perfect.'

'What does he mean by that?'

'He doesn't know. It's just that he always felt that there was something wrong.'

'That he wasn't French?'

'Exactly. Two facts of interest there. He's always whistling a funny little tune. Gaston picked it up because he plays accordion. He says Rocard told him once that it was Irish.'

'Now that is interesting.'

'A further point. When he was assembling the machine gun in the back of the Renault at Valenton he told the boys it was a Kalashnikov. Not just bullets. Tracer, armour piercing, the lot. He said he'd seen one take out a Land Rover full of British paratroopers. Pierre didn't like to ask him where.'

'So, you smell IRA here, Inspector? And what have you done about it?'

'Got your people to get the picture books out, Colonel. The Joberts are looking through them right now.'

35

'Excellent.' Hernu got up and this time refilled his coffee cup himself. 'What do you make of the hotel business? Do you think he's been alerted?'

'Perhaps, but not necessarily,' Savary said. 'I mean what have we got here, sir? A real pro out to make the hit of a lifetime. Maybe he was just being extra careful, just to make sure he wasn't followed to his real destination. I mean, I wouldn't trust the Joberts an inch, so why should he?'

He shrugged and Max Hernu said shrewdly, 'There's more. Spit it out.'

'I got a bad feeling about this guy, Colonel. I think he's special. I think he may have used the hotel thing because he suspected that Gaston might follow him, but then he'd want to know why. Was it the Joberts just being curious or was there more to it?'

'So you think he could have been up the street watching our people arrive?'

'Very possibly. On the other hand, maybe he didn't know Gaston was tailing him. Maybe the hotel thing was a usual precaution. An old Resistance trick from the war.'

Hernu nodded. 'Right, let's see if they've finished. Have them in.'

Savary went out and returned with the Jobert brothers. They stood there looking worried and Hernu said, 'Well?'

'No luck, Colonel. He wasn't in any of the books.'

'All right,' Hernu said. 'Wait downstairs. You'll be taken home. We'll collect you again later.'

'But what for, Colonel?' Pierre asked.

'So that your brother can go to Valenton in the Renault and you can follow in the car just like Rocard told you. Now get out.' They hurriedly left and Hernu said to Savary,

'We'll see Mrs Thatcher is spirited to safety by another route, but a pity to disappoint our friend Rocard.'

'If he turns up, Colonel.'

'You never know, he just might. You've done well, Inspector. I think I'll have to requisition you for Section Five. Would you mind?'

Would he mind? Savary almost choked with emotion. 'An honour, sir.'

'Good. Go and get a shower then and some breakfast. I'll see you later.'

'And you, Colonel.'

'Me, Inspector.' Hernu laughed and looked at his watch. 'Five-fifteen. I'm going to ring British intelligence in London. Disturb the sleep of a very old friend of mine. If anyone can help us with our mystery man it should be he.'

The Directorate General of the British Security Service occupies a large white and red brick building not far from the Hilton Hotel in Park Lane, although many of its departments are housed in various locations throughout London. The special number that Max Hernu rang was of a section known as Group Four, located on the third floor of the Ministry of Defence. It had been set up in 1972 to handle matters concerning terrorism and subversion in the British Isles. It was responsible only to the Prime Minister. It had been administered by only one man since its inception, Brigadier Charles Ferguson. He was asleep in his flat in Cavendish Square when the telephone beside his bed awakened him.

'Ferguson,' he said, immediately wide awake, knowing it had to be important.

'Paris, Brigadier,' an anonymous voice said. 'Priority one. Colonel Hernu.'

'Put him through and scramble.'

Ferguson sat up, a large, untidy man of sixty-five with rumpled grey hair and a double chin.

'Charles?' Hernu said in English.

'My dear Max. What brings you on the line at such a disgusting hour? You're lucky I'm still on the phone. The powers that be are trying to make me redundant along with Group Four.'

'What nonsense.'

'I know, but the Director General was never happy with my freebooter status all these years. What can I do for you?'

'Mrs Thatcher overnighting at Choisy. We've details of a plot to hit her on the way to the airfield at Valenton tomorrow.'

'Good God!'

'All taken care of. The lady will now take a different route home. We're still hoping the man concerned will show up, though I doubt it. We'll be waiting though, this afternoon.'

'Who is it? Anyone we know?'

'From what our informants say, we suspect he's Irish though his French is good enough to pass as a native. The thing is, the people involved have looked through all our IRA pictures with no success.'

'Have you a description?'

Hernu gave it to him. 'Not much to go on, I'm afraid.'

'I'll have a computer check done and get back to you. Tell me the story.' Which Hernu did. When he was finished Ferguson said, 'You've lost him, old chap. I'll bet you dinner on it at the Savoy Grill next time you're over.'

'I've a feeling about this one. I think he's special,' Hernu said.

'And yet not on your books and we always keep you up to date.'

'I know,' Hernu said. 'And you're the expert on the IRA, so what do we do?'

'You're wrong there,' Ferguson said. 'The greatest expert on the IRA is right there in Paris, Martin Brosnan, our Irish-American friend. After all, he carried a gun for them till nineteen seventy-five. I heard he was a Professor of Political Philosophy at the Sorbonne.'

'You're right,' Hernu said. 'I'd forgotten about him.'

'Very respectable these days. Writes books and lives rather well on all that money his mother left him when she died in Boston five years ago. If you've a mystery on your hands he might be the man to solve it.'

'Thanks for the suggestion,' Hernu said. 'But first we'll see what happens at Valenton. I'll be in touch.'

Ferguson put down the phone, pressed a button on the wall and got out of bed. A moment later the door opened and his manservant, an ex-Gurkha came in, putting a dressing-gown over his pyjamas.

'Emergency, Kim. I'll ring Captain Tanner and tell her to get round here, then I'll have a bath. Breakfast when she arrives.'

The Gurkha withdrew. Ferguson picked up the phone and dialled a number. 'Mary? Ferguson here. Something big. I want you at Cavendish Square within the hour. Oh, better wear your uniform. We've got that thing at the

Ministry of Defence at eleven. You always impress them in full war paint.'

He put the phone down and went into the bathroom feeling wide awake and extremely cheerful.

It was six-thirty when the taxi picked up Mary Tanner on the steps of her Lowndes Square flat. The driver was impressed, but then most people were. She wore the uniform of a captain in the Women's Royal Army Corps, the wings of an Army Air Corps pilot on her left breast. Below them the ribbon of the George Medal, a gallantry award of considerable distinction and campaign ribbons for Ireland and for service with the United Nations peace-keeping force in Cyprus.

She was a small girl, black hair cropped short, twenty-nine years of age and a lot of service under the belt. A doctor's daughter who'd taken an English degree at London University, tried teaching and hated it. After that came the army. A great deal of her service had been with the Military Police. Cyprus for a while, but three tours of duty in Ulster. It had been the affair in Derry that had earned her the George Medal and left her with the scar on her left cheek which had brought her to Ferguson's attention. She'd been his aide for two years now.

She paid off the taxi, hurried up the stairs to the flat on the first floor and let herself in with her own key. Ferguson was sitting on the sofa beside the fireplace in the elegant drawing room, a napkin under his chin while Kim served his poached eggs.

'Just in time,' he said. 'What would you like?'

'Tea, please. Earl Grey, Kim, and toast and honey.'

'Got to watch our figure.'

'Rather early in the day for sexist cracks, even for you, Brigadier. Now what have we got?'

He told her while he ate and Kim brought her tea and toast and she sat opposite, listening.

When he finished she said, 'This Brosnan, I've never heard of him.'

'Before your time, my love. He must be about forty-five now. You'll find a file on him in my study. He was born in Boston. One of those filthy rich American families. Very high society. His mother was a Dubliner. He did all the right things, went to Princeton, took his degree then went and spoiled it all by volunteering for Viet Nam and as an enlisted man. I believe that was nineteen sixty-six. Airborne Rangers. He was discharged a sergeant and heavily decorated.'

'So what makes him so special?'

'He could have avoided Viet Nam by staying at university, but he didn't. He also enlisted in the ranks. Quite something for someone with his social standing.'

'You're just an old snob. What happened to him after that?'

'He went to Trinity College, Dublin, to work on a doctorate. He's a Protestant, by the way, but his mother was a devout Catholic. In August sixty-nine, he was visiting an uncle on his mother's side, a priest in Belfast. Remember what happened? How it all started?'

'Orange mobs burning Catholics out?' she said.

'And the police not doing too much about it. The mob burned down Brosnan's uncle's church and started on the Falls Road. A handful of old IRA hands with a few rifles and handguns held them off and when one of them was shot, Brosnan picked up his rifle. Instinctive, I suppose. I mean Viet Nam and all that.'

'And from then on he was committed?'

'Very much so. You've got to remember that in those early days, there were plenty of men like him in the movement. Believers in Irish freedom and all that sort of thing.'

'Sorry, sir, I've seen too much blood on the streets of Derry to go for that one.'

'Yes, well I'm not trying to whitewash him. He's killed a few in his time, but always up front, I'll say that for him. He became quite famous. There was a French war photographer called Anne-Marie Audin. He saved her life in Viet Nam after a helicopter crash. Quite a romantic story. She turned up in Belfast and Brosnan took her underground for a week. She got a series out of it for *Life* magazine. The gallant Irish struggle. You know the sort of thing.'

'What happened after that?'

'In nineteen seventy-five he went to France to negotiate an arms deal. As it turned out it was a set-up and the police were waiting. Unfortunately he shot one of them dead. They gave him life. He escaped from prison in seventy-nine, at my instigation, I might add.'

'But why?'

'Someone else before your time, a terrorist called Frank Barry. Started off in Ulster with a splinter group called the Sons of Erin, then joined the European terrorist circuit, an evil genius if ever there was one. Tried to get Lord Carrington on a trip to France when he was Foreign Secretary. The French hushed it up, but the Prime Minister was furious. Gave me direct orders to hunt Barry down whatever the cost.'

'Oh, I see now. You needed Brosnan to do that?'

'Set a thief to catch a thief and so forth, and he got him for us.'

42

'And afterwards?'

'He went back to Ireland and took that doctorate.'

'And this Anne-Marie Audin, did they marry?'

'Not to my knowledge, but she did him a bigger favour than that. Her family is one of the oldest in France and enormously powerful politically and he had been awarded the Legion of Honour for saving her in Viet Nam. Anyway, her pressure behind the scenes bore fruit five years ago. President Mitterrand granted him a pardon. Wiped the slate clean.'

'Which is how he's at the Sorbonne now? He must be the only professor they've had who shot a policeman dead.'

'Actually one or two after the war had done just that when serving with the Resistance.'

'Does the leopard ever change its spots?' she asked.

'Oh, ye of little faith. As I say, you'll find his file in the study if you want to know more.' He passed her a piece of paper. 'That's the description of the mystery man. Not much to go on, but run it through the computer anyway.'

She went out.

Kim entered with a copy of *The Times*. Ferguson read the headlines briefly then turned to page two where his attention was immediately caught by the same item concerning Mrs Thatcher's visit to France as had appeared in *Paris Soir*.

'Well, Max,' he said softly, 'I wish you luck,' and he poured himself another cup of coffee.

3

It was much warmer in Paris later that morning, most of the snow clearing by lunchtime. It was clear in the country-side too, only a bit here and there on the hedgerows as Dillon moved towards Valenton keeping to the back roads. He was riding the BMW motorcycle from the garage and was dressed as a CRS policeman, helmet, goggles, a MAT49 machine gun slung across the front of the dark uniform raincoat.

Madness to have come, of course, but he couldn't resist the free show. He pulled off a narrow country lane by a farm gate after consulting his map, followed a track through a small wood on foot and came to a low stone wall on a hill. Way below, some two hundred yards on, was the railway crossing, the black Renault still parked where he had left it. There wasn't a soul about. Perhaps fifteen minutes later, a train passed through.

He checked his watch. Two-fifteen. He focused his Zeiss glasses on the scene below again and then the white Renault came down the road half-turning to block the crossing. There was a Peugeot behind it, Pierre at the wheel and he was already reversing, turning the car as Gaston ran towards him. It was an old model, painted scarlet and cream.

'Very pretty,' Dillon said softly as the Peugeot disappeared up the road.

'Now for the cavalry,' he said and lit a cigarette.

It was perhaps ten minutes later that a large truck came down the road and braked to a halt unable to progress further. It had high canvas sides on which was emblazoned 'Steiner Electronics'.

'Electronics my arse,' Dillon said.

A heavy machine gun opened up from inside the truck firing through the side, raking the Renault. As the firing stopped Dillon took a black plastic electronic detonator from his pocket, switched on and pulled out the aerial.

A dozen men in black overalls and riot helmets, all clutching machine carbines, jumped out. As they approached the Renault, Dillon pressed the detonator. The self-destruct charge in the second black box, the one he had told Pierre contained extra ammunition, exploded instantly, the vehicle disintegrating, parts of the panelling lifting into the air in slow motion. There were several men on the ground, others running for cover.

'There you are, chew on that, gentlemen,' Dillon said.

He walked back through the wood, pushed the BMW off its stand, swung a leg over and rode away.

He opened the door of the warehouse on rue de Helier, got back on the BMW, rode inside and parked it. As he turned to close the door, Makeev called from above, 'It went wrong, I presume?'

Dillon took off his helmet. 'I'm afraid so. The Jobert brothers turned me in.'

As he went up the stairs Makeev said, 'The disguise, I like that. A policeman is just a policeman to people. Nothing to describe.'

'Exactly. I worked for a great Irishman called Frank Barry for a while years ago. Ever heard of him?'

'Certainly. A veritable Carlos.'

'He was better than Carlos. Got knocked off in seventy-nine. I don't know who by. He used the CRS copper on a motorcycle a lot. Postmen are good too. No one ever notices a postman.'

He followed the Russian into the sitting room. 'Tell me,' Makeev said.

Dillon brought him up to date. 'It was a chance using those two and it went wrong, that's all there is to it.'

'Now what?'

'As I said last night, I'll provide an alternative target. I mean, all that lovely money. I've got to think of my old age.'

'Nonsense, Sean, you don't give a damn about your old age. It's the game that excites you.'

'You could be right.' Dillon lit a cigarette. 'I know one thing. I don't like to be beaten. I'll think of something for you and I'll pay my debts.'

'The Joberts? Are they worth it?'

'Oh, yes,' Dillon said. 'A matter of honour, Josef.'

Makeev sighed. 'I'll go and see Aroun, give him the bad news. I'll be in touch.'

'Here or at the barge.' Dillon smiled. 'Don't worry, Josef. I've never failed yet, not when I set my mind to a thing.'

Makeev went down the stairs. His footsteps echoed across the warehouse, the Judas gate banged behind him.

Dillon turned and went back into the long room, whistling softly.

'But I don't understand,' Aroun said. 'There hasn't been a word on television.'

'And there won't be.' Makeev turned from the French windows overlooking the Avenue Victor Hugo. 'The affair never happened, that is the way the French will handle it. The idea that Mrs Thatcher could have in any way been at risk on French soil would be considered a national affront.'

Aroun was pale with anger. 'He failed, this man of yours. A great deal of talk, Makeev, but nothing at the end of it. A good thing I didn't transfer that million to his Zurich account this morning.'

'But you agreed,' Makeev said. 'In any case, he may ring at any time to check the money has been deposited.'

'My dear Makeev, I have five hundred million dollars on deposit at that bank. Faced with the possibility of me transferring my business, the managing director was more than willing to agree to a small deception when Rashid spoke to him this morning. When Dillon phones to check on the situation, the deposit will be confirmed.'

'This is a highly dangerous man you are dealing with,' Makeev said. 'If he found out . . .'

'Who's going to tell him? Certainly not you and he'll get paid in the end, but only if he produces a result.'

Rashid poured him a cup of coffee and said to Makeev, 'He promised an alternative target, mentioned the British Prime Minister. What does he intend?'

'He'll be in touch when he's decided,' Makeev said.

'Talk,' Aroun walked to the window and stood sipping his coffee. 'All talk.'

'No, Michael,' Josef Makeev told him. 'You could not be more mistaken.'

Martin Brosnan's apartment was by the river on the Quai de Montebello opposite the Île de la Cité and had one of the finest views of Notre Dame in Paris. It was within decent walking distance of the Sorbonne which suited him perfectly.

It was just after four as he walked towards it, a tall man with broad shoulders in an old-fashioned trenchcoat, dark hair that still had no grey in it in spite of his forty-five years and was far too long, giving him the look of some sixteenth-century bravo. Martin Aodh Brosnan. The Aodh was Gaelic for Hugh and his Irishness showed in the high cheekbones and grey eyes.

It was getting colder again and he shivered as he turned the corner into the Quai de Montebello and hurried along to the apartment block. He owned it all, as it happened, which gave him the apartment on the corner of the first floor, the most favoured location. Scaffolding ran up the corner of the building to the fourth floor where some sort of building work was taking place.

As he was about to go up the steps to the ornate entrance, a voice called, 'Martin?'

He glanced up and saw Anne-Marie Audin leaning over the balustrade of the terrace. 'Where in the hell did you spring from?' he asked in astonishment.

'Cuba. I just got in.'

He went up the stairs two at a time and she had the door open as he got there. He lifted her up in his arms in an enormous hug and carried her back into the hall. 'How marvellous to see you. Why Cuba?'

She kissed him and helped him off with the trenchcoat.

'Oh, I had a rather juicy assignment for *Time* magazine. Come in the kitchen. I'll make your tea.'

A standing joke for years, the tea. Surprising in an American, but he couldn't stand coffee. He lit a cigarette and sat at the table and watched her move around the kitchen, her short hair as dark as his own, this supremely elegant woman who was the same age as himself and looked twelve years younger.

'You look marvellous,' he told her as she brought the tea. He sampled it and nodded in approval. 'That's grand. Just the way you learned to make it back in South Armagh in nineteen seventy-one with me and Liam Devlin showing you the hard way how the IRA worked.'

'How is the old rogue?'

'Still living in Kilrea outside Dublin. Gives the odd lecture at Trinity College. Claims to be seventy, but that's a wicked lie.'

'He'll never grow old, that one.'

'Yes, you really do look marvellous,' Brosnan said. 'Why didn't we get married?'

It was a ritual question he had asked for years, a joke now. There was a time when they had been lovers, but for some years now, just friends. Not that it was by any means the usual relationship. He would have died for her, almost had in a Viet Nam swamp the first time they had met.

'Now that we've got that over, tell me about the new book,' she said.

'A philosophy of terrorism,' he told her. 'Very boring. Not many people will buy a copy.'

'A pity,' she said, 'coming from such an expert in the field.'

'Doesn't really matter,' he said. 'Knowing the reasons still won't make people act any differently.'

'Cynic. Come on, let's have a real drink.' She opened the fridge and took out a bottle of Krug.

'Non-vintage?'

'What else?'

They went into the magnificent long drawing room. There was an ornate gold mirror over the marble fireplace, plants everywhere, a grand piano, comfortable, untidy sofas and a great many books. She had left the French windows to the balcony standing ajar. Brosnan went to close them as she opened the Krug at the sideboard and got two glasses. At the same moment, the bell sounded outside.

When Brosnan opened the door he found Max Hernu and Jules Savary standing there, the Jobert brothers behind them.

'Professor Brosnan?' Hernu said. 'I am Colonel Max Hernu.'

'I know very well who you are,' Brosnan said. 'Action Service, isn't it? What's all this? My wicked past catching up with me?'

'Not quite, but we do need your assistance. This is Inspector Savary and these two are Gaston and Pierre Jobert.'

'You'd better come in then,' Brosnan said, interested in spite of himself.

The Jobert brothers stayed in the hall, on Hernu's orders when he and Savary followed Brosnan into the drawing room. Anne-Marie turned, frowning slightly and Brosnan made the introductions.

'A great pleasure.' Hernu kissed her hand. 'I'm a long-time admirer.'

'Martin?' She looked worried now. 'You're not getting involved in anything?'

'Of course not,' he assured her. 'Now what can I do for you, Colonel?'

'A matter of national security, Professor. I hesitate to mention the fact, but Mademoiselle Audin is a photojournalist of some distinction.'

She smiled. 'Total discretion, you have my word, Colonel.'

'We're here because Brigadier Charles Ferguson in London suggested it.'

'That old Devil? And why should he suggest you see me?'

'Because you are an expert in matters relating to the IRA, Professor. Let me explain.'

Which he did, covering the whole affair as rapidly as possible. 'You see, Professor,' he said as he concluded, 'the Jobert brothers have combed our IRA picture books without finding him and Ferguson has had no success with the brief description we were able to give.'

'You've got a real problem.'

'My friend, this man is not just anybody. He must be special to attempt such a thing, but we know nothing more than that we think he's Irish and he speaks fluent French.'

'So what do you want me to do?'

'Speak to the Joberts.'

Brosnan glanced at Anne-Marie, then shrugged. 'All right, wheel them in.'

He sat on the edge of the table drinking champagne while they stood before him, awkward in such circumstances. 'How old is he?'

'Difficult, monsieur,' Pierre said. 'He changes from one minute to the next. It's like he's more than one person. I'd say late thirties.'

'And description?'

'Small with fair hair.'

'He looks like nothing,' Gaston put in. 'We thought he was a no-no and then he half-killed some big ape in our café one night.'

'All right. He's small, fair-haired, late thirties and he can handle himself. What makes you think he's Irish?'

'When he was assembling the Kalashnikov he made a crack about seeing one take out a Land Rover full of English paratroopers.'

'Is that all?'

Pierre frowned. Brosnan took the bottle of Krug from the bucket and Gaston said, 'No, there's something else. He's always whistling a funny sort of tune. A bit eerie. I managed to follow it on my accordion. He said it was Irish.'

Brosnan's face had gone quite still. He stood there, holding the bottle in one hand, a glass in the other.

'And he likes that stuff, monsieur,' Pierre said.

'Champagne?' Brosnan asked.

'Well, yes, any champagne is better than nothing, but Krug is his favourite.'

'Like this, non-vintage?'

'Yes, monsieur. He told us he preferred the grape mix,' Pierre said.

'The bastard always did.'

Anne-Marie put a hand on Brosnan's arm. 'You know him, Martin?'

'Almost certainly. Could you pick that tune out on the piano?' he asked Gaston.

'I'll try, monsieur.'

He lifted the lid, tried the keyboard gently, then played the beginning of the tune with one finger.

'That's enough.' Brosnan turned to Hernu and Savary. 'An old Irish folk song, "The Lark in the Clear Air", and you've got trouble, gentlemen, because the man you're looking for is Sean Dillon.'

'Dillon?' Hernu said. 'Of course. The man of a thousand faces someone once called him.'

'A slight exaggeration,' Brosnan said, 'but it will do.'

They sent the Jobert brothers home and Brosnan and Anne-Marie sat on a sofa opposite Hernu and Savary. The inspector made notes as the American talked.

'His mother died in childbirth. I think that was nineteen fifty-two. His father was an electrician. Went to work in London so Dillon went to school there. He had an incredible talent for acting, a genius really. He can change before your eyes, hunch his shoulders, put on fifteen years. It's astonishing.'

'So you knew him well?' Hernu asked.

'In Belfast in the bad old days, but before that he won a scholarship to the Royal Academy of Dramatic Art. Only stayed a year. They couldn't teach him anything. He did one or two things at the National Theatre. Nothing much. He was very young remember. Then in nineteen seventy-one his father, who'd returned home to Belfast, was killed by a British Army patrol. Caught in crossfire. An accident.'

'And Dillon took it hard?'

'You could say that. He offered himself to the Provisional IRA. They liked him. He had brains, an aptitude for languages. They sent him to Libya to one of those terrorist training camps for a couple of months. A fast course in weaponry. That's all it took. He never looked back. God knows how many he's killed.'

'So, he still operates for the IRA?'

Brosnan shook his head. 'Not for years. Oh, he still counts himself as a soldier, but he thinks the leadership are a bunch of old women and they couldn't handle him. He'd have killed the Pope if he'd thought it was needed. He was too happy to do things that were counter-productive. The word is that he was involved in the Mountbatten affair.'

'And since those days?' Hernu asked.

'Beirut, Palestine. He's done a lot for the PLO. Most terrorist groups have used his services.' Brosnan shook his head. 'You're going to have trouble here.'

'Why exactly?'

'The fact that he used a couple of crooks like the Joberts. He always does that. All right, it didn't work this time, but he knows the weakness of all revolutionary movements. That they're ridden with either hotheads or informers. You called him the faceless man, and that's right because I doubt if you'll find a photo of him on any file, and frankly it wouldn't matter if you did.'

'Why does he do it?' Anne-Marie asked. 'Not for any political ends?'

'Because he likes it,' Brosnan said. 'Because he's hooked. He's an actor, remember. This is for real and he's good at it.'

'I get the impression that you don't care for him very much,' Hernu said. 'In personal terms, I mean.'

'Well, he tried to kill me and a good friend of mine a

long time ago,' Brosnan told him. 'Does that answer your question?'

'It's certainly reason enough.' Hernu got up and Savary joined him. 'We must be going. I want to get all this to Brigadier Ferguson as soon as possible.'

'Fine,' Brosnan said.

'We may count on your help in this thing, I hope, Professor?'

Brosnan glanced at Anne-Marie whose face was set. 'Look,' he said, 'I don't mind talking to you again if that will help, but I don't want to be personally involved. You know what I was, Colonel. Whatever happens I won't go back to anything like that. I made someone a promise a long time ago.'

'I understand perfectly, Professor.' Hernu turned to Anne-Marie. 'Mademoiselle, a distinct pleasure.'

'I'll see you out,' she said and led the way.

When she returned Brosnan had the French windows open and was standing looking across the river smoking a cigarette. He put an arm around her. 'All right?'

'Oh, yes,' she said. 'Perfect,' and laid her head against his chest.

At that precise moment Ferguson was sitting by the fire in the Cavendish Square flat when the phone rang. Mary Tanner answered it in the study. After a while she came out. 'That was Downing Street. The Prime Minister wants to see you.'

'When?'

'Now, sir.'

Ferguson got up and removed his reading glasses. 'Call the car. You come with me and wait.'

She picked up the phone, spoke briefly, then put it down. 'What do you think it's about, Brigadier?'

'I'm not sure. My imminent retirement or your return to more mundane duties. Or this business in France. He'll have been told all about it by now. Anyway, let's go and see,' and he led the way out.

They were checked through the security gates at the end of Downing Street. Mary Tanner stayed in the car while Ferguson was admitted through the most famous door in the world. It was rather quiet compared to the last time he'd been there, a Christmas party given by Mrs Thatcher for the staff in the Pillared Room. Cleaners, typists, office workers. Typical of her, that. The other side of the Iron Lady.

He regretted her departure, that was a fact, and sighed as he followed a young aide up the main staircase lined with replicas of portraits of all those great men of history. Peel, Wellington, Disraeli and many more. They reached the corridor, the young man knocked on the door and opened it.

'Brigadier Ferguson, Prime Minister.'

The last time Ferguson had been in that study it had been a woman's room, the feminine touches unmistakably there, but things were different now, a little more austere in a subtle way, he was aware of that. Darkness was falling fast outside and John Major was checking some sort of report, the pen in his hand moving with considerable speed.

'Sorry about this. It will only take a moment,' he said.

It was the courtesy that astounded Ferguson, the sheer basic good manners that one didn't experience too often from heads of state. Major signed the report, put it on one side and sat back, a pleasant, grey-haired man in horn-rimmed glasses, the youngest Prime Minister of the twentieth century. Almost unknown to the general public on his succession to Margaret Thatcher and yet his handling of the crisis in the Gulf had already marked him out as a leader of genuine stature.

'Please sit down, Brigadier. I'm on a tight schedule, so I'll get right to the point. The business affecting Mrs Thatcher in France. Obviously very disturbing.'

'Indeed so, Prime Minister. Thank God it all turned out as it did.'

'Yes, but that seems to have been a matter of luck more than anything else. I've spoken to President Mitterrand and he's agreed that in all our interests and especially with the present situation in the Gulf there will be a total security clampdown.'

'What about the press, Prime Minister?'

'Nothing will reach the press, Brigadier,' John Major told him. 'I understand the French failed to catch the individual concerned?'

'I'm afraid that is so according to my latest information, but Colonel Hernu of Action Service is keeping in close touch.'

'I've spoken to Mrs Thatcher and it was she who alerted me to your presence, Brigadier. As I understand it, the intelligence section known as Group Four was set up in nineteen seventy-two, responsible only to the Prime Minister, its purpose to handle specific cases of terrorism and subversion?'

'That is correct.'

'Which means you will have served five prime ministers if we include myself.'

'Actually, Prime Minister, that's not quite accurate,' Ferguson said. 'We do have a problem at the moment.'

'Oh, I know all about that. The usual security people have never liked your existence, Brigadier, too much like the Prime Minister's private army. That's why they thought a changeover at Number Ten was a good time to get rid of you.'

'I'm afraid so, Prime Minister.'

'Well, it wasn't and it isn't. I've spoken to the Director General of Security Services. It's taken care of.'

'I couldn't be more delighted.'

'Good. Your first task quite obviously is to run down whoever was behind this French affair. If he's IRA, then he's our business, wouldn't you agree?'

'Absolutely.'

'Good. I'll let you go and get on with it then. Keep me informed of every significant development on an eyes only basis.'

'Of course, Prime Minister.'

The door behind opened as if by magic, the aide appeared to usher Ferguson out, the Prime Minister was already working over another sheaf of papers as the door closed and Ferguson was led downstairs.

As the limousine drove away, Mary Tanner reached forward to close the screen. 'What happened? What was it about?'

'Oh, the French business.' Ferguson sounded curiously remote. 'You know, he's really got something about him this one.'

'Oh, come off it, sir,' Mary said. 'I mean, don't you honestly think we could do with a change, after all these years of Tory government?'

'Wonderful spokesperson for the workers you make,' he said. 'Your dear old Dad, God rest him, was a Professor of Surgery at Oxford, your mother owns half of Herefordshire. That flat of yours in Lowndes Square, a million, would you say? Why is it the children of the rich are always so depressingly left-wing while still insisting on dining at the Savoy?'

'A gross exaggeration.'

'Seriously, my dear, I've worked for Labour as well as Conservative prime ministers. The colour of the politician doesn't matter. The Marquess of Salisbury when he was Prime Minister, Gladstone, Disraeli, had very similar problems to those we have today. Fenians, anarchists, bombs in London, only dynamite instead of Semtex and how many attempts were there on Queen Victoria's life?' He gazed out at the Whitehall traffic as they moved towards the Ministry of Defence. 'Nothing changes.'

'All right, end of lecture, but what happened?' she demanded.

'Oh, we're back in business, that's what happened,' he said. 'I'm afraid we'll have to cancel your transfer back to the Military Police.'

'Damn you!' she cried and flung her arms around his neck.

Ferguson's office on the third floor of the Ministry of Defence was on a corner at the rear overlooking Horseguards Avenue with a view of the Victoria Embankment and the river at the far end. He had hardly got settled behind his desk when Mary hurried in.

'Coded fax from Hernu. I've put it through the machine. You're not going to like it one little bit.'

It contained the gist of Hernu's meeting with Martin Brosnan, the facts on Sean Dillon – everything.

'Dear God,' Ferguson said. 'Couldn't be worse. He's like a ghost, this Dillon chap. Does he exist or doesn't he? As bad as Carlos in international terrorist terms, but totally unknown to the media or the general public and nothing to go on.'

'But we do have one thing, sir.'

'What's that?'

'Brosnan.'

'True, but will he help?' Ferguson got up and moved to the window. 'I tried to get Martin to do something for me the other year. He wouldn't touch it with a bargepole.' He turned and smiled. 'It's the girlfriend, you see, Anne-Marie Audin. She has a horror of him becoming what he once was.'

'Yes, I can understand that.'

'But never mind. We'd better get a report on their latest developments to the Prime Minister. Let's keep it brief.'

She produced a pen and took notes as he dictated. 'Anything else, sir?' she asked when he had finished.

'I don't think so. Get it typed. One copy for the file, the other for the PM. Send it straight round to Number Ten by messenger. Eyes only.'

Mary did a rough type of the report herself then went along the corridor to the typing and copying room. There was one on each floor and the clerks all had full security clearance. The copier was clattering as she went in. The man standing in front of it was in his mid-fifties, white hair, steel-rimmed army glasses, his shirt sleeves rolled up.

'Hello, Gordon,' she said. 'A priority one here. Your

very best typing. One copy for the personal file. You'll do it straight away?'

'Of course, Captain Tanner.' He glanced at it briefly. 'Fifteen minutes. I'll bring it along.'

She went out and he sat down at his typewriter, taking a deep breath to steady himself as he read the words. *For the eyes of the Prime Minister only.* Gordon Brown had served in the Intelligence Corps for twenty-five years, reaching the rank of warrant officer. A worthy, if unspectacular career, culminating in the award of an MBE and the offer of employment at the Ministry of Defence on his retirement from the army. And everything had been fine until the death of his wife from cancer the previous year. They were childless, which left him alone in a cold world at fifty-five years of age, and then something miraculous happened.

There were invitation cards flying around at the Ministry all the time to receptions at the various embassies in London. He often helped himself to one. It was just something to do and at an art display at the German Embassy he'd met Tania Novikova, a secretary-typist at the Soviet Embassy.

They'd got on so well together. She was thirty and not particularly pretty, but when she'd taken him to bed on their second meeting at his flat in Camden it was like a revelation. Brown had never known sex like it, was hooked instantly. And then it had started. The questions about his job, anything and everything about what went on at the Ministry of Defence. Then there was a cooling off. He didn't see her and was distracted, almost out of his mind. He'd phoned her at her flat. She was cold at first, distant and then she'd asked him if he'd been doing anything interesting.

He knew then what was happening, but didn't care. There was a series of reports passing through on British Army changes in view of political changes in Russia. It was easy to run off spare copies. When he took them round to her flat, it was just as it had been and she took him to heights of pleasure such as he had never known.

From then on he would do anything, providing copies of everything that might interest her. *For the eyes of the Prime Minister only*. How grateful would she be for that? He finished typing, ran off two extra copies, one for himself. He had a file of them now in one of his bedroom drawers. The other was for Tania Novikova, who was, of course, not a secretary-typist at the Soviet Embassy as she had informed Brown, but a captain in the KGB.

Gaston opened the door of the lock-up garage opposite *Le Chat Noir* and Pierre got behind the wheel of the old cream and red Peugeot. His brother got in the rear seat and they drove away.

'I've been thinking,' Gaston said. 'I mean, what if they don't get him? He could come looking for us, Pierre.'

'Nonsense,' Pierre told him. 'He's long gone, Gaston. What kind of fool would hang around after what's happened? No, light me a cigarette and shut up. We'll have a nice dinner and go on to the *Zanzibar* afterwards. They've still got those Swedish sisters stripping.'

It was just before eight, the streets at that place quiet and deserted, people inside because of the extreme cold. They came to a small square and as they started to cross it a CRS man on his motorcycle came up behind them, flashing his lights.

'There's a cop on our tail,' Gaston said.

The policeman pulled up alongside, anonymous in his helmet and goggles and waved them down.

'A message from Savary, I suppose,' Pierre said, and pulled over to the pavement.

'Maybe they've got him,' Gaston said excitedly.

The CRS man halted behind them, pushed his bike up on its stand and approached. Gaston got the rear door open and leaned out. 'Have they caught the bastard?'

Dillon took a Walther with a Carswell silencer from inside the flap of his raincoat and shot him twice in the heart. He pushed up his goggles and turned. Pierre crossed himself. 'It's you.'

'Yes, Pierre. A matter of honour.'

The Walther coughed twice more, Dillon pushed it back inside his raincoat, got on the BMW and rode away. It started to snow a little, the square very quiet. It was perhaps half an hour later that a policeman on foot patrol, caped against the cold, found them.

Tania Novikova's flat was just off the Bayswater Road not far from the Soviet Embassy. She'd had a hard day, had intended an early night. It was just before ten-thirty when her doorbell rang. She was towelling herself down after a nice relaxing bath. She pulled on a robe, and went downstairs.

Gordon Brown's evening shift had finished at ten. He couldn't wait to get to her and had had the usual difficulty parking his Ford Escort. He stood at the door, ringing the bell impatiently, hugely excited. When she opened the door and saw who it was she was immediately angry and drew him inside.

'I told you never to come here, Gordon, under any circumstances.'

'But this is special,' he pleaded. 'Look what I've brought you.'

In the living room she took the large envelope from him, opened it and slipped out the report. *For the eyes of the Prime Minister only.* Her excitement was intense as she read through it. Incredible that this fool could have delivered her such a coup. His arms were around her waist, sliding up to her breasts and she was aware of his excitement.

'It's good stuff, isn't it?' he demanded.

'Excellent, Gordon. You *have* been a good boy.'

'Really?' His grip tightened. 'I can stay over then?'

'Oh, Gordon, it's such a pity. I'm on the night shift.'

'Please, darling.' He was shaking like a leaf. 'Just a few minutes then.'

She had to keep him happy, she knew that, put the report on the table and took him by the hand. 'Quarter of an hour, Gordon, that's all and then you'll have to go,' and she led him into the bedroom.

After she'd got rid of him, she dressed hurriedly, debating what to do. She was a hard, committed Communist. That was how she had been raised and how she would die. More than that, she served the KGB with total loyalty. It had nurtured her, educated her, given her whatever status she had in their world. For a young woman, she was surprisingly old-fashioned. Had no time for Gorbachev or the Glasnost fools who surrounded him. Unfortunately, many in the KGB did support him and one of those was her boss at the London Embassy, Colonel Yuri Gatov.

What would his attitude be to such a report, she wondered as she let herself out into the street and started to walk. What would Gorbachev's attitude be to the failed attempt to assassinate Mrs Thatcher? Probably the same outrage the British Prime Minister must feel and if Gorbachev felt that way, so would Colonel Gatov. So, what to do?

It came to her then as she walked along the frosty pavement of the Bayswater Road, that there was someone who might very well be interested and not only because he thought as she did, but because he was himself right in the centre of all the action – Paris. Her old boss, Colonel Josef Makeev. That was it. Makeev would know how best to use such information. She turned into Kensington Palace Gardens and went into the Soviet Embassy.

By chance, Makeev was working late in his office that night when his secretary looked in and said, 'A call from London on the scrambler. Captain Novikova.'

Makeev picked up the red phone. 'Tania,' he said, a certain affection in his voice for they had been lovers during the three years she'd worked for him in Paris. 'What can I do for you?'

'I understand there was an incident affecting Empire over there earlier today?' she said.

It was an old KGB coded phrase, current for years, always used when referring to assassination attempts of any kind at high government level where Britain was concerned.

Makeev was immediately alert. 'That's correct. The usual kind of it-didn't-happen affair.'

'Have you an interest?'

'Very much so.'

'There's a coded fax on the way. I'll stand by in my office if you want to talk.'

Tania Novikova put down the phone. She had her own fax coding machine at a second desk. She went to it, tapping the required details out quickly, checking on the screen to see that she had got it right. She added Makeev's personal number, inserted the report and waited. A few moments later, she got a message received okay signal. She got up, lit a cigarette and went and stood by the window, waiting.

The jumbled message was received in the radio and coding room at the Paris Embassy. Makeev stood waiting impatiently for it to come through. The operator handed it to him and the Colonel inserted it into the decoder and tapped in his personal key. He couldn't wait to see the contents, was reading it as he went along the corridor, as excited as Tania Novikova when he saw the line *For the eyes of the Prime Minister only*. He sat behind his desk and read it through again. He thought about it for a while, then reached for the red phone.

'You've done well, Tania. This one was my baby.'

'I'm so pleased.'

'Does Gatov know about this?'

'No, Colonel.'

'Good, let's keep it that way.'

'Is there anything else I can do?'

'Very much so. Cultivate your contact. Let me have anything else on the instant. There could be more for you. I have a friend coming to London. The particular friend you've been reading about.'

'I'll wait to hear.'

She put down the phone, totally elated, and went along to the canteen.

In Paris, Makeev sat there for a moment, frowning, then he picked up the phone and rang Dillon. There was a slight delay before the Irishman answered.

'Who is it?'

'Josef, Sean, I'm on my way there. Utmost importance.'

Makeev put down the phone, got his overcoat and went out.

4

Brosnan had taken Anne-Marie to the cinema that evening and afterwards to a small restaurant in Montmartre called *La Place Anglaise*. It was an old favourite because, and in spite of the name, one of the specialities of the house was Irish stew. It wasn't particularly busy and they had just finished the main course when Max Hernu appeared, Savary standing behind him.

'Snow in London, snow in Brussels and snow in Paris.' Hernu brushed it from his sleeve and opened his coat.

'Do I deduce from your appearance here that you've had me followed?' Brosnan asked.

'Not at all, Professor. We called at your apartment where the porter told us you had gone to the cinema. He was also kind enough to mention three or four restaurants he thought you might be at. This is the second.'

'Then you'd better sit down and have a cognac and some coffee,' Anne-Marie told him. 'You both look frozen.'

They took off their coats and Brosnan nodded to the head waiter who hurried over and took the order.

'I'm sorry, mademoiselle, to spoil your evening, but

this is most important,' Hernu said. 'An unfortunate development.'

Brosnan lit a cigarette. 'Tell us the worst.'

It was Savary who answered. 'About two hours ago the bodies of the Jobert brothers were found by a beat policeman in their car in a small square not far from *Le Chat Noir*.'

'Murdered, is that what you are saying?' Anne-Marie put in.

'Oh, yes, mademoiselle,' he said. 'Shot to death.'

'Two each in the heart?' Brosnan said.

'Why, yes, Professor, the pathologist was able to tell us that at the start of his examination. We didn't stay for the rest. How did you know?'

'Dillon, without a doubt. It's a real pro's trick, Colonel, you should know that. Never one shot, always two in case the other man manages to get one off at you as a reflex.'

Hernu stirred his coffee. 'Did you expect this, Professor?'

'Oh, yes. He'd have come looking for them sooner or later. A strange man. He always keeps his word, never goes back on a contract and he expects the same from those he deals with. What he calls a matter of honour. At least he did in the old days.'

'Can I ask you something?' Savary said. 'I've been on the street fifteen years. I've known killers in plenty and not just the gangsters who see it as part of the job, but the poor sod who's killed his wife because she's been unfaithful. Dillon seems something else. I mean, his father was killed by British soldiers so he joined the IRA. I can see that, but everything that's happened since. Twenty years of it. All those hits and not even in his own country. Why?'

'I'm not a psychiatrist,' Brosnan said. 'They'd give you all the fancy names starting with psychopath and working down. I knew men like him in the army in Viet Nam in Special Forces and good men, some of them, but once they started, the killing, I mean, it seemed to take over like a drug. They became driven men. The next stage was always to kill when it wasn't necessary. To do it without emotion. Back there in Nam it was as if people had become, how can I put it, just things.'

'And this, you think, happened to Dillon?' Hernu asked.

'It happened to me, Colonel,' Martin Brosnan said bleakly.

There was silence. Finally, Hernu said, 'We must catch him, Professor.'

'I know.'

'Then you'll join us in hunting him down?'

Anne-Marie put a hand on his arm, dismay on her face and she turned to the two men, a kind of desperate anger there. 'That's your job, not Martin's.'

'It's all right,' Martin soothed her. 'Don't worry.' He said to Hernu, 'Any advice I can give, any information that might help, but no personal involvement. I'm sorry, Colonel, that's the way it has to be.'

Savary said, 'You told us he tried to kill you once. You and a friend.'

'That was in seventy-four. He and I both worked for this friend of mine, a man named Devlin, Liam Devlin. He was what you might call an old-fashioned revolutionary. Thought you could still fight it out like the old days, an undercover army against the troops. A bit like the Resistance in France during the war. He didn't like bombs, soft target bits, that kind of stuff.'

'What happened?' the Inspector asked.

'Dillon disobeyed orders and the bomb that was meant for the police patrol killed half a dozen children. Devlin and I went after him. He tried to take us out.'

'Without success, obviously?'

'Well, we weren't exactly kids off the street.' His voice had changed in a subtle way. Harder, more cynical. 'Left me with a groove in one shoulder and I gave him one in the arm himself. That was when he first dropped out of sight into Europe.'

'And you didn't see him again?'

'I was in prison for over four years from nineteen seventy-five, Inspector. Belle Isle. You're forgetting your history. He worked with a man called Frank Barry for a while, another refugee from the IRA who turned up on the European scene. A really bad one, Barry. Do you remember him?'

'I do, indeed, Professor,' Hernu said. 'As I recall, he tried to assassinate Lord Carrington, the British Foreign Secretary, on a visit to France in nineteen seventy-nine in very similar circumstances to this recent affair.'

'Dillon was probably doing a copy-cat of that operation. He worshipped Barry.'

'Who you killed, on behalf of British intelligence, I understand?'

Anne-Marie said, 'Excuse me.'

She got up and walked down to the powder room. Hernu said, 'We've upset her.'

'She worries about me, Colonel, worries that some circumstances might put a gun in my hand again and send me sliding all the way back.'

'Yes, I can see that, my friend.' Hernu got up and buttoned

71

his coat. 'We've taken up enough of your time. My apologies to Mademoiselle Audin.'

Savary said, 'Your lectures at the Sorbonne, Professor, the students must love you. I bet you get a full house.'

'Always,' Brosnan said.

He watched them go and Anne-Marie returned. 'Sorry about that, my love,' he told her.

'Not your fault.' She looked tired. 'I think I'll go home.'

'You're not coming back to my place?'

'Not tonight. Tomorrow perhaps.'

The head waiter brought the bill which Brosnan signed, then helped them into their coats and ushered them to the door. Outside, snow sprinkled the cobbles. She shivered and turned to Brosnan. 'You changed, Martin, back there when you were talking to them. You started to become the other man again.'

'Really?' he said and knew that it was true.

'I'll get a taxi.'

'Let me come with you.'

'No, I'd rather not.'

He watched her go down the street, then turned and went the other way. Wondering about Dillon, where he was and what he was doing.

Dillon's barge was moored in a small basin on the Quai St Bernard. There were mainly motor cruisers there, pleasure craft with canvas hoods over them for the winter. The interior was surprisingly luxurious, a stateroom lined with mahogany, two comfortable sofas, a television. His sleeping quarters were in a cabin beyond with a divan bed and a small shower-room adjacent. The kitchen was on the other side of the passageway, small, but very modern.

Everything a good cook could want. He was in there now, waiting for the kettle to boil when he heard the footfalls on deck. He opened a drawer, took out a Walther, cocked it and slipped it into his waistband at the rear. Then he went out.

Makeev came down the companionway and entered the stateroom. He shook snow from his overcoat and took it off. 'What a night. Filthy weather.'

'Worse in Moscow,' Dillon told him. 'Coffee?'

'Why not.'

Makeev helped himself to a cognac from a bottle on the sideboard and the Irishman came back with a china mug in each hand. 'Well, what's happened?'

'First of all, my sources tell me the Jobert brothers have turned up very dead indeed. Was that wise?'

'To use an immortal phrase from one of those old James Cagney movies, they had it coming. Now what else has happened?'

'Oh, an old friend from your dim past has surfaced. One Martin Brosnan.'

'Holy Mother of God!' Dillon seemed transfixed for a moment. 'Martin? Martin Brosnan? Where in the hell did he turn up from?'

'He's living right here in Paris, just up the river from you on the Quai de Montebello, the block on the corner opposite Notre Dame. Very ornate entrance. Within walking distance of here. You can't miss it. Has scaffolding on the front. Some sort of building work going on.'

'All very detailed.' Dillon took a bottle of Bushmills from the cupboard and poured one. 'Why?'

'I've had a look on my way here.'

'What's all this got to do with me?'

So Makeev told him, Max Hernu, Savary, Tania Novikova in London, everything. 'So,' he said as he finished. 'At least we know what our friends are up to.'

'This Novikova girl could be very useful to me,' Dillon said. 'Will she play things our way?'

'No question. She worked for me for some years. A very clever young woman. Like me, she isn't happy with present changes back home. Her boss is a different matter. Colonel Yuri Gatov. All for change. One of those.'

'Yes, she could be important,' Dillon said.

'Do I take it this means you want to go to London?'

'When I know, I'll let you know.'

'And Brosnan?'

'I could pass him on the street and he wouldn't recognise me.'

'You're sure?'

'Josef, I could pass you and you wouldn't recognise me. You've never really seen me change, have you? Have you come in your car?'

'Of course not. Taxi. I hope I can get one back.'

'I'll get my coat and walk some of the way with you.'

He went out and Makeev buttoned his coat and poured another brandy. There was a slight sound behind him and when he turned, Dillon stood there in cap and reefer coat, hunched over in some strange way. Even the shape of his face seemed different. He looked fifteen years older. The change in body language was incredible.

'My God, it's amazing,' Makeev said.

Dillon straightened up and grinned, 'Josef, my old son, if I'd stuck to the stage I'd have been a theatrical knight by now. Come on, let's get going.'

* * *

The snow was only a light powdering on the ground, barges passed on the river and Notre Dame, floodlit, floated in the night. They reached the Quai de Montebello without seeing a taxi.

Makeev said, 'Here we are, Brosnan's place. He owns the block. It seems his mother left him rather well off.'

'Is that a fact?'

Dillon looked across at the scaffolding and Makeev said, 'Apartment Four, the one on the corner on the first floor.'

'Does he live alone?'

'Not married. Has a woman friend, Anne-Marie Audin . . .'

'The war photographer? I saw her once back in seventy-one in Belfast. Brosnan and Liam Devlin, my boss at the time, were giving her a privileged look at the IRA.'

'Did you meet her?'

'Not personally. Do they live together?'

'Apparently not.' A taxi came out of a side turning and moved towards them and Makeev raised an arm. 'We'll speak tomorrow.'

The taxi drove off and Dillon was about to turn away when Brosnan came round the corner. Dillon recognised him instantly.

'Now then, Martin, you old bastard,' he said softly.

Brosnan went up the steps and inside. Dillon turned, smiling, and walked away, whistling to himself softly.

At his flat in Cavendish Square, Ferguson was just getting ready to go to bed when the phone rang. Hernu said, 'Bad news. He's knocked off the Jobert brothers.'

'Dear me,' Ferguson said. 'He doesn't mess about, does he?'

75

'I've been to see Brosnan to ask him to come in with us on this. I'm afraid he's refused. Offered to give us his advice and so on, but he won't become actively involved.'

'Nonsense,' Ferguson said. 'We can't have that. When the ship is sinking it's all hands to the pumps and this ship is sinking very fast indeed.'

'What do you suggest?'

'I think it might be an idea if I came over to see him. I'm not sure of the time. I've things to arrange. Possibly this afternoon. We'll let you know.'

'Excellent. I couldn't be more pleased.'

Ferguson sat there thinking about it for a while and then he phoned Mary Tanner at her flat. 'I suppose like me, you'd hoped for a relatively quiet night after your early rise this morning?' he said.

'It had crossed my mind. Has something happened?'

He brought her up to date. 'I think it might be an idea to go over tomorrow, have a chat with Hernu then speak to Brosnan. He must be made to realise how serious this is.'

'Do you want me to come?'

'Naturally. I can't even make sense of a menu over there whereas we all know that one of the benefits of your rather expensive education is fluency in the French language. Get in touch with the transport officer at the Ministry and tell him I want the Lear jet standing by tomorrow.'

'I'll handle it. Anything else?'

'No, I'll see you at the office in the morning and don't forget your passport.'

Ferguson put down the phone, got into bed and switched off the light.

*　　*　　*

Back on the barge, Dillon boiled the kettle, then poured a little Bushmills whiskey into a mug, added some lemon juice, sugar and the boiling water and went back into the stateroom, sipping the hot toddy. *My God, Martin Brosnan after all these years*. His mind went back to the old days with the American and Liam Devlin, his old commander. Devlin, the living legend of the IRA. Wild, exciting days, taking on the might of the British Army, face to face. Nothing would ever be the same as that.

There was a stack of London newspapers on the table. He'd bought them all at the Gare de Lyon newsstand earlier. There was the *Daily Mail*, the *Express*, *The Times*, and the *Telegraph*. It was the political sections that interested him most and all the stories were similar. The Gulf crisis, the air strikes on Baghdad, speculation on when the land war would start. And photos, of course. Prime Minister John Major outside Number Ten Downing Street. The British press was wonderful. There were discussions about security, speculation as to possible Arab terrorist attacks and articles that even included maps and street plans of the immediate area around Downing Street. And more photos of the Prime Minister and cabinet ministers arriving for the daily meetings of the War Cabinet. London, that was where the action was, no doubt about it. He put the papers away neatly, finished his toddy and went to bed.

One of the first things Ferguson did on reaching his office was to dictate a further brief report to the Prime Minister bringing him up to date and informing him of the Paris trip. Mary took the draft along to the copy room. The duty clerk just coming to the end of the night shift was a woman, a Mrs Alice Johnson, a war widow whose husband had been killed in the Falklands. She got on with the typing of the report instantly, had just finished putting it through the copier when Gordon Brown entered. He was on a split shift. Three hours from ten until one and six until ten in the evening. He put his briefcase down and took off his jacket.

'You go whenever you like, Alice. Anything special?'

'Just this report for Captain Tanner. It's a Number Ten job. I said I'd take it along.'

'I'll take it for you,' Brown said. 'You get going.'

She passed him both copies of the report and started to clear her desk. No chance to make an extra copy, but at least he could read it which he did as he went along the corridor to Mary Tanner's office. She was sitting at her desk when he went in.

'That report you wanted, Captain Tanner. Shall I arrange a messenger?'

'No thanks, Gordon. I'll see to it.'

'Anything else, Captain?'

'No, I'm just clearing the desk. Brigadier Ferguson and I are going to Paris.' She glanced at her watch. 'I'll have to get moving. We're due out of Gatwick at eleven.'

'Well, I hope you enjoy yourself.'

When he went back to the copy room Alice Johnson was still there. 'I say, Alice,' he said, 'would you mind hanging on for a little while? Only something's come up. I'll make it up to you.'

'That's all right,' she said. 'You get off.'

He put on his coat, hurried downstairs to the canteen and went into one of the public telephone booths. Tania Novikova was only at the flat because of the lateness of the hour when she had left the Embassy the previous night.

'I've told you not to ring me here. I'll ring you,' she told him.

'I must see you. I'm free at one.'

'Impossible.'

'I've seen another report. The same business.'

'I see. Have you got a copy?'

'No, that wasn't possible, but I've read it.'

'What did it say?'

'I'll tell you at lunchtime.'

She realised then that control on her part, severe control, was necessary. Her voice was cold and hard when she said, 'Don't waste my time, Gordon, I'm busy. I think I'd better bring this conversation to an end. I may give you a ring sometime, but then I may not.'

He panicked instantly. 'No, let me tell you. There wasn't much. Just that the two French criminals involved had been murdered, they presumed by the man Dillon. Oh, and Brigadier Ferguson and Captain Tanner are flying over to Paris in the Lear jet at noon.'

'Why?'

'They're hoping to persuade this man Martin Brosnan to help them.'

'Good,' she said. 'You've done well, Gordon. I'll see you tonight at your flat. Six o'clock and bring your work schedule for the next couple of weeks.' She rang off.

Brown went upstairs, full of elation.

Ferguson and Mary Tanner had an excellent flight and touched down at Charles de Gaulle Airport just after one. By two o'clock they were being ushered into Hernu's office at DGSE headquarters in Boulevard Mortier.

He embraced Ferguson briefly. 'Charles, you old rogue, it's far too long.'

'Now then, none of your funny French ways,' Ferguson told him. 'You'll be kissing me on both cheeks next. Mary Tanner, my aide.'

She was wearing a rather nice Armani trouser suit of dark brown and a pair of exquisite ankle boots by Manolo Blahnik, diamond stud earrings and a small gold Rolex divers' watch completed the picture. For a girl who was not supposed to be particularly pretty, she looked stunning. Hernu, who knew class when he saw it, kissed her hand. 'Captain Tanner, your reputation precedes you.'

'Only in the nicest way, I hope,' she replied in fluent French.

'Good,' Ferguson said. 'So now we've got all that stuff over, let's get down to brass tacks. What about Brosnan?'

'I have spoken to him this morning and he's agreed to see us at his apartment at three. Time for a late lunch. We have excellent canteen facilities here. Everyone mixes in from the Director downwards.' He opened the door. 'Just follow me. It may not be quite the best food in Paris, but it's certainly the cheapest.'

In the stateroom at the barge, Dillon was pouring a glass of Krug and studying a large-scale map of London. Around him, pinned to the mahogany walls, were articles and reports from all the newspapers specifically referring to affairs at Number Ten, the Gulf War and how well John Major was doing. There were photos of the youngest Prime Minister of the century, several of them. In fact, the eyes seemed to follow him about. It was as if Major was watching him.

'And I've got my eye on you, too, fella,' Dillon said softly.

The things that intrigued him were the constant daily meetings of the British War Cabinet at Number Ten. All those bastards, all together in the same spot. What a target. Brighton all over again and that affair had come close to taking out the entire British Government. But Number Ten as a target? That didn't seem possible. Fortress Thatcher it had been dubbed by some after that redoubtable lady's security improvements. There were footsteps on the deck overhead. He opened a drawer in the table casually revealing a Smith & Wesson .38 revolver, closed it again as Makeev came in.

'I could have telephoned, but I thought I'd speak to you personally,' the Russian said.

'What now?'

'I've brought you some photos we've had taken of Brosnan as he is now. Oh, and that's the girlfriend, Anne-Marie Audin.'

'Good. Anything else?'

'I've heard from Tania Novikova again. It seems Brigadier Ferguson and his aide, a Captain Mary Tanner, have flown over. They were due out of Gatwick at eleven.' He glanced at his watch. 'I'd say they'll be with Hernu right now.'

'To what end?'

'The real purpose of the trip is to see Brosnan. Try and persuade him to help actively in the search for you.'

'Really?' Dillon smiled coldly. 'Martin's becoming a serious inconvenience. I might have to do something about that.'

Makeev nodded at the clippings on the walls. 'Your own private gallery?'

81

'I'm just getting to know the man,' Dillon said. 'Do you want a drink?'

'No thanks.' Suddenly Makeev felt uncomfortable. 'I've things to do. I'll be in touch.'

He went up the companionway. Dillon poured himself a little more champagne, sipped a little then stopped, walked into the kitchen and poured the whole bottle down the sink. Conspicuous waste, but he felt like it. He went back into the stateroom, lit a cigarette and looked at the clippings again, but all he could think about was Martin Brosnan. He picked up the photos Makeev had brought and pinned them up beside the clippings.

Anne-Marie was in the kitchen at the Quai de Montebello, Brosnan going over a lecture at the table, when the doorbell rang. She hurried out, wiping her hands on a cloth.

'That will be them,' she said. 'I'll get it. Now don't forget your promise.'

She touched the back of his neck briefly and went out. There was a sound of voices in the hall and she returned with Ferguson, Hernu and Mary Tanner.

'I'll make some coffee,' Anne-Marie said and went into the kitchen.

'My dear Martin.' Ferguson held out his hand. 'It's been too long.'

'Amazing,' Brosnan said. 'We only ever meet when you want something.'

'Someone you haven't met, my aide, Captain Mary Tanner.'

Brosnan looked her over quickly, the small, dark girl with the scar on the left cheek, and liked what he saw.

'Couldn't you find a better class of work than what this old sod has to offer?' he demanded.

Odd that she should feel slightly breathless faced with this forty-five-year-old man with the ridiculously long hair and the face that had seen rather too much of the worst of life.

'There's a recession on. You have to take what's going these days,' she said, her hand light in his.

'Right. We've had the cabaret act so let's get down to business,' Ferguson said. Hernu went to the window, Ferguson and Mary took the sofa opposite Brosnan.

'Max tells me he spoke to you last night after the murder of the Jobert brothers?'

Anne-Marie came in with coffee on a tray. Brosnan said, 'That's right.'

'He tells me you've refused to help us?'

'That's putting it a bit strongly. What I said was that I'd do anything I could except become actively involved myself and if you've come to attempt to change my mind, you're wasting your time.'

Anne-Marie poured coffee. Ferguson said, 'You agree with him, Miss Audin?'

'Martin slipped out of that life a long time ago, Brigadier,' she said carefully. 'I would not care to see him step back in for whatever reason.'

'But surely you can see that a man like Dillon must be stopped?'

'Then others must do the stopping. Why Martin, for God's sake?' She was distressed now and angry. 'It's your job, people like you. This sort of thing is how you make your living.'

Max Hernu came across and picked up a cup of coffee.

'But Professor Brosnan is in a special position as regards this business, you must see that, mademoiselle. He knew Dillon intimately, worked with him for years. He could be of great help to us.'

'I don't want to see him with a gun in his hand,' she said, 'and that's what it would come to. Once his foot is on that road again, there can only be one end.'

She was very distressed, turned and went through into the kitchen. Mary Tanner went after her and closed the door. Anne-Marie was leaning against the sink, arms folded as if holding herself in, agony on her face.

'They don't see, do they? They don't understand what I mean.'

'I do,' Mary said simply. 'I understand exactly what you mean,' and as Anne-Marie started to sob quietly, went and put her arms around her.

Brosnan opened the French windows and stood on the terrace by the scaffolding taking in lungsful of cold air. Ferguson joined him. 'I'm sorry for the distress we've caused her.'

'No you're not, you only see the end in view. You always did.'

'He's a bad one, Martin.'

'I know,' Brosnan nodded. 'A real can of worms the little bastard has opened this time. I must get a smoke.'

He went inside. Hernu was sitting by the fire. Brosnan found a packet of cigarettes, hesitated, then opened the kitchen door. Anne-Marie and Mary were sitting opposite each other, holding hands across the table.

Mary turned. 'She'll be fine. Just leave us for a while.'

Brosnan went back to the terrace. He lit a cigarette and

leaned against the balustrade. 'She seems quite a lady, that aide of yours. That scar on her left cheek. Shrapnel. What's her story?'

'She was doing a tour of duty as a lieutenant with the Military Police in Londonderry. Some IRA chap was delivering a car bomb when the engine failed. He left it at the kerb and did a runner. Unfortunately it was outside an old folks' home. Mary was driving past in a Land Rover when a civilian alerted her. She got in the car, released the brake and managed to freewheel down the hill on to some waste land. It exploded as she made a run for it.'

'Good God!'

'Yes, I'd agree on that occasion. When she came out of hospital she received a severe reprimand for breaking standing orders and the George Medal for the gallantry of her action. I took her on after that.'

'A lot of still waters there.' Brosnan sighed and tossed his cigarette out into space as Mary Tanner joined them.

'She's gone to lie down in the bedroom.'

'All right,' Brosnan said. 'Let's go back in.' They went and sat down again and he lit another cigarette. 'Let's get this over with. What did you want to say?'

Ferguson turned to Mary. 'Your turn, my dear.'

'I've been through the files, checked out everything the computer can tell us.' She opened her brown handbag and took out a photo. 'The only likeness of Dillon we can find. It's from a group photo taken at RADA twenty years ago. We had an expert in the department blow it up.'

There was a lack of definition, the texture grainy and the face was totally anonymous. Just another young boy.

Brosnan gave it back. 'Useless. I didn't even recognise him myself.'

'Oh, it's him all right. The man on his right became quite successful on television. He's dead now.'

'Not through Dillon?'

'Oh, no, stomach cancer, but he was approached by one of our people back in nineteen eighty-one and confirmed that it was Dillon standing next to him in the photo.'

'The only likeness we have,' Ferguson said. 'And no bloody use at all.'

'Did you know that he took a pilot's licence and a commercial one at that?' Mary said.

'No, I never knew that,' Brosnan said.

'According to one of our informants, he did it in the Lebanon some years ago.'

'Why were your people on his case in eighty-one?' Brosnan asked.

'Yes, well that's interesting,' she told him. 'You told Colonel Hernu that he'd quarrelled with the IRA, had dropped out and joined the international terrorist circuit.'

'That's right.'

'It seems they took him back in nineteen eighty-one. They were having trouble with their active service units in England. Too many arrests, that kind of thing. Through an informer in Ulster we heard that he was operating in London for a time. There were at least three or four incidents attributed to him. Two car bombs and the murder of a police informant in Ulster who'd been relocated with his family in Maida Vale.'

'And we didn't come within spitting distance of catching him,' Ferguson said.

'Well, you wouldn't,' Brosnan told him. 'Let me go over

it again. He's an actor of genius. He really can change before your eyes, just by use of body language. You'd have to see it to believe it. Imagine what he can do with make-up, hair colouring changes. He's only five feet five, remember. I've seen him dress as a woman and fool soldiers on foot patrol in Belfast.'

Mary Tanner was leaning forward intently. 'Go on,' she said softly.

'You want to know another reason why you've never caught him? He works out a series of aliases. Changes hair colour, uses whatever tricks of make-up are necessary, then takes his photo. That's what goes on his false passport or identity papers. He keeps a collection, then when he needs to move, makes himself into the man on the photo.'

'Ingenious,' Hernu said.

'Exactly, so no hope of any help from television or newspaper publicity of the have-you-seen-this-man type. Wherever he goes, he slips under the surface. If he was working in London and needed anything at all, help, weapons, whatever, he'd simply pretend to be an ordinary criminal and use the underworld.'

'You mean he wouldn't go near any kind of IRA contact at all?' Mary said.

'I doubt it. Maybe someone who'd been in very deep cover for years, someone he could really trust and people like that are thin on the ground.'

'There is a point in all this which no one has touched on,' Hernu said. 'Who is he working for?'

'Well it certainly isn't the IRA,' Mary said. 'We did an instant computer check and we have links with both the RUC computer and British Army intelligence at Lisburn. Not a smell from anyone about the attempt on Mrs Thatcher.'

'Oh, I believe that,' Brosnan said, 'although you can never be sure.'

'There are the Iraqis, of course,' Ferguson said. 'Saddam would dearly love to blow everyone up at the moment.'

'True, but don't forget Hizbollah, PLO, Wrath of Allah and a few others in between. He's worked for them all,' Brosnan reminded him.

'Yes,' Ferguson said, 'and checking our sources through that lot would take time and I don't think we've got it.'

'You think he'll try again?' Mary asked.

'Nothing concrete, my dear, but I've been in this business a lifetime. I always go by my instincts and this time my instincts tell me there's more to it.'

'Well, I can't help you there. I've done all I can.' Brosnan stood up.

'All you're prepared to, you mean?' Ferguson said.

They moved into the hall and Brosnan opened the door. 'I suppose you'll be going back to London?'

'Oh, I don't know. I thought we might stay over and sample the delights of Paris. I haven't stayed at the Ritz since the refurbishment.'

Mary Tanner said, 'That will give the expenses a bashing.' She held out her hand. 'Goodbye, Professor Brosnan, it was nice to be able to put a face to the name.'

'And you,' he said. 'Colonel,' he nodded to Hernu and closed the door.

When he went into the drawing room, Anne-Marie came in from the bedroom. Her face was drawn and pale. 'Did you come to any decision?' she asked.

'I gave you my word. I've helped them all I can. Now they've gone and that's an end to it.'

She opened the table drawer. Inside there was an assortment of pens, envelopes, writing paper, stamps. There was also a Browning High Power 9-mm pistol, one of the most deadly handguns in the world, preferred by the SAS above all others.

She didn't say a word, simply closed the drawer and looked at him calmly. 'I'll make some coffee,' she said and went into the kitchen.

In the limousine Hernu said, 'You've lost him. He won't do any more.'

'I wouldn't be too sure of that. We'll discuss it over dinner at the Ritz later. You'll join us, I hope? Eight o'clock all right?'

'Delighted,' Hernu said. 'Group Four must be rather more generous with its expenses than my own poor department.'

'Oh, it's all on dear Mary here,' Ferguson said. 'Flashed this wonderful piece of plastic at me the other day which American Express had sent her. The Platinum Card. Can you believe that, Colonel?'

'Damn you!' Mary said.

Hernu lay back and laughed helplessly.

Tania Novikova came out of the bathroom of Gordon Brown's Camden flat combing her hair. He pulled on a dressing-gown.

'You've got to go?' he said.

'I must. Come into the living room.' She pulled on her coat and turned to face him. 'No more coming to the Bayswater flat, no more telephones. The work schedule you showed me. All split shifts for the next month. Why?'

'They're not popular, especially for people with families. That isn't a problem for me, so I agreed to do it for the moment. And it pays more.'

'So, you usually finish at one o'clock and start again at six in the evening?'

'Yes.'

'You have an answering machine, the kind where you can phone home and get your messages?'

'Yes.'

'Good. We can keep in touch that way.'

She started for the door and he caught her arm. 'But when will I see you?'

'Difficult at the moment, Gordon, we must be careful. If you've nothing better to do, always come home between shifts. I'll do what I can.'

He kissed her hungrily. 'Darling.'

She pushed him away. 'I must go now, Gordon.'

She opened the door, went downstairs and let herself out of the street entrance. It was still very cold and she pulled up her collar.

'My God, the things I do for Mother Russia,' she said, went down to the corner and hailed a cab.

5

It was colder than ever in the evening, a front from Siberia sweeping across Europe, too cold for snow even. In the apartment, just before seven, Brosnan put some more logs on the fire.

Anne-Marie, lying full length on the sofa, stirred and sat up. 'So we stay in to eat?'

'I think so,' he said. 'A vile night.'

'Good. I'll see what I can do in the kitchen.'

He put on the television news programme. More air strikes against Baghdad, but still no sign of a land war. He switched the set off and Anne-Marie emerged from the kitchen and picked up her coat from the chair where she had left it.

'Your fridge, as usual, is almost empty. Unless you wish me to concoct a meal based on some rather stale cheese, one egg, and half a carton of milk, I'll have to go round the corner to the delicatessen.'

'I'll come with you.'

'Nonsense,' she said. 'Why should we both suffer? I'll see you soon.'

She blew him a kiss and went out. Brosnan went and opened the French windows. He stood on the terrace, shivering and lit a cigarette, watching for her. A moment later, she emerged from the front door and started along the pavement.

'Goodbye, my love,' he called dramatically. 'Parting is such sweet sorrow.'

'Idiot!' she called back. 'Go back in before you catch pneumonia.' She moved away, careful on the frozen pavement, and disappeared round the corner.

At that moment, the phone rang. Brosnan turned and hurried in, leaving the French windows open.

Dillon had an early meal at a small café he often frequented. He was on foot and his route back to the barge took him past Brosnan's apartment block. He paused on the other side of the road, cold in spite of the reefer coat and the knitted cap pulled down over his ears. He stood there, swinging his arms vigorously, looking up at the lighted windows of the apartment.

When Anne-Marie came out of the entrance, he recognised her instantly and stepped back into the shadows. The street was silent, no traffic movement at all and when Brosnan leaned over the balustrade and called down to her, Dillon heard every word he said. It gave him a totally false impression. That she was leaving for the evening. As she disappeared round the corner, he crossed the road quickly. He checked the Walther in his waistband at the rear, had a quick glance each way to see that no one was about, then started to climb the scaffolding.

* * *

It was Mary Tanner on the phone. 'Brigadier Ferguson wondered whether we could see you again in the morning before going back?'

'It won't do you any good,' Brosnan told her.

'Is that a yes or a no?'

'All right,' he said reluctantly. 'If you must.'

'I understand,' she said, 'I really do. Has Anne-Marie recovered?'

'A tough lady, that one,' he said. 'She's covered more wars than we've had hot dinners. That's why I've always found her attitude about such things where I'm concerned strange.'

'Oh, dear,' she said. 'You men can really be incredibly stupid on occasions. She loves you, Professor, it's as simple as that. I'll see you in the morning.'

Brosnan put the phone down. There was a draught of cold air, the fire flared up. He turned and found Sean Dillon standing in the open French windows, the Walther in his left hand.

'God bless all here,' he said.

The delicatessen in the side street, as with so many such places these days, was run by an Indian, a Mr Patel. He was most assiduous where Anne-Marie was concerned, carried the basket for her as they went round the shelves. Delicious French bread sticks, milk, eggs, Brie cheese, a beautiful quiche.

'Baked by my wife with her own hands,' Mr Patel assured her. 'Two minutes in the microwave and a perfect meal.'

She laughed. 'Then all we need is a very large tin of caviar and some smoked salmon to complement it.'

He packed the things carefully for her. 'I'll put them on Professor Brosnan's account as usual.'

'Thank you,' she said.

He opened the door for her. 'A pleasure, mademoiselle.'

She started back along the frosty pavement feeling suddenly unaccountably cheerful.

'Jesus, Martin, and the years have been good to you,' Dillon pulled the glove off his right hand with his teeth and found a pack of cigarettes in his pocket. Brosnan, a yard from the table drawer and the Browning High Power, made a cautious move. 'Naughty.' Dillon gestured with the Walther. 'Sit on the arm of the sofa and put your hands behind your head.'

Brosnan did as he was told. 'You're enjoying yourself, Sean.'

'I am so. How's that old sod Liam Devlin these days?'

'Alive and well. Still in Kilrea outside Dublin, but then you know that.'

'And that's a fact.'

'The job at Valenton, Mrs Thatcher,' Brosnan said. 'Very sloppy, Sean. I mean, to go with a couple of bums like the Joberts. You really must be losing your touch.'

'You think so?'

'Presumably it was a big pay day?'

'Very big,' Dillon said.

'I hope you got your money in advance.'

'Very funny.' Dillon was beginning to get annoyed.

'One thing does intrigue me,' Brosnan said. 'What you want with me after all these years?'

'Oh, I know all about you,' Dillon said. 'How they're pumping you for information about me. Hernu, the Action

Service colonel, that old bastard Ferguson and this girl sidekick of his, this Captain Tanner. Nothing I don't know. I've got the right friends, you see, Martin, the kind of people who can access anything.'

'Really, and were they happy when you failed with Mrs Thatcher?'

'Just a try-out, that, just a perhaps. I've promised them an alternative target. You know how this game works.'

'I certainly do and one thing I do know is that the IRA don't pay for hits. Never have.'

'Who said I was working for the IRA?' Dillon grinned. 'Plenty of other people with enough reason to hit the Brits these days.'

Brosnan saw it then, or thought he did. 'Baghdad?'

'Sorry, Martin, you can go to your maker puzzling over that one for all eternity.'

Brosnan said, 'Just indulge me. A big hit for Saddam. I mean, the war stinks. He needs something badly.'

'Christ, you always did run on.'

'President Bush stays back in Washington so that leaves the Brits. You fail on the best-known woman in the world, so what's next? The Prime Minister?'

'Where you're going it doesn't matter, son.'

'But I'm right, aren't I?'

'Damn you, Brosnan, you always were the clever bastard!' Dillon exploded angrily.

'You'll never get away with it,' Brosnan said.

'You think so? I'll just have to prove you wrong then.'

'As I said, you must be losing your touch, Sean. This bungled attempt to get Mrs Thatcher. Reminds me of a job dear old Frank Barry pulled back in seventy-nine when he tried to hit the British Foreign Secretary, Lord Carrington, when he was passing through St Etienne. I'm rather surprised you used the same ground plan, but then you always did think Barry was special, didn't you?'

'He was the best.'

'And at the end of things, very dead,' Brosnan said.

'Yes, well whoever got him must have given it to him in the back,' Dillon said.

'Not true,' Brosnan told him. 'We were face to face as I recall.'

'You killed Frank Barry?' Dillon whispered.

'Well somebody had to,' Brosnan said. 'It's what usually happens to mad dogs. I was working for Ferguson, by the way.'

'You bastard.' Dillon raised the Walther, took careful aim and the door opened and Anne-Marie walked in with the shopping bags.

Dillon swung towards her. Brosnan called, 'Look out!' and went down and Dillon fired twice at the sofa.

Anne-Marie screamed, not in terror, but in fury, dropped her bags and rushed at him. Dillon tried to fend her off, staggered back through the French windows. Inside, Brosnan crawled towards the table and reached for the drawer. Anne-Marie scratched at Dillon's face. He cursed, pushing her away from him. She fell against the balustrade and went over backwards.

Brosnan had the drawer open now, knocked the lamp on the table sideways, plunging the room into darkness and reached for the Browning. Dillon fired three times very fast and ducked for the door. Brosnan fired twice, too late. The door banged. He got to his feet, ran to the terrace and looked over. Anne-Marie lay on the pavement below. He turned and ran through the drawing room into the hall, got the door open and went downstairs two at a time. It was snowing when he went out on the steps. Of Dillon there was no sign, but the night porter was kneeling beside Anne-Marie.

He looked up. 'There was a man, Professor, with a gun. He ran across the road.'

'Never mind.' Brosnan sat down and cradled her in his arms. 'An ambulance and hurry.'

The snow was falling quite fast now. He held her close and waited.

Ferguson, Mary and Max Hernu were having a thoroughly enjoyable time in the magnificent dining room at the Ritz. They were already on their second bottle of Louis Roederer Crystal champagne and the Brigadier was in excellent form.

'Who was it who said that when a man tires of champagne he's tired of life?' he demanded.

'He must certainly have been a Frenchman,' Hernu told him.

'Very probably, but I think the time has come when we should toast the provider of this feast.' He raised his glass. 'To you, Mary, my love.'

She was about to respond when she saw in the mirror on the wall Inspector Savary at the entrance speaking to the head waiter. 'I think you're being paged, Colonel,' she told Hernu.

He glanced round. 'What's happened now?' He got up, threaded his way through the tables and approached Savary. They talked for a few moments, glancing towards the table.

Mary said, 'I don't know about you, sir, but I get a bad feeling.'

Before he could reply, Hernu came back to them, his face grave. 'I'm afraid I've got some rather ugly news.'

'Dillon?' Ferguson asked.

'He paid a call on Brosnan a short while ago.'

'What happened?' Ferguson demanded. 'Is Brosnan all right?'

'Oh, yes. There was some gunplay. Dillon got away.' He sighed heavily. 'But Mademoiselle Audin is at the Hôpital St-Louis. From what Savary tells me, it doesn't look good.'

Brosnan was in the waiting room on the second floor when they arrived, pacing up and down smoking a cigarette. His eyes were wild, such a rage there as Mary Tanner had never seen.

She was the first to reach him. 'I'm so sorry.'

Ferguson said, 'What happened?'

Briefly, coldly, Brosnan told them. As he finished, a tall, greying man in surgeon's robes came in. Brosnan turned to him quickly. 'How is she, Henri?' He said to the others, 'Professor Henri Dubois, a colleague of mine at the Sorbonne.'

'Not good, my friend,' Dubois told him. 'The injuries to the left leg and spine are bad enough, but even more worrying is the skull fracture. They're just preparing her for surgery now. I'll operate straight away.'

He went out. Hernu put an arm around Brosnan's shoulders. 'Let's go and get some coffee, my friend. I think it's going to be a long night.'

'But I only drink tea,' Brosnan said, his face bone white, his eyes dark. 'Never could stomach coffee. Isn't that the funniest thing you ever heard?'

*　　*　　*

There was a small café for visitors on the ground floor. Not many customers at that time of night. Savary had gone off to handle the police side of the business, the others sat at a table in the corner.

Ferguson said, 'I know you've got other things on your mind, but is there anything you can tell us? Anything he said to you?'

'Oh yes – plenty. He's working for somebody and definitely not the IRA. He's being paid for this one and from the way he boasted, it's big money.'

'Any idea who?'

'When I suggested Saddam Hussein he got angry. My guess is you wouldn't have to look much further. An interesting point. He knew about all of you.'

'All of us?' Hernu said. 'You're sure?'

'Oh, yes, he boasted about that.' He turned to Ferguson. 'Even knew about you and Captain Tanner being in town to pump me for information, that's how he put it. He said he had the right friends.' He frowned, trying to remember the phrase exactly. 'The kind of people who can access anything.'

'Did he indeed?' Ferguson glanced at Hernu. 'Rather worrying, that.'

'And you've got another problem. He spoke of the Thatcher affair as being just a try-out, that he had an alternative target.'

'Go on,' Ferguson said.

'I managed to get him to lose his temper by needling him about what a botch-up the Valenton thing was. I think you'll find he intends to have a crack at the British Prime Minister.'

Mary said, 'Are you certain?'

'Oh, yes.' He nodded. 'I baited him about that, told him he'd never get away with it. He lost his temper. Said he'd just have to prove me wrong.'

Ferguson looked at Hernu and sighed. 'So now we know. I'd better go along to the Embassy and alert all our people in London.'

'I'll do the same here,' Hernu said. 'After all, he has to leave the country sometime. We'll alert all airports and ferries. The usual thing, but discreetly, of course.'

They got up and Brosnan said, 'You're wasting your time. You won't get him, not in any usual way. You don't even know what you're looking for.'

'Perhaps, Martin,' Ferguson said. 'But we'll just have to do our best, won't we?'

Mary Tanner followed them to the door. 'Look, if you don't need me, Brigadier, I'd like to stay.'

'Of course, my dear. I'll see you later.'

She went to the counter and got two cups of tea. 'The French are wonderful,' she said. 'They always think we're crazy to want milk in our tea.'

'Takes all sorts,' he said and offered her a cigarette. 'Ferguson told me how you got that scar.'

'Souvenir of old Ireland,' she shrugged.

He was desperately trying to think of something to say. 'What about your family? Do they live in London?'

'My father was a Professor of Surgery at Oxford. He died some time ago. Cancer. My mother's still alive. Has an estate in Herefordshire.'

'Brothers and sisters?'

'I had one brother. Ten years older than me. He was shot dead in Belfast in nineteen-eighty. Sniper got him from the Divis Flats. He was a Marine Commando captain.'

'I'm sorry.'

'A long time ago.'·

'It can't make you particularly well disposed towards a man like me.'

'Ferguson explained to me how you became involved with the IRA after Viet Nam.'

'Just another bloody Yank sticking his nose in, is that what you think?' he sighed. 'It seemed the right thing to do at the time, it really did and don't let's pretend. I was up to my neck in it for five long and bloody years.'

'And how do you see it now?'

'Ireland?' he laughed harshly. 'The way I feel I'd see it sink into the sea with pleasure.' He got up. 'Come on, let's stretch our legs,' and he led the way out.

Dillon was in the kitchen in the barge heating the kettle when the phone rang. Makeev said, 'She's in the Hôpital St-Louis. We've had to be discreet in our enquiries, but from what my informant can ascertain, she's on the critical list.'

'Sod it,' Dillon said. 'If only she'd kept her hands to herself.'

'This could cause a devil of a fuss. I'd better come and see you.'

'I'll be here.'

Dillon poured hot water into a basin then he went into the bathroom. First he took off his shirt, then he got a briefcase from the cupboard under the sink. It was exactly as Brosnan had forecast. Inside he had a range of passports, all of himself suitably disguised. There was also a first-class make-up kit.

Over the years he had travelled backwards and forwards

to England many times, frequently through Jersey in the Channel Islands. Jersey was British soil. Once there, a British citizen didn't need a passport for the flight to the English mainland. So, a French tourist holidaying in Jersey. He selected a passport in the name of Henri Jacaud, a car salesman from Rennes.

To go with it, he found a Jersey driving licence in the name of Peter Hilton with an address in the Island's main town of St Helier. Jersey driving licences, unlike the usual British mainland variety, carry a photo. It was always useful to have positive identification on you, he'd learned that years ago. Nothing better than for people to be able to check the face with a photo and the photos on the driving licence and on the French passport were identical. That was the whole point.

He dissolved some black hair dye into the warm water and started to brush it into his fair hair. Amazing what a difference it made, just changing the hair colour. He blow-dried it and brilliantined it back in place, then he selected from a range in his case, a pair of horn-rimmed spectacles, slightly tinted. He closed his eyes, thinking about the role and when he opened them again, Henri Jacaud stared out of the mirror. It was quite extraordinary. He closed the case, put it back in the cupboard, pulled on his shirt and went into the stateroom carrying the passport and the driving licence.

At that precise moment Makeev came down the companionway. 'Good God!' he said. 'For a moment I thought it was someone else.'

'But it is,' Dillon said. 'Henri Jacaud, car salesman from Rennes on his way to Jersey for a winter break. Hydrofoil from St Malo.' He held up the driving licence.

'Who is also Jersey resident Peter Hilton, accountant in St Helier.'

'You don't need a passport to get to London?'

'Not if you're a Jersey resident, it's British territory. The driving licence just puts a face to me. Always makes people feel happier. Makes them feel they know who you are, even the police.'

'What happened tonight, Sean? What really happened?'

'I decided the time had come to take care of Brosnan. Come on, Josef, he knows me too damned well. Knows me in a way no one else does and that could be dangerous.'

'I can see that. A clever one, the Professor.'

'There's more to it than that, Josef. He understands how I make my moves, how I think. He's the same kind of animal as I am. We inhabited the same world and people don't change. No matter how much he thinks he has he's still the same underneath, the same man who was the most feared enforcer the IRA had in the old days.'

'So you decided to eliminate him?'

'It was an impulse. I was passing his place, saw the woman leaving. He called to her. The way it sounded I thought she was gone for the night so I took a chance and went up the scaffolding.'

'What happened?'

'Oh, I had the drop on him.'

'But didn't kill him?'

Dillon laughed, went out to the kitchen and returned with a bottle of Krug and two glasses. As he uncorked it he said, 'Come on, Josef, face to face after all those years. There were things to be said.'

'You didn't tell him who you were working for?'

'Of course not,' Dillon lied cheerfully and poured the champagne. 'What do you take me for?'

He toasted Makeev who said, 'I mean, if he knew you had an alternative target, that you intended to go for Major . . .' He shrugged. 'That would mean that Ferguson would know. It would render your task in London impossible. Aroun, I'm sure, would want to abort the whole business.'

'Well he doesn't know.' Dillon drank some more champagne. 'So Aroun can rest easy. After all, I want that second million. I checked with Zurich, by the way. The first million has been deposited.'

Makeev shifted uncomfortably. 'Of course. So, when do you intend to leave?'

'Tomorrow or the next day. I'll see. Meanwhile something you can organise for me. This Tania Novikova in London. I'll need her help.'

'No problem.'

'First, my father had a second cousin, a Belfast man living in London called Danny Fahy.'

'IRA?'

'Yes, but not active. A deep-cover man. Brilliant with his hands. Worked in light engineering. Could turn his hand to anything. I used him in nineteen eighty-one when I was doing a few jobs for the organisation in London. In those days he lived at number ten Tithe Street in Kilburn. I want Novikova to trace him.'

'Anything else?'

'Yes, I'll need somewhere to stay. She can organise that for me too. She doesn't live in the Embassy, I suppose?'

'No, she has a flat off the Bayswater Road.'

'I wouldn't want to stay there, not on a regular basis.

She could be under surveillance. Special Branch at Scotland Yard have a habit of doing that with employees of the Soviet Embassy, isn't that so?'

'Oh, it's not like the old days,' Makeev smiled. 'Thanks to that fool Gorbachev, we're all supposed to be friends these days.'

'I'd still prefer to stay somewhere else. I'll contact her at her flat, no more than that.'

'There is one problem,' Makeev said. 'As regards hardware, explosives, weapons, anything like that you might need, I'm afraid she won't be able to help you there. A handgun perhaps, but no more. As I mentioned when I first told you about her, her boss, Colonel Yuri Gatov, the commander of KGB station in London, is a Gorbachev man, and very well disposed to our British friends.'

'That's all right,' Dillon said, 'I have my own contacts for that kind of thing, but I will need more working capital. If I am checked going through customs on the Jersey to London flight, I couldn't afford to be caught with large sums of money in my briefcase.'

'I'm sure Aroun can fix that for you.'

'That's all right then. I'd like to see him again before I go. Tomorrow morning, I think. Arrange that, will you?'

'All right.' Makeev fastened his coat. 'I'll keep you posted on the situation at the hospital.' He reached the bottom of the companionway and turned. 'There is one thing. Say you managed to pull this thing off. It would lead to the most ferocious manhunt. How would you intend to get out of England?'

Dillon smiled. 'That's exactly what I'm going to give some thought to now. I'll see you in the morning.'

Makeev went up the companionway. Dillon poured

another glass of Krug, lit a cigarette and sat at the table, looking at the clippings on the walls. He reached for the pile of newspapers and sorted through them and finally found what he wanted. An old copy of the magazine *Paris Match* from the previous year. Michael Aroun was featured on the front cover. Inside was a seven-page feature about his lifestyle and habits. Dillon lit a cigarette and started going through it.

It was one o'clock in the morning and Mary Tanner was sitting alone in the waiting room when Professor Henri Dubois came in. He was very tired, shoulders bowed, sank wearily into a chair and lit a cigarette.

'Where is Martin?' he asked her.

'It seems Anne-Marie's only close relative is her grandfather. Martin is trying to contact him. Do you know him?'

'Who doesn't, mademoiselle? One of the richest and most powerful industrialists in France. Very old. Eighty-eight, I believe. He was once a patient of mine. He had a stroke last year. I don't think Martin will get very far there. He lives on the family estate, Château Vercors. It's about twenty miles outside Paris.'

Brosnan came in, looking incredibly weary, but when he saw Dubois he said eagerly, 'How is she?'

'I won't pretend, my friend. She's not good. Not good at all. I've done everything that I possibly can. Now we wait.'

'Can I see her?'

'Leave it for a while. I'll let you know.'

'You'll stay?'

'Oh, yes. I'll grab a couple of hours' sleep on my office couch. How did you get on with Pierre Audin?'

'I didn't. Had to deal with his secretary, Fournier. The old man's confined to a wheelchair now. Doesn't know the time of day.'

Dubois sighed. 'I suspected as much. I'll see you later.'

When he'd gone, Mary said, 'You could do with some sleep yourself.'

He managed a dark smile. 'The way I feel now, I don't think I could ever sleep again. All my fault, in a way.' There was despair on his face.

'How can you say that?'

'Who I am or to put it another way, what I was. If it hadn't been for that, none of this would have happened.'

'You can't talk like that,' she said. 'Life doesn't work like that.'

The phone on the table rang and she answered it, spoke for a few brief moments, then put it down. 'Just Ferguson checking.' She put a hand on his shoulder. 'Come on, lie down on the couch. Just close your eyes. I'll be here. I'll wake you the moment there's word.'

Reluctantly, he lay back and did as he was told and surprisingly did fall into a dark dreamless sleep. Mary Tanner sat there, brooding, listening to his quiet breathing.

It was just after three when Dubois came in. As if sensing his presence, Brosnan came awake with a start and sat up. 'What is it?'

'She's regained consciousness.'

'Can I see her?' Brosnan got up.

'Yes, of course.' As Brosnan made for the door, Dubois put a hand on his arm. 'Martin, it's not good. I think you should prepare for the worst.'

'No,' Brosnan almost choked. 'It's not possible.'

107

He ran along the corridor, opened the door of her room and went in. There was a young nurse sitting beside her. Anne-Marie was very pale, her head so swathed in bandages that she looked like a young nun.

'I'll wait outside, monsieur,' the nurse said and left.

Brosnan sat down. He reached for her hand and Anne-Marie opened her eyes. She stared vacantly at him and then recognition dawned and she smiled.

'Martin, is that you?'

'Who else?' He kissed her hand.

Behind them, the door clicked open slightly as Dubois peered in.

'Your hair. Too long. Ridiculously too long.' She put up a hand to touch it. 'In Viet Nam, in the swamp, when the Viet Cong were going to shoot me. You came out of the reeds like some medieval warrior. Your hair was too long then and you wore a headband.'

She closed her eyes and Brosnan said, 'Rest now, don't try to talk.'

'But I must.' She opened them again. 'Let him go, Martin. Give me your promise. It's not worth it. I don't want you going back to what you were.' She grabbed at his hand with surprising strength. 'Promise me.'

'My word on it,' he said.

She lay back, staring up at the ceiling. 'My lovely wild Irish boy. Always loved you, Martin, no one else.'

Her eyes closed gently, the monitoring machine beside the bed changed its tone. Henri Dubois was in the room in a second. 'Outside, Martin – wait.'

He pushed Brosnan out and closed the door. Mary was standing in the corridor. 'Martin?' she said.

He stared at her vacantly and then the door opened

and Dubois appeared. 'I'm so sorry, my friend. I'm afraid she's gone.'

On the barge, Dillon came awake instantly when the phone rang. Makeev said, 'She's dead, I'm afraid.'

'That's a shame,' Dillon said. 'It was never intended.'

'What now?' Makeev asked.

'I think I'll leave this afternoon. A good idea in the circumstances. What about Aroun?'

'He'll see us at eleven o'clock.'

'Good. Does he know what's happened?'

'No.'

'Let's keep it that way. I'll meet you outside the place just before eleven.'

He replaced the phone, propped himself up against the pillows. Anne-Marie Audin. A pity about that. He'd never gone in for killing women. An informer once in Derry, but she deserved it. An accident this time, but it smacked of bad luck and that made him feel uneasy. He stubbed out his cigarette and tried to go to sleep again.

It was just after ten when Mary Tanner admitted Ferguson and Hernu to Brosnan's apartment. 'How is he?' Ferguson asked.

'He's kept himself busy. Anne-Marie's grandfather is not well so Martin's been making all the necessary funeral arrangements with his secretary.'

'So soon?' Ferguson said.

'Tomorrow, in the family plot at Vercors.'

She led the way in. Brosnan was standing at the window staring out. He turned to meet them, hands in pockets, his face pale and drawn. 'Well?' he demanded.

'Nothing to report,' Hernu told him. 'We've notified all ports and airports, discreetly, of course.' He hesitated. 'We feel it would be better not to go public on this, Professor, Mademoiselle Audin's unfortunate death, I mean.'

Brosnan seemed curiously indifferent. 'You won't get him. London's the place to look and sooner rather than later. Probably on his way now and for London you'll need me.'

'You mean you'll help us? You'll come in on this thing?' Ferguson said.

'Yes.'

Brosnan lit a cigarette, opened the French windows and stood on the terrace. Mary joined him. 'But you can't, Martin, you promised Anne-Marie.'

'I lied,' he said calmly, 'just to make her going easier. There's nothing out there. Only darkness.'

His face was rock hard, the eyes bleak. It was the face of a stranger. 'Oh, my God,' she whispered.

'I'll have him,' Brosnan said. 'If it's the last thing I do on this earth I'll see him dead.'

6

It was just before eleven when Makeev drew up before Michael Aroun's apartment in the Avenue Victor Hugo. His chauffeur drew in beside the kerb and as he switched off the engine, the door opened and Dillon climbed into the rear seat.

'You'd better not be wearing designer shoes,' he said. 'Slush everywhere.'

He smiled and Makeev reached over to close the partition. 'You seem in good form considering the situation.'

'And why shouldn't I be? I just wanted to make sure you hadn't told Aroun about the Audin woman.'

'No, of course not.'

'Good.' Dillon smiled. 'I wouldn't like anything to spoil things. Now let's go and see him.'

Rashid opened the door to them. A maid took their coats. Aroun was waiting in the magnificent drawing room.

'Valenton, Mr Dillon. A considerable disappointment.'

Dillon said, 'Nothing's ever perfect in this life, you

should know that. I promised you an alternative target and I intend to go for it.'

'The British Prime Minister?' Rashid asked.

'That's right.' Dillon nodded. 'I'm leaving for London later today. I thought we'd have a chat before I go.'

Rashid glanced at Aroun who said, 'Of course, Mr Dillon. Now how can we help you?'

'First, I'm going to need operating money again. Thirty thousand dollars. I want you to arrange that from someone in London. Cash, naturally. Colonel Makeev can finalise details.'

'No problem,' Aroun said.

'Secondly, there's the question of how I get the hell out of England after the successful conclusion of the venture.'

'You sound full of confidence, Mr Dillon,' Rashid told him.

'Well, you have to travel hopefully, son,' Dillon said. 'The thing with any major hit, as I've discovered during the years, is not so much achieving it as moving on with a whole skin afterwards. I mean, if I get the British Prime Minister for you, the major problem for me is getting out of England and that's where you come in, Mr Aroun.'

The maid entered with coffee on a tray. Aroun waited while she laid the cups out on a table and poured. As she withdrew he said, 'Please explain.'

'One of my minor talents is flying. I share that with you, I understand. According to an old *Paris Match* article I was reading, you bought an estate in Normandy called Château St Denis about twenty miles south of Cherbourg on the coast?'

'That's correct.'

'The article mentioned how much you loved the place,

how remote and unspoiled it was. A time capsule from the eighteenth century.'

'Exactly what are we getting at here, Mr Dillon?' Rashid demanded.

'It also said it had its own landing strip and that it wasn't unknown for Mr Aroun to fly down there from Paris when he feels like it, piloting his own plane.'

'Quite true,' Aroun said.

'Good. This is how it will go then. When I'm close to, how shall we put it, the final end of things, I'll let you know. You'll fly down to this St Denis place. I'll fly out from England and join you there after the job is done. You can arrange my onwards transportation.'

'But how?' Rashid demanded. 'Where will you find a plane?'

'Plenty of flying clubs, old son, and planes to hire. I'll simply fly off the map. Disappear, put it any way you like. As a pilot yourself you must know that one of the biggest headaches the authorities have is the vast amount of uncontrolled air space. Once I land at St Denis, you can torch the bloody thing up.' He looked from Rashid to Aroun. 'Are we agreed?'

It was Aroun who said, 'Absolutely, and if there is anything else we can do.'

'Makeev will let you know. I'll be going now.' Dillon turned to the door.

Outside, he stood on the pavement beside Makeev's car, the snow falling lightly. 'That's it then. We shan't be seeing each other, not for a while anyway.'

Makeev passed him an envelope. 'Tania's home address and telephone number.' He glanced at his watch. 'I couldn't get her earlier this morning. I left a message to say I wanted to speak to her at noon.'

113

'Fine,' Dillon said. 'I'll speak to you from St Malo before I get the hydrofoil for Jersey, just to make sure everything is all right.'

'I'll drop you off,' Makeev told him.

'No thanks. I feel like the exercise.' Dillon held out his hand. 'To our next merry meeting.'

'Good luck, Sean.'

Dillon smiled. 'Oh, you always need that as well,' and he turned and walked away.

Makeev spoke to Tania on the scrambler at noon. 'I have a friend calling to see you,' he said. 'Possibly late this evening. The one we've spoken of.'

'I'll take care of him, Colonel.'

'You've never handled a more important business transaction,' he said, 'believe me. He'll need alternative accommodation, by the way. Make it convenient to your own place.'

'Of course.'

'And I want you to put a trace out on this man.'

He gave her Danny Fahy's details. When he was finished, she said, 'There should be no problem. Anything else?'

'Yes, he likes Walthers. Take care, my dear, I'll be in touch.'

When Mary Tanner went into the suite at the Ritz, Ferguson was having afternoon tea by the window.

'Ah, there you are,' he said. 'Wondered what was keeping you. We've got to get moving.'

'To where?' she demanded.

'Back to London.'

She took a deep breath. 'Not me, Brigadier, I'm staying.'

114

'Staying?' he said.

'For the funeral at Château Vercors at eleven o'clock tomorrow morning. After all, he's going to do what you want him to. Don't we owe him some support?'

Ferguson put up a hand defensively. 'All right, you've made your point. However, I need to go back to London now. You can stay if you want and follow tomorrow afternoon. I'll arrange for the Lear jet to pick you up, both of you. Will that suffice?'

'I don't see why not.' She smiled brightly and reached for the teapot. 'Another cup, Brigadier?'

Sean Dillon caught the express to Rennes and changed trains for St Malo at three o'clock. There wasn't much tourist traffic, the wrong time of the year for that and the atrocious weather all over Europe had killed whatever there was. There couldn't have been more than twenty passengers on the hydrofoil to Jersey. He disembarked in St Helier just before six o'clock on the Albert Quay and caught a cab to the airport.

He knew he was in trouble before he arrived, for the closer they got, the thicker the fog was. It was an old story in Jersey, but not the end of the world. He confirmed that both evening flights to London were cancelled, went out of the airport building, caught another taxi and told the driver to take him to a convenient hotel.

It was thirty minutes later that he phoned Makeev in Paris. 'Sorry I didn't have a chance to phone from St Malo. The train was late. I might have missed the hydrofoil. Did you contact Novikova?'

'Oh, yes,' Makeev told him. 'Everything is in order. Looking forward to meeting you. Where are you?'

'A place called Hotel L'Horizon in Jersey. There was fog at the airport. I'm hoping to get out in the morning.'

'I'm sure you will. Stay in touch.'

'I'll do that.'

Dillon put down the phone, then he put on his jacket and went downstairs to the bar. He'd heard somewhere that the hotel's grill was a quite exceptional restaurant. After a while he was approached by a handsome, energetic Italian who introduced himself as the head waiter, Augusto. Dillon took a menu from him gratefully, ordered a bottle of Krug and relaxed.

It was at roughly the same time that the doorbell sounded at Brosnan's apartment on the Quai de Montebello. When he opened the door, a large glass of Scotch in one hand, Mary Tanner stood there.

'Hello,' he said. 'This is unexpected.'

She took the glass of Scotch and emptied it into the potted plant that stood by the door. 'That won't do you any good at all.'

'If you say so. What do you want?'

'I thought you'd be alone. I didn't think that was a good idea. Ferguson spoke to you before he left?'

'Yes, he said you were staying over. Suggested we followed him tomorrow afternoon.'

'Yes, well that doesn't take care of tonight. I expect you haven't eaten a thing all day so I suggest we go out for a meal and don't start saying no.'

'I wouldn't dream of it, Captain.' He saluted.

'Don't fool around. There must be somewhere close by that you like.'

'There is indeed. Let me get a coat and I'll be right with you.'

It was a typical little side-street bistro, simple and unpretentious, booths to give privacy and cooking smells from the kitchen that were out of this world. Brosnan ordered champagne.

'Krug?' she said when the bottle came.

'They know me here.'

'Always champagne with you?'

'I was shot in the stomach years ago. It gave me problems. The doctors said no spirits under any circumstances, no red wine. Champagne was okay. Did you notice the name of this place?'

'*La Belle Aurore.*'

'Same as the café in Casablanca. Humphrey Bogart? Ingrid Bergman?' He raised his glass. 'Here's looking at you, kid.'

They sat there in companionable silence for a while and then she said, 'Can we talk business?'

'Why not? What do you have in mind?'

'What happens next? I mean, Dillon just fades into the woodwork, you said that yourself. How on earth do you hope to find him?'

'One weakness,' Brosnan said. 'He won't go near any IRA contacts for fear of betrayal. That leaves him with only one choice. The usual one he makes. The underworld. Anything he needs, weaponry, explosives, even physical help, he'll go to the obvious place and you know where that is?'

'The East End of London?'

'Yes, just about as romantic as Little Italy in New York or the Bronx. The Kray brothers, the nearest thing England ever had to cinema gangsters, the Richardson gang. Do you know much about the East End?'

'I thought all that was history.'

'Not at all. A lot of the big men, the governors as they call them, have gone legitimate to a certain degree, but all the old-fashioned crimes, hold-ups, banks, security vans, are committed by roughly the same group. All family men, who just look upon it as business, but they'll shoot you if you get in the way.'

'How nice.'

'Everyone knows who they are, including the police. It's in that fraternity Dillon will look for help.'

'Forgive me,' she said. 'But that must be rather a close-knit community.'

'You're absolutely right, but as it happens, I've got what you might call the entrée.'

'And how on earth do you have that?'

He poured her another glass of champagne. 'Back in Viet Nam in nineteen sixty-eight, during my wild and foolish youth, I was a paratrooper, Airborne Rangers. I formed part of a Special Forces detachment to operate in Cambodia, entirely illegally, I might add. It was recruited from all branches of the services. People with specialist qualifications. We even had a few Marines and that's how I met Harry Flood.'

'Harry Flood?' she said and frowned. 'For some reason, that name's familiar.'

'Could be. I'll explain. Harry's the same age as me. Born in Brooklyn. His mother died when he was born. He grew up with his father who died when Harry was eighteen.

He joined the Marines for something to do, went to Nam which is where I met him.' He laughed. 'I'll never forget the first time. Up to our necks in a stinking swamp in the Mekong Delta.'

'He sounds quite interesting.'

'Oh, that and more. Silver Star, Navy Cross. In sixty-nine when I was getting out, Harry still had a year of his enlistment to do. They posted him to London. Embassy Guard duty. He was a sergeant then and that's when it happened.'

'What did?'

'He met a girl at the old Lyceum Ballroom one night, a girl called Jean Dark. Just a nice, pretty twenty-year-old in a cotton frock only there was one difference. The Dark family were gangsters, what they call in the East End real villains. Her old man had his own little empire down by the river, was in his own way as famous as the Kray brothers. He died later that year.'

'What happened?' She was totally fascinated.

'Jean's mother tried to take over. Ma Dark everyone called her. There were differences. Rival gangs. That sort of thing. Harry and Jean got married, he took his papers in London, stayed on and just got sucked in. Sorted the rivals out and so on.'

'You mean he became a gangster?'

'Not to put too fine a point on it, yes, but more than that, much more. He became one of the biggest governors in the East End of London.'

'My God, now I remember. He has all those casinos. He's the man doing all that riverside development on the Thames.'

'That's right. Jean died of cancer about five or six

years ago. Her mother died ages before that. He just carried on.'

'Is he British now?'

'No, never gave up his American nationality. The authorities could never toss him out because he has no criminal record. Never served a single day in gaol.'

'And he's still a gangster?'

'That depends on your definition of the term. There's plenty he got away with, or his people did, in the old days. What you might call old-fashioned crime.'

'Oh, you mean nothing nasty like drugs or prostitution? Just armed robbery, protection, that sort of thing?'

'Don't be bitter. He has the casinos, business interests in electronics and property development. He owns half of Wapping. Nearly all the river frontage. He's extremely legitimate.'

'And still a gangster?'

'Let's say, he's still the governor to a lot of East Enders. The Yank, that's what they call him. You'll like him.'

'Will I?' She looked surprised. 'And when are we going to meet?'

'As soon as I can arrange it. Anything that moves in the East End and Harry or his people know about it. If anyone can help me catch Sean Dillon, he can.' The waiter appeared and placed bowls of French onion soup before them. 'Good,' he said. 'Now let's eat, I'm starving.'

Harry Flood crouched in one corner of the pit, arms folded to conserve his body heat. He was naked to the waist, barefooted, clad only in a pair of camouflage pants. The pit was only a few feet square and rain poured down relentlessly through the bamboo grid high above his head. Sometimes the Viet Cong would peer down at him, visitors being shown the Yankee dog who squatted in his own foulness although he'd long since grown used to the stench.

It seemed as if he'd been there for ever and time no longer had any meaning. He had never felt such total despair. It was raining faster now, pouring over the edge of the pit in a kind of waterfall, the water rising rapidly. He was on his feet and yet suddenly it was up to his chest and he was struggling. It poured over his head relentlessly and he no longer had a footing and struggled and kicked to keep afloat, fighting for breath, clawing at the side of the pit. Suddenly a hand grabbed his, a strong hand, and it pulled him up through the water and he started to breathe again.

He came awake with a start and sat upright. He'd had that dream for years on and off, ever since Viet Nam and that was a hell of a long time ago. It usually ended with him drowning. The hand pulling him out was something new.

He reached for his watch. It was almost ten. He always had a nap early evening before visiting one of the clubs later, but this time he'd overslept. He put his watch on, hurried into the bathroom, and had a quick shower. There was grey in his black hair now, he noticed that as he shaved.

'Comes to us all, Harry,' he said softly and smiled.

In fact he smiled most of the time, although anyone who observed closely would have noticed a certain world-weariness to it. The smile of a man who had found life on the whole, disappointing. He was handsome enough in a rather hard way, muscular with good shoulders. In fact not bad for forty-six which he usually told himself at least once a day if only for encouragement. He dressed in a black silk shirt buttoned at the neck without a tie and a loose-fitting Armani suit in dark brown raw silk. He checked his appearance in the mirror.

'Here we go again, baby,' he said and went out.

His apartment was enormous, part of a warehouse development on Cable Wharf. The brick walls of the sitting room were painted white, the wooden floor lacquered, Indian rugs scattered everywhere. Comfortable sofas, a bar, bottles of every conceivable kind ranged behind. Only for guests. He never drank alcohol. There was a large desk in front of the rear wall and the wall itself was lined with books.

He opened French windows and went onto the balcony overlooking the river. It was very cold. Tower Bridge was to his right, the Tower of London just beyond it, floodlit. A ship passed down from the Pool of London in front of him, its lights clear in the darkness so that he could see crew members working on deck. It always gave him a lift and he took a great lungful of that cold air.

The door opened at the far end of the sitting room and Mordecai Fletcher came in. He was six feet tall with iron-grey hair and a clipped moustache and wore a well-cut, double-breasted blazer and a Guards tie. The edge was rather taken off his conventional appearance by the scar tissue round the eyes and the flattened nose that had been broken more than once.

'You're up,' he said flatly.

'Isn't that what it looks like?' Flood asked.

Mordecai had been his strong right arm for the best part of fifteen years, a useful heavy-weight boxer who'd had the sense to get out of the ring before his brains were scrambled. He went behind the bar, poured a Perrier water, added ice and lemon and brought it over.

Flood took it without thanking him. 'God, how I love this old river. Anything come up?'

'Your accountant called. Some papers to sign on that market development. I told him to leave them till the morning.'

'Was that all?'

'Maurice was on the phone from the *Embassy*. He says Jack Harvey was in for a bite to eat with that bitch of a niece of his.'

'Myra?' Flood nodded. 'Anything happen?'

'Maurice said Harvey asked if you'd be in later. Said he'd come back and have a go at the tables.' He hesitated. 'You know what the bastard's after, Harry, and you've been avoiding him.'

'We aren't selling, Mordecai, and we certainly aren't going into partnership. Jack Harvey's the worst hood in the East End. He makes the Kray brothers look like kindergarten stuff.'

'I thought that was you, Harry.'

'I never did drugs, Mordecai, didn't run girls, you know that. Okay, I was a right villain for a few years, we both were.' He walked into the sitting room to the desk and picked up the photo in its silver frame that always stood there. 'When Jean was dying, for all those lousy months.' He shook his head. 'Nothing seemed important and you know the promise she made me give her towards the end. To get out.'

Mordecai closed the window. 'I know, Harry. She was a woman and a half, Jean.'

'That's why I made us legitimate, and wasn't I right? You know what the firm's net worth is? Nearly fifty million. Fifty million.' He grinned. 'So let Jack Harvey and others like him keep dirtying their hands if they want.'

'Yes, but to most people in the East End you're still the governor, Harry, you're still the Yank.'

'I'm not complaining.' Flood opened a cupboard and took out a dark overcoat. 'There's times when it helps a deal along, I know that. Now let's get moving. Who's driving tonight?'

'Charlie Salter.'

'Good.'

Mordecai hesitated. 'Shall I carry a shooter, Harry?'

'For God's sake, Mordecai, we're legit now, I keep telling you.'

'But Jack Harvey isn't, that's the trouble.'

'Leave Jack Harvey to me.'

They went down in the old original freight elevator to the warehouse where the black Mercedes saloon waited, Charlie Salter leaning against it reading a paper, a small, wiry man in a grey chauffeur's uniform. He folded the paper quickly and got the rear door open.

'Where to, Harry?'

'The *Embassy* and drive carefully. A lot of frost around tonight and I'll have the paper.'

Salter got behind the wheel and Mordecai got in beside him and reached for the electronic door control. The warehouse doors opened and they turned on to the wharf. Flood opened the paper, leaned back and started catching up on how the Gulf War was progressing.

*   *   *

The *Embassy* club was only half a mile away, just off Wapping High Street. It had only been open six months, another of Harry Flood's developments of old warehouse property. The car park was up a side street at the rear and was already quite full. There was an old negro in charge who sat in a small hut.

'Kept your place free, Mr Flood,' he said, coming out.

Flood got out of the car with Mordecai and took out his wallet as Salter went off to park. He extracted a five-pound note and gave it to the old man. 'Don't go crazy, Freddy.'

'With this?' The old man smiled. 'Wouldn't even buy me a woman at the back of the pub these days. Inflation's a terrible thing, Mr Flood.'

Flood and Mordecai were laughing as they went up the side street and Salter caught up with them as they turned the corner and reached the entrance. Inside it was warm and luxurious, black and white tiles on the floor, oak panelling, oil paintings. As the cloakroom girl took their coats, a small man in evening dress hurried to meet them. His accent was unmistakably French.

'Ah, Mr Flood, a great pleasure. Will you be dining?'

'I should think so, Maurice. We'll just have a look round first. Any sign of Harvey?'

'Not yet.'

They went down the steps into the main dining room. The club atmosphere continued, panelled walls, paintings, table booths with leather seats. The place was almost full, waiters working busily. A trio played on a small dais in one corner and there was a dance floor, though not large.

Maurice threaded his way through the tables by the floor and opened a door in quilted leather that led to the casino part of the premises. It was just as crowded in there people jostling each other at the roulette wheel, the chairs occupied at most of the tables.

'We losing much?' Flood asked Maurice.

'Swings and roundabouts, Mr Flood. It all balances out as usual.'

'Plenty of punters, anyway.'

'And not an Arab in sight,' Mordecai said.

'They're keeping their heads down,' Maurice told him, 'what with the Gulf business.'

'Wouldn't you?' Flood grinned. 'Come on, let's go and eat.'

He had his own booth in a corner to one side of the band overlooking the floor. He ordered smoked salmon and scrambled eggs and more Perrier water. He took a Camel cigarette from an old silver case. English cigarettes were something he'd never been able to come to terms with. Mordecai gave him a light and leant against the wall. Flood sat there, brooding, surveying the scene, experiencing one of those dark moments when you wondered what life was all about, and Charlie Salter came down the steps from the entrance and hurried through the tables.

'Jack Harvey and Myra – just in,' he said.

Harvey was fifty years of age, of medium height and overweight, a fact that the navy-blue barathea suit failed to hide in spite of having been cut in Savile Row. He was balding, hardly any hair there at all, and he had the fleshy decadent face of the wrong sort of Roman emperor.

His niece, Myra, was thirty and looked younger, her jet-black hair caught up in a bun and held in place by a diamond comb. There was little make-up on her face except for the lips and they were blood red. She wore a sequinned jacket and black mini-skirt by Gianni Versace and very high-heeled black shoes for she was only a little over five feet tall. She looked immensely attractive, men turning to stare at her. She was also her uncle's right hand, had a degree in business studies from London University and was just as ruthless and unscrupulous as he was.

Flood didn't get up, just sat there waiting. 'Harry, my old son,' Harvey said and sat down. 'Don't mind if we join you, do you?'

Myra leaned down and kissed Flood on the cheek. 'Like my new perfume, Harry? Cost a fortune, but Jack says it's like an aphrodisiac, the smell's so good.'

'That's a big word for you, isn't it?' Flood said.

She sat on his other side and Harvey took out a cigar. He clipped it and looked up at Mordecai. 'Come on, where's your bleeding lighter then?'

Mordecai took out his lighter and flicked it without a change of expression and Myra said, 'Any chance of a drink? We know you don't, Harry, but think about the rest of us poor sods.'

Her voice had a slight cockney accent, not too much and it had its own attraction. She put a hand on his knee and Flood said, 'Champagne cocktail, isn't that what you like?'

'It'll do to be going on with.'

'Not me, can't drink that kind of piss,' Harvey said. 'Scotch and water. A big one.'

Maurice, who had been hovering, spoke to a waiter, then whispered in Flood's ear, 'Your scrambled eggs, Mr Flood.'

127

'I'll have them now,' Flood told him.

Maurice turned away and a moment later, a waiter appeared with a silver salver. He removed the dome and put the plate in front of Flood who got to work straight away.

Harvey said, 'I've never seen you eat a decent meal yet, Harry. What's wrong with you?'

'Nothing really,' Flood told him. 'Food doesn't mean much to me, Jack. When I was a kid in Viet Nam, the Viet Cong had me prisoner for a while. I learnt you could get by on very little. Later on I was shot in the gut. Lost eighteen inches of my intestines.'

'You'll have to show me your scar sometime,' Myra said.

'There's always a silver lining. If I hadn't been shot, the Marine Corps wouldn't have posted me to that nice soft job as a guard at the London Embassy.'

'And you wouldn't have met Jean,' Harvey said. 'I remember the year you married her, Harry, the year her old Dad died. Sam Dark.' He shook his head. 'He was like an uncrowned king in the East End after the Krays got put inside. And Jean.' He shook his head again. 'What a goer. The boys were queuing for her. There was even a Guards officer, a lord.' He turned to Myra. 'Straight up.'

'And instead she married me,' Flood said.

'Could have done worse, Harry. I mean, you helped her keep things going a treat, especially after her Mum died, we all know that.'

Flood pushed his plate away and wiped his mouth with a napkin. 'Compliments night is it, Jack? Now what have you really come for?'

'You know what I want, Harry, I want in. The casinos, four of them now and how many clubs, Myra?'

'Six,' she said.

'And all this development on the river,' Harvey went on. 'You've got to share the cake.'

'There's only one trouble with that, Jack,' Flood told him. 'I'm a legitimate businessman, have been for a long time, whereas you . . .' He shook his head. 'Once a crook, always a crook.'

'You Yank bastard,' Harvey said. 'You can't talk to me like that.'

'I just did, Jack.'

'We're in, Harry, whether you like it or not.'

'Try me,' Flood said.

Salter had drifted across the room and leaned against the wall beside Mordecai. The big man whispered to him and Salter moved away.

Myra said, 'He means it, Harry, so be reasonable. All we're asking for is a piece of the action.'

'You come in with me you're into computers, building development, clubs and gambling,' Flood told her. 'Which means I'm in with you into pimps, whores, drugs and protection. I shower three times a day, sweetness, and it still wouldn't make me feel clean.'

'You Yank bastard!' She raised her hand and he grabbed her wrist.

Harvey stood up. 'Let it go, Myra, let it go. Come on. I'll be seeing you, Harry.'

'I hope not,' Flood told him.

They went out and Mordecai leaned down. 'He's a disgusting piece of slime. Always turned my stomach, him and his boyfriends.'

129

'Takes all sorts,' Flood said. 'Don't let your prejudices show, Mordecai, and get me a cup of coffee.'

'The swine,' Jack Harvey said as he and Myra walked along the pavement towards the car park. 'I'll see him in hell, talking to me that way.'

'I told you we were wasting our time,' she said.

'Right.' He eased his gloves over his big hands. 'Have to show him we mean business then, won't we?'

A dark van was parked at the end of the street. As they approached, the sidelights were turned on. The young man who leaned out from behind the wheel was about twenty-five, hard and dangerous-looking in a black leather bomber jacket and flat cap.

'Mr Harvey,' he said.

'Good boy, Billy, right on time.' Harvey turned to his niece. 'I don't think you've met Billy Watson, Myra.'

'No, I don't think I have,' she said, looking him over.

'How many have you got in the back?' Harvey demanded.

'Four, Mr Harvey. I heard this Mordecai Fletcher was a bit of an animal.' He picked up a baseball bat. 'This should cool him.'

'No shooters, like I told you?'

'Yes, Mr Harvey.'

'Flesh on flesh, that's all it needs and maybe a couple of broken legs. Get on with it. He'll have to come out sooner or later.'

Harvey and Myra continued along the pavement. 'Five?' she said. 'You think that's enough?'

'Enough?' he laughed harshly. 'Who does he think he is, Sam Dark? Now he was a man, but this bloody Yank

. . . They'll cripple him. Put him on sticks for six months. They're hard boys, Myra.'

'Really?' she said.

'Now come on and let's get out of this bleeding cold,' and he turned into the car park.

It was an hour later that Harry Flood got ready to leave. As the cloakroom girl helped him on with his coat, he said to Mordecai, 'Where's Charlie?'

'Oh, I gave him the nod a couple of minutes ago. He went ahead to get the car warmed up. I mean it's spawn of the north time out there, Harry, we'll have the bleeding Thames freezing over next.'

Flood laughed and they went down the steps and started along the pavement. When it happened, it was very quick, the rear doors of the van parked on the other side of the road swinging open, the men inside rushing out and crossing the road on the run. They all carried baseball bats. The first to reach them swung hard, Mordecai ducked inside, blocked the blow and pitched him over his hip down the steps of the basement area behind.

The other four paused and circled, bats ready. 'That won't do you any good,' Billy Watson said. 'It's leg-breaking time.'

There was a shot behind them, loud in the frosty air and then another. As they turned Charlie Salter moved out of the darkness reloading a sawn-off shotgun. 'Now drop 'em,' he said. 'Unless you want to be jam all over the pavement.'

They did as they were told and stood there waiting for what was to come. Mordecai moved close and looked them over then he grabbed the nearest one by the hair. 'Who are you working for, sonny?'

'I don't know, mister.'

Mordecai turned him and ran him up against the railings, holding his face just above the spikes. 'I said who are you working for?'

The youth cracked instantly, 'Jack Harvey. It was just a wages job. It was Billy who pulled us in.'

Billy said, 'You bastard. I'll get you for that.'

Mordecai glanced at Flood who nodded. The big man said to Billy, 'You stay. The rest of you, piss off.'

They turned and ran for it. Billy Watson stood looking at them, his face wild. Salter said, 'He needs a good slapping this one.'

Billy suddenly picked up one of the baseball bats and raised it defensively. 'All right, let's be having you. Harry Flood – big man. No bloody good on your own are you, mate?'

Mordecai took a step forward and Flood said, 'No,' and moved in himself. 'All right, son.'

Billy swung, Flood swayed to one side, found the right wrist, twisting. Billy cried out and dropped the baseball bat and in the same moment, the American half-turned, striking him hard across the face with his elbow, sending him down on one knee.

Mordecai picked up the baseball bat. 'No, he's got the point, let's get going,' Flood said.

He lit a cigarette as they went along the street. Mordecai said, 'What about Harvey? You going to stitch him up?'

'I'll think about it,' Flood said and they moved across to the car park.

Billy Watson got himself together, held on to the railings for a while. It was snowing a little as he turned and limped across the road to the van. As he went round to the driver's side, Myra Harvey stepped out of the entrance of a narrow alley, holding the collar of her fur coat up around her neck.

'Well that didn't go too well, did it?'

'Miss Harvey,' he croaked. 'I thought you'd gone.'

'After my uncle dropped me off, I got a taxi back. I wanted to see the fun.'

'Here,' he said, 'are you telling me you expected it to go like it did?'

'I'm afraid so, sunshine. My uncle gets it wrong sometimes. Lets his emotions get the better of him. You really think five young punks like you could walk all over Harry Flood?' She opened the driver's door and pushed him in. 'Go on, get over. I'll drive.'

She climbed behind the wheel, the fur coat opened and the mini-skirt went about as high as it could.

Billy said, 'But where are we going?'

'Back to my place. What you need is a nice hot bath, sunshine.' Her left hand squeezed his thigh hard and she switched on and drove away.

7

The flight from Jersey got into Heathrow Terminal One just after eleven the following morning. It took half an hour for Dillon's case to come through and he sat smoking and reading the paper while he waited. The war news was good for the coalition forces. A few pilots down in Iraq, but the airstrikes were having a terrible effect.

His case came and he walked through. There was a rush of customers as several planes had come in at around the same time. Customs didn't seem to be stopping anyone that morning, not that they'd have found anything on him. His suitcase contained a change of clothes and toilet articles, no more, and there were only a couple of newspapers in the briefcase. He also had two thousand dollars in his wallet which was in twenty hundred-dollar bills. Nothing wrong with that. He'd destroyed the French passport at the hotel in Jersey. No turning back now. When he went back to France it would be very definitely a different route and until then the Jersey driving licence in the name of Peter Hilton was all the identification he needed.

He took the escalator to the upper concourse and joined

the queue at one of the bank counters, changing five hundred dollars for sterling. He repeated the exercise at three other banks, then went downstairs to get a taxi, whistling softly to himself.

He told the driver to drop him at Paddington Station where he left the suitcase in a locker. He phoned Tania Novikova on the number Makeev had given him, just on the chance she was at home, and got her answering machine. He didn't bother to leave a message, but went out and hailed a cab and told the driver to take him to Covent Garden.

In his tinted glasses, striped tie and navy-blue Burberry trenchcoat he looked thoroughly respectable.

The driver said, 'Terrible weather, guv. I reckon we're going to see some real heavy snow soon.'

'I shouldn't be surprised.' Dillon's accent was impeccable public school English.

'You live in London, guv?'

'No, just in town for a few days on business. I've been abroad for some time,' Dillon said glibly. 'New York. Haven't been in London for years.'

'A lot of changes. Not like it used to be.'

'So I believe. I was reading the other day that you can't take a walk up Downing Street any more.'

'That's right, guv. Mrs Thatcher had a new security system installed, gates at the end of the street.'

'Really?' Dillon said. 'I'd like to see that.'

'We'll go that way if you like. I can take you down to Whitehall then cut back to Covent Garden.'

'Suits me.'

Dillon sat back, lit a cigarette and watched. They

moved down Whitehall from Trafalgar Square past Horse Guards with the two Household Cavalrymen on mounted duty, wearing greatcoats against the cold, sabres drawn.

'Must be bleeding cold for the horses,' the cabby said and then added, 'Here we are, guv, Downing Street.' He slowed a little. 'Can't stop. If you do, the coppers come up and ask you what you're doing.'

Dillon looked across at the end of the street. 'So those are the famous gates?'

'Thatcher's folly, some twerps call it, but if you ask me, she was usually right. The bloody IRA have pulled off enough stunts in London during the past few years. I'd shoot the lot of them, I would. If I drop you in Long Acre, will that do, guv?'

'Fine,' Dillon told him and sat back, thinking about those rather magnificent gates at the end of Downing Street.

The taxi pulled into the kerb and Dillon gave him a ten-pound note. 'Keep it,' he said, turned and walked briskly away along Langley Street. The whole Covent Garden area was as busy as usual, people dressed for the extreme cold, more like Moscow than London. Dillon went with the throng and finally found what he wanted in an alley near Neal's Yard, a small theatrical shop, the window full of old costume masks and make-up. A bell tinkled when he went in. The man who appeared through a curtain at the rear was about seventy with snow-white hair and a round fleshy face.

'And what can I do for you?' he asked.

'Some make-up, I think. What have you got in boxes?'

'Some very good kits here,' the old boy said. He took one down and opened it on the counter. 'They use these at the National Theatre. In the business, are you?'

'Amateur, that's all, I'm afraid, church players.' Dillon checked the contents of the box. 'Excellent. I'll take an extra lipstick, bright red, some black hair dye and also some solvent.'

'You *are* going to town. Clayton's my name, by the way. I'll give you my card in case you ever need anything else.' He got the required items and put them inside the make-up box and closed it. 'Thirty quid for cash and don't forget, anything you need . . .'

'I won't,' Dillon said and went out whistling.

In the village of Vercors it was snowing as the cortège drove down from the château. In spite of the weather, villagers lined the street, men with their caps off, as Anne-Marie Audin went to her final rest. There were only three cars behind the hearse, old Pierre Audin and his secretary in the first, a number of servants in the other. Brosnan and Mary Tanner with Max Hernu following, walked up through the tombstones and paused as the old man was lifted from the car into his wheelchair. He was pushed inside, the rest followed.

It was very old, a typical village church, whitewashed walls, the stations of the Cross and it was cold, very cold. In fact Brosnan had never felt so cold and sat there, shaking slightly, hardly aware of what was being said, rising and kneeling obediently with everyone else. It was only when the service ended and they stood as the pallbearers carried the coffin down the aisle that he realised that Mary Tanner was holding his hand.

They walked through the graveyard to the family mausoleum. It was the size of a small chapel built in grey granite and marble with a steep Gothic roof. The oaken doors stood open. The priest paused to give the final benediction, the coffin was taken inside. The secretary turned the wheelchair and pushed it down the path past them, the old man huddled over, a rug across his knees.

'I feel so sorry for him,' Mary said.

'No need, he doesn't know what time of day it is,' Brosnan told her.

'That's not always true.'

She walked to the car, and put a hand on the old man's shoulder as he sat there in his wheelchair. Then she returned.

'So, my friends, back to Paris,' Hernu said.

'And then London,' Brosnan said.

Mary took his arm as they walked towards the car. 'Tomorrow, Martin, tomorrow morning will be soon enough and I won't take no for an answer.'

'All right,' he said, 'tomorrow it is,' and he got in the rear of the car and leaned back, suddenly drained and closed his eyes, Mary sitting beside him as Hernu drove away.

It was just after six when Tania Novikova heard the doorbell. She went downstairs and opened the door. Dillon stood there, suitcase in one hand, briefcase in the other. 'Josef sends his regards.'

She was amazed. Since Makeev had spoken to her she had accessed KGB files in London to discover as much about Dillon as she could and had been astonished at his record. She had expected some kind of dark hero. Instead she had a small man in a trenchcoat with tinted glasses and a college tie.

'You are Sean Dillon?' she said.

'As ever was.'

'You'd better come in.'

Women had never been of great importance to Dillon. They were there to satisfy a need on occasions, but he had never felt the slightest emotional involvement with one. Following Tania Novikova up the stairs, he was aware that she had a good figure and that the black trouser suit became her. Her hair was caught up at the nape of the neck in a velvet bow, but, when she turned to him in the full light of her sitting room, he realised that she was really rather plain.

'You had a good trip?' she asked.

'All right. I was delayed in Jersey last night because of fog.'

'Would you like a drink?'

'Tea would be fine.'

She opened a drawer, produced a Walther, two spare clips and a Carswell silencer. 'Your preferred weapon according to Josef.'

'Definitely.'

'Also I thought this might come in useful.' She handed him a small bundle. 'They say it can stop a .45 bullet at point-blank range. Nylon and titanium.'

Dillon unfolded it. Nothing like as bulky as a flak jacket, it was designed like a small waistcoat and fastened with Velcro tabs.

'Excellent,' he said and put it in his briefcase together with the Walther and the silencer. He unbuttoned his trenchcoat, lit a cigarette and stood in the kitchen door and watched her make the tea. 'You're very convenient for the Soviet Embassy here?'

'Oh, yes, walking distance.' She brought the tea out on a tray. 'I've fixed you up with a room in a small hotel just round the corner in the Bayswater Road. It's the sort of place commercial travellers overnight at.'

'Fine.' He sipped his tea. 'To business. What about Fahy?'

'No luck so far. He moved from Kilburn a few years ago to a house in Finchley. Only stayed there a year and moved again. That's where I've drawn a blank. But I'll find him, I've got someone on his case.'

'You must. It's essential. Does KGB's London station still have a forgery department?'

'Of course.'

'Good.' He took out his Jersey driving licence. 'I want a private pilot's licence in the same name and address. You'll need a photo.' He slipped a finger inside the plastic cover of the licence and pulled out a couple of identical prints. 'Always useful to have a few of these.'

She took one of them. 'Peter Hilton, Jersey. Can I ask why this is necessary?'

'Because when the right time comes, time to get the hell out of it, I want to fly and they won't hire a plane to you unless you have a licence issued by the Civil Aviation Authority.' He helped himself to some more tea. 'Tell your expert I want full instrument rating and twin-engine.'

'I'll write that down.' She opened her handbag, took out an envelope, slipped the photo inside and made a note on the cover. 'Is there anything else?'

'Yes, I'd like full details of the present security system at Number Ten Downing Street.'

She caught her breath. 'Am I to take it that is your target?'

'Not as such. The man inside, but that's a different thing. The Prime Minister's daily schedule, how easy is it to access that?'

'It depends what you want. There are always fixed points in the day. Question time in the House of Commons, for example. Of course, things are different because of the Gulf. The War Cabinet meets every morning at ten o'clock.'

'At Downing Street?'

'Oh, yes, in the Cabinet Room. But he has other appointments during the day. Only yesterday he did a broadcast on British Forces Network to the troops in the Gulf.'

'Was that from the BBC?'

'No, they have their own headquarters at Bridge House. That's near Paddington Station and not too far from here.'

'Interesting. I wonder what his security was like?'

'Not much, believe me. A few detectives, no more than that. The British are crazy.'

'A damn good job they are. This informant of yours, the one who got you all the information on Ferguson. Tell me about him.' Which she did and when she was finished he nodded. 'You've got him well and truly by the cobblers then?'

'I think you could say that.'

'Let's keep it that way.' He got up and buttoned his coat. 'I'd better go and book in at this hotel.'

'Have you eaten?' she asked.

'No.'

'I have a suggestion. Just along from the hotel is an excellent Italian restaurant, Luigi's. One of those little family-owned places. You get settled in at the hotel and I'll walk along to the Embassy. I'll check on what we have on the Downing Street defences and see if anything's turned up on Fahy.'

'And the flying licence?'

'I'll put that in hand.'

'Twenty-four hours.'

'All right.'

She got a coat and scarf, went downstairs with him and they left together. The pavements were frosty and she carried his briefcase for him and held on to his arm until they reached the hotel.

'I'll see you in an hour,' she said and moved on.

It was the sort of place which had been a thriving pub and hotel in late Victorian times. The present owners had done their best with it and that wasn't very much. The dining room to the left of the foyer was totally uninviting, no more than half a dozen people eating there. The desk clerk was an old man with a face like a skull who wore a faded brown uniform. He moved with infinite slowness, booking Dillon in and gave him his key. Guests were obviously expected to carry their own cases.

The room was exactly what he'd expected. Twin beds, cheap coverings, a shower room, a television with a slot for coins and a kettle, a little basket beside it containing sachets of coffee, teabags and powdered milk. Still, it wouldn't be for long and he opened his suitcase and unpacked.

Among Jack Harvey's interests was a funeral business in Whitechapel. It was a sizeable establishment and did well for, as he liked to joke, the dead were always with us. It was an imposing three-storeyed Victorian building which he'd had renovated. Myra had the top floor as a penthouse and took an interest in the running of the place. Harvey had an office on the first floor.

Harvey told his driver to wait, went up the steps and rang the bell. The night porter answered.

'My niece in?' Harvey demanded.

'I believe so, Mr Harvey.'

Harvey moved through the main shop with coffins on display and along the passage with the little chapels of rest on each side where relatives could view the bodies. He went up two flights of stairs and rang the bell on Myra's door.

She was ready for him, alerted by a discreet call from the porter, let him wait for a moment, then opened the door. 'Uncle Jack.'

He brushed past her. She was wearing a gold sequinned mini-dress, black stockings and shoes. 'You going out or something?' he demanded.

'A disco, actually.'

'Well, never mind that now. You saw the accountants? Is there any way I can get at Flood legally? Any problems with leases? Anything?'

'Not a chance,' Myra said. 'We've gone through the lot with a fine-tooth comb. There's nothing.'

'Right, then I'll just have to get him the hard way.'

'That didn't exactly work last night, did it?'

'I used rubbish, that's why, a bunch of young jerks who didn't deserve the time of day.'

'So what do you intend?'

'I'll think of something.' As he turned to the door, he heard a movement in the bedroom. 'Here, who's in there?' He flung the door open and revealed Billy Watson standing there, looking hunted. 'Jesus!' Harvey said to Myra. 'Disgusting. All you can ever think of is a bit of the other.'

'At least we do it the right way,' she told him.

'Screw you!' he said.

'No, he'll do that.'

Harvey stormed downstairs. Billy said, 'You don't give a monkey's for anyone, do you?'

'Billy love, this is the house of the dead,' she said and picked up her fur coat and handbag. 'They're lying in their coffins downstairs and we're alive. Simple as that, so make the most of it. Now let's get going.'

Dillon was sitting in a small booth in the corner at Luigi's drinking the only champagne available, a very reasonable Bollinger non-vintage, when Tania came in. Old Luigi greeted her personally and as a favoured customer and she sat down.

'Champagne?' Dillon asked.

'Why not?' She looked up at Luigi. 'We'll order later.'

'One thing that hasn't been mentioned is my operating money. Thirty thousand dollars. Aroun was to arrange that,' Dillon said.

'It's taken care of. The man in question will be in touch with me tomorrow. Some accountant of Aroun's in London.'

'Okay, so what have you got for me?' he asked.

'Nothing on Fahy yet. I've set the wheels in motion as regards the flying licence.'

'And Number Ten?'

'I've had a look at the file. The public always had a right of way along Downing Street. The IRA coming so close to blowing up the whole cabinet at the Tory Party Conference in Brighton the other year made for a change in thinking about security. The bombing campaign in London and attacks on individuals accelerated things.'

'So?'

'Well, the public used to be able to stand at the opposite

side of the road from Number Ten watching the great and the good arrive and depart, but no longer. In December eighty-nine Mrs Thatcher ordered new security measures. In effect the place is now a fortress. The steel railings are ten feet high. The gates, by the way, are neo-Victorian, a nice touch that, from the Iron Lady.'

'Yes, I saw them today.'

Luigi hovered anxiously and they broke off and ordered minestrone, veal chops, sauté potatoes and a green salad.

Tania carried on, 'There were accusations in some quarters that she's become the victim of paranoid delusions. Nonsense, of course. That lady has never been deluded about anything in her life. Anyway, on the other side of the gates there's a steel screen designed to come up fast if an unauthorised vehicle tries to get through.'

'And the building itself?'

'The windows have specially strengthened glass and that includes the Georgian windows. Oh, and the net curtains are definitely a miracle of modern science. They're blast-proof.'

'You certainly have the facts.'

'Incredibly, everything I've told you has been reported in either a British newspaper or magazine. The British press puts its own right to publish above every other consideration. They just refuse to face up to security implications. On file at the clippings library of any major British newspaper you'll find details of the interior of Number Ten or the Prime Minister's country home, Chequers, or even Buckingham Palace.'

'What about getting in as ancillary staff?'

'That used to be a real loophole. Most catering for functions is done by outside firms and some of the cleaning, but they're very tough about security clearance for these people. There are always slip-ups, of course. There was a plumber working on the Chancellor of the Exchequer's home at Number Eleven who opened a door and found himself wandering about Number Ten trying to get out.'

'It sounds like a French farce.'

'Only recently staff from one of the outside firms employed to offer cleaning services of one kind or another, staff who had security clearance, were found to be operating under false identities. Some of them had clearance for the Home Office and other ministries.'

'Yes, but all you're saying is mistakes occur.'

'That's right.' She hesitated. 'Have you anything particular in mind?'

'You mean potshots with a sniper's rifle from a rooftop two hundred yards away as he comes out of the door? I don't think so. No, I really have no firm idea at the moment, but I'll come up with something. I always do.' The waiter brought their soup. Dillon said, 'Now that smells good enough to eat. Let's do just that.'

Afterwards, he walked her round to her door. It was snowing just a little and very cold. He said, 'Must remind you of home, this weather?'

'Home?' She looked blank for a moment then laughed. 'Moscow, you mean?' She shrugged. 'It's been a long time. Would you like to come up?'

'No thanks. It's late and I could do with the sleep. I'll stay at the hotel tomorrow morning. Let's say till noon. From what I saw I don't think I could stand the thought of lunch there. I'll be back after two so you'll know where I'll be.'

'Fine,' she said.

'I'll say goodnight then.'

She closed the door, Dillon turned and walked away. It was only after he rounded the corner into the Bayswater Road that Gordon Brown moved out of the shadows of a doorway opposite and looked up at Tania's window. The light came on. He stayed there for a while longer then turned and walked away.

In Paris the following morning the temperature went up three or four degrees and it started to thaw. Mary and Hernu in the Colonel's black Citroën picked Brosnan up just before noon. He was waiting for them in the entrance of the Quai de Montebello apartment block. He wore his trenchcoat, a tweed cap and carried a suitcase. The driver put the case in the boot and Brosnan got in the rear with the other two.

'Any news?' he asked.

'Not a thing,' the Colonel told him.

'Like I said, he's probably there already. What about Ferguson?'

Mary glanced at her watch. 'He's due to see the Prime Minister now, to alert him as to the seriousness of this whole business.'

'About all he can do,' Brosnan said. 'That and spread the word to the other branches of the security services.'

'And how would you handle it, my friend?' Hernu asked.

'We know he worked in London for the IRA in nineteen eighty-one. As I told Mary, he must have used underworld contacts to supply his needs. He always does and it will be the same this time. That's why I must see my old friend Harry Flood.'

'Ah, yes, the redoubtable Mr Flood. Captain Tanner was telling me about him, but what if he can't help?'

'There's another way. I have a friend in Ireland just outside Dublin at Kilrea, Liam Devlin. There's nothing he doesn't know about IRA history in the last few years and who did what. It's a thought.' He lit a cigarette and leaned back. 'But I'll get the bastard, one way or another. I'll get him.'

The driver took them to the end of the Charles de Gaulle terminal where the private planes parked. The Lear was waiting on the tarmac. There was no formality. Everything had been arranged. The driver took their cases across to where the second pilot waited.

Hernu said, 'Captain, if I may presume.' He kissed Mary lightly on both cheeks. 'And you, my friend.' He held out his hand. 'Always remember that when you set out on a journey with revenge at the end of it, it is necessary to first dig two graves.'

'Philosophy now?' Brosnan said. 'And at your time of life? Goodbye, Colonel.'

They strapped themselves into their seats, the second pilot pulled up the stairs, locked the door and went and joined his companion in the cockpit.

'Hernu is right, you know,' Mary said.

'I know he is,' Brosnan answered. 'But there's nothing I can do about that.'

'I understand, believe me, I do,' she said as the plane rolled forward.

When Ferguson was shown into the study at Number Ten the Prime Minister was standing at the window drinking a cup of tea. He turned and smiled. 'The cup that refreshes, Brigadier.'

'They always say it was tea that got us through the war, Prime Minister.'

'Well as long as it gets me through my present schedule. We've a meeting of the War Cabinet at ten every morning as you know, and all the other pressing matters to do with the Gulf.'

'And the day-to-day running of the country,' Ferguson said.

'Yes, well we do our best. No one ever said politics was easy, Brigadier.' He put down the cup. 'I've read your latest report. You think it likely the man Dillon is here somewhere in London?'

'From what he said to Brosnan, I think we must assume that, Prime Minister.'

'You've alerted all branches of the security services?'

'Of course, but we can't put a face to him, you see. Oh, there's the description. Small, fair-haired and so on, but as Brosnan says, he'll look entirely different by now.'

'It's been suggested to me that perhaps some press coverage might be useful.'

Ferguson said, 'Well, it's a thought, but I doubt it would achieve anything. What could they say? In furtherance of an enquiry the police would like to contact a man named Sean Dillon who isn't called that any more? As regards a description, we don't know what he looks like and if we did, he wouldn't look like that anyway.'

'My goodness, you carried that off beautifully, Brigadier.' The Prime Minister roared with laughter.

'Of course there could be more lurid headlines. IRA jackal stalks the Prime Minister.'

'No, I'm not having any of that nonsense,' the Prime Minister said firmly. 'By the way, as regards the suggestion that Saddam Hussein might be behind this affair, I must tell you your other colleagues in the intelligence services disagree. They are firmly of the opinion this is an IRA matter and I must tell you that is how they are pursuing it.'

'Well, if Special Branch think they'll find him by visiting Irish pubs in Kilburn, that's their privilege.'

There was a knock at the door, an aide came in. 'We're due at the Savoy in fifteen minutes, Prime Minister.'

John Major smiled with great charm. 'Another of those interminable luncheons, Brigadier. Prawn cocktail to start . . .'

'And chicken salad to follow,' Ferguson said.

'Find him, Brigadier,' the Prime Minister told him. 'Find him for me,' and the aide showed Ferguson out.

Tania, with good news for Dillon, knew there was no point in calling at the hotel before two so she went to her flat. As she was looking for her key in her handbag Gordon Brown crossed the road.

'I was hoping I might catch you,' he said.

'For God's sake, Gordon, you must be crazy.'

'And what happens when something important comes up and you need to know? Can't wait for you to get in touch. It might be too late, so I'd better come in, hadn't I?'

'You can't. I'm due back at the Embassy in thirty minutes. I'll have a drink with you, that's all.'

She turned and walked down to the pub on the corner before he could argue. They sat in a corner of the snug which was empty, aware of the noise from the main bar. Brown had a beer and Tania a vodka and lime.

'What have you got for me?' she asked.

'Shouldn't the question be the other way about?' She got up at once and he put a hand on her arm. 'I'm sorry. Don't go.'

'Then behave yourself.' She sat down again. 'Now get on with it.'

'Ferguson had a meeting with the Prime Minister just before twelve. He was back in the office at twelve-thirty before I finished the first half of my shift. He dictated a report to Alice Johnson, she's one of the confidential typists who works with me. The report was for the file.'

'Did you get a copy?'

'No, but I did the same as last time. Took it along to his office for her and read it on the way. Captain Tanner stayed in Paris with Brosnan for the funeral of a French woman.'

'Anne-Marie Audin?' she prompted him.

'They're flying in today. Brosnan has promised full co-operation. Oh, all the other branches of the intelligence services have been notified about Dillon. No newspaper coverage on the PM's instructions. The impression I got was he's told Ferguson to get on with it.'

'Good,' she said. 'Very good, but you must stay on the case, Gordon. I have to go.'

She started to get up and he caught her wrist. 'I saw you last night, about eleven it was, coming back to your flat with a man.'

'You were watching my flat?'

'I often do on my way home.'

Her anger was very real, but she restrained it. 'Then if you were there you'll know that the gentleman in question, a colleague from the Embassy, didn't come in. He simply escorted me home. Now let me go, Gordon.'

She pulled free and walked out and Brown, thoroughly depressed, went to the bar and ordered another beer.

When she knocked on the door of Dillon's room just after two he opened it at once. She brushed past him and went inside.

'You look pleased with yourself,' he said.

'I should do.'

Dillon lit a cigarette. 'Go on, tell me.'

'First, I've had words with my mole at Group Four. Ferguson's just been to see the Prime Minister. They believe you're here and all branches of intelligence have been notified. Brosnan and the Tanner woman are coming in from Paris. Brosnan's offered full co-operation.'

'And Ferguson?'

'The Prime Minister said no press publicity. Just told him to go all out to get you.'

'It's nice to be wanted.'

'Second.' She opened her handbag and took out a pass-port-style booklet. 'One pilot's licence as issued by the Civil Aviation Authority to one Peter Hilton.'

'That's bloody marvellous,' Dillon said and took it from her.

'Yes, the man who does this kind of thing pulled out all the stops. I told him all your requirements. He said he'd give you a commercial licence. Apparently you're also an instructor.'

Dillon checked his photo and riffled through the pages. 'Excellent. Couldn't be better.'

'And that's not the end,' she said. 'You wanted to know the whereabouts of one Daniel Maurice Fahy?'

'You've found him?'

'That's right, but he doesn't live in London. I've brought you a road map.' She unfolded it. 'He has a farm here at a place called Cadge End in Sussex. It's twenty-five to thirty miles from London. You take the road through Dorking towards Horsham then head into the wilds.'

'How do you know all this?'

'The operative I put on the job managed to trace him late yesterday afternoon. By the time he'd looked the place over, then dropped into the pub in the local village to make a few enquiries, it was very late. He didn't get back to London until after midnight. I got his report this morning.'

'And?'

'He says the farm is very out of the way near a river called the Arun. Marsh country. The village is called Doxley. The farm is a mile south of it. There's a signpost.'

'He is efficient, your man.'

'Well he's young and trying to prove himself. From what he heard in the pub, Fahy runs a few sheep and dabbles in agricultural machinery.'

Dillon nodded. 'That makes sense.'

'One thing that might come as a surprise. He has a girl staying with him, his grandniece, it seems. My man saw her.'

'And what did he say?'

'That she came into the pub for some bottles of beer. About twenty. Angel, they called her, Angel Fahy. He said she looked like a peasant.'

'Wonderful.' He got up and reached for his jacket. 'I must get down there right away. Do you have a car?'

'Yes, but it's only a Mini. Easier parking in London.'

'No problem. As you said, thirty miles at the most. I can borrow it then?'

'Of course. It's in the garage at the end of my street. I'll show you.'

He put on his trenchcoat, opened the briefcase, took out the Walther, rammed a clip in the butt and put it in his left-hand pocket. The silencer he put in the right. 'Just in case,' he said and they went out.

The car was in fact a Mini Cooper which meant performance, jet black with a gold trim. 'Excellent,' he said, 'I'll get moving.'

He got behind the wheel and she said, 'What's so important about Fahy?'

'He's an engineer who can turn his hand to anything, a bomb maker of genius and he's been in deep cover for years. He helped me when I last operated here in eighty-one, helped me a lot. It also helps that he was my father's second cousin. I knew him when I was a kid over here. You haven't mentioned the cash from Aroun, by the way.'

'I've to pick it up this evening at six. All very dramatic. A Mercedes stops at the corner of Brancaster Street and Town Drive. That's not far from here. I say, "It's cold, even for this time of the year," and the driver hands me a briefcase.'

'God help us, he must have been seeing too much television,' Dillon said. 'I'll be in touch,' and he drove away.

Ferguson had stopped off at his office at the Ministry of Defence after Downing Street to bring the report on the Dillon affair file up to date and clear his desk generally. As always, he preferred to work at the flat so he returned to Cavendish Square, had Kim prepare him a late lunch of scrambled eggs and bacon and was browsing through his *Times* when the doorbell rang. A moment later Kim showed in Mary Tanner and Brosnan.

'My dear Martin,' Ferguson got up and shook hands. 'So here we are again.'

'So it would seem,' Brosnan said.

'Everything go off all right at the funeral?' Ferguson asked.

'As funerals go, it went,' Brosnan said harshly and lit a cigarette. 'So where are we? What's happening?'

'I've seen the Prime Minister again. There's to be no press publicity.'

'I agree with him there,' Brosnan said. 'It would be pointless.'

'All relevant intelligence agencies, plus Special Branch, of course, have been notified. They'll do what they can.'

'Which isn't very much,' Brosnan said.

'Another point,' Mary put in. 'I know he's threatened the Prime Minister but we don't have a clue what he intends or when. He could be up to something this very evening for all we know.'

Brosnan shook his head. 'No, I think there'll be more to it than that. These things take time. I should know.'

'So where will you start?' Ferguson asked.

'With my old friend Harry Flood. When Dillon was here in eighty-one he probably used underworld contacts to supply his needs. Harry may be able to dig something out.'

'And if not?'

'Then I'll borrow that Lear jet of yours again, fly to Dublin and have words with Liam Devlin.'

'Ah, yes,' Ferguson said, 'who better?'

'When Dillon went to London in nineteen eighty-one he must have been under someone's orders. If Devlin could find out who, that could be a lead to all sorts.'

'Sounds logical to me. So you'll see Flood tonight?'

'I think so.'

'Where are you staying?'

'With me,' Mary said.

'At Lowndes Square?' Ferguson's eyebrows went up. 'Really?'

'Come on, Brigadier, don't be an old fuddy-duddy. I've got four bedrooms remember, each with its own bathroom and Professor Brosnan can have one with a lock on the inside of his door.'

Brosnan laughed. 'Come on, let's get out of here. See you later, Brigadier.'

They used Ferguson's car. She closed the sliding window between them and the driver and said, 'Don't you think you'd better ring your friend, let him know you'd like to see him?'

'I suppose so. I'll need to check his number.'

She took a notebook from her handbag. 'I have it here. It's ex-directory. There you go. Cable Wharf. That's in Wapping.'

'Very efficient.'

'And here's a phone.'

She handed him the car phone. 'You do like to be in charge,' he said and dialled the number.

It was Mordecai Fletcher who answered. Brosnan said, 'Harry Flood, please.'

'Who wants him?'

'Martin Brosnan.'

'The Professor? This is Mordecai. We haven't heard

from you for what – three or four years? Christ, but he's going to be pleased.'

A moment later a voice said, 'Martin?'

'Harry?'

'I don't believe it. You've come back to haunt me, you bastard.'

8

For Dillon in the Mini Cooper, the run from London went easily enough. Although there was a light covering of snow on the fields and hedgerows the roads were perfectly clear and not particularly busy. He was in Dorking within half an hour. He passed straight through and continued towards Horsham, finally pulling into a petrol station about five miles outside.

As the attendant was topping up the tank Dillon got his road map out. 'Place called Doxley, you know it?'

'Half a mile up the road on your right a signpost says Grimethorpe. That's the airfield, but before you get there you'll see a sign to Doxley.'

'So it's not far from here?'

'Three miles maybe, but it might as well be the end of the world.' The attendant chuckled as he took the notes Dillon gave him. 'Not much there, mister.'

'Thought I'd take a look. Friend told me there might be a weekend cottage going.'

'If there is, I haven't heard of it.'

Dillon drove away, came to the Grimethorpe sign within

a few minutes, followed the narrow road and found the Doxley sign as the garage man had indicated. The road was even narrower, high banks blocking the view until he came to the brow of a small hill and looked across a desolate landscape, powdered with snow. There was the occasional small wood, a scattering of hedged fields and then flat marshland drifting towards a river which had to be the Arun. Beside it, perhaps a mile away, he saw houses, twelve or fifteen, with red pantiled roofs and there was a small church, obviously Doxley. He started down the hill to the wooded valley below and as he came to it, saw a five-barred gate standing open and a decaying wooden sign with the legend 'Cadge End Farm'.

The track led through the wood and brought him almost at once to a farm complex. There were a few chickens running here and there, a house and two large barns linked to it so that the whole enclosed a courtyard. It looked incredibly run-down as if nothing had been done to it for years, but then, as Dillon knew, many country people preferred to live like that. He got out of the Mini and crossed to the front door, knocked and tried to open it. It was locked. He turned and went to the first barn. Its old wooden doors stood open. There was a Morris van in there and a Ford car jacked up on bricks, no wheels, agricultural implements all over the place.

Dillon took out a cigarette. As he lit it in cupped hands, a voice behind said, 'Who are you? What do you want?'

He turned and found a girl in the doorway. She wore baggy trousers tucked into a pair of rubber boots, a heavy roll-neck sweater under an old anorak and a knitted beret like a tam-o'-shanter, the kind of thing you found in fishing villages on the west coast of Ireland. She was holding a double-barrelled shotgun threateningly. As he took a step towards her, she thumbed back the hammer.

'You stay there.' The Irish accent was very pronounced.

'You'll be the one they call Angel Fahy?' he said.

'Angela if it's any of your business.'

Tania's man had been right. She did look like a little peasant. Broad cheekbones, upturned nose and a kind of fierceness there. 'Would you really shoot with that thing?'

'If I had to.'

'A pity that and me only wanting to meet my father's cousin, once removed, Danny Fahy.'

She frowned. 'And who in the hell might you be, mister?'

'Dillon's the name. Sean Dillon.'

She laughed harshly. 'That's a damn lie. You're not even Irish and Sean Dillon is dead, everyone knows that.'

Dillon dropped into the hard distinctive accent of Belfast. 'To steal a great man's line, girl dear, all I can say is reports of my death have been greatly exaggerated.'

The gun went slack in her hands. 'Mother Mary, are you Sean Dillon?'

'As ever was. Appearances can be deceiving.'

'Oh, God,' she said. 'Uncle Danny talks about you all the time, but it was always like stories, nothing real to it at all and here you are.'

'Where is he?'

'He did a repair on a car for the landlord of the local pub, took it down there an hour ago. Said he'd walk back, but he'll be there a while yet drinking, I shouldn't wonder.'

'At this time? Isn't the pub closed until evening?'

'That might be the law, Mr Dillon, but not in Doxley. They never close.'

'Let's go and get him then.'

She left the shotgun on a bench and got into the Mini beside him. As they drove away, he said, 'What's your story then?'

'I was raised on a farm in Galway. My Da was Danny's nephew, Michael. He died six years ago when I was fourteen. After a year, my mother married again.'

'Let me guess,' Dillon said. 'You didn't like your stepfather and he didn't like you?'

'Something like that. Uncle Danny came over for my father's funeral so I'd met him and liked him. When things got too heavy, I left home and came here. He was great about it. Wrote to my mother and she agreed I could stay. Glad to get rid of me.'

There was no self-pity at all and Dillon warmed to her. 'They always say some good comes out of everything.'

'I've been working it out,' she said. 'If you're Danny's second cousin and I'm his great-niece, then you and I are blood related, isn't that a fact?'

Dillon laughed. 'In a manner of speaking.'

She looked ecstatic as she leaned back. 'Me, Angel Fahy, related to the greatest gunman the Provisional IRA ever had.'

'Well, now, there would be some who would argue about that,' he said as they reached the village and pulled up outside the pub.

It was a small, desolate sort of place, no more than fifteen rather dilapidated cottages and a Norman church with a tower and an overgrown graveyard. The pub was called the Green Man and even Dillon had to duck to enter the door. The ceiling was very low and beamed. The floor was constructed of heavy stone flags worn with the years, the walls were whitewashed. The man behind the bar in his shirt sleeves was at least eighty.

He glanced up and Angel said, 'Is he here, Mr Dalton?'

'By the fire, having a beer,' the old man said.

A fire burned in a wide stone hearth and there was a wooden bench and a table in front of it. Danny Fahy sat there reading the paper, a glass in front of him. He was sixty-five with an untidy grizzled beard and wore a cloth cap and an old Harris Tweed suit.

Angel said, 'I've brought someone to see you, Uncle Danny.'

He looked up at her and then at Dillon, puzzlement on his face. 'And what can I do for you, sir?'

Dillon removed his glasses. 'God bless all here!' he said in his Belfast accent, 'and particularly you, you old bastard.'

Fahy turned very pale, the shock was so intense. 'God save us, is that you, Sean, and me thinking you were in your box long ago?'

'Well, I'm not and I'm here.' Dillon took a five-pound note from his wallet and gave it to Angel. 'A couple of whiskeys, Irish for preference.'

She went back to the bar and Dillon turned. Danny Fahy actually had tears in his eyes and he flung his arms around him. 'Dear God, Sean, but I can't tell you how good it is to see you.'

The sitting room at the farm was untidy and cluttered, the furniture very old. Dillon sat on a sofa while Fahy built up the fire. Angel was in the kitchen cooking a meal. It was open to the sitting room and Dillon could see her moving around.

'And how's life been treating you, Sean?' Fahy stuffed a pipe and lit it. 'Ten years since you raised Cain in London town. By God, boy, you gave the Brits something to think about.'

'I couldn't have done it without you, Danny.'

'Great days. And what happened after?'

'Europe, the Middle East. I kept on the move. Did a lot for the PLO. Even learned to fly.'

'Is that a fact?'

Angel came and put plates of bacon and eggs on the table. 'Get it while it's hot.' She returned with a tray laden with teapot and milk, three mugs and a plate piled high with bread and butter. 'I'm sorry there's nothing fancier, but we weren't expecting company.'

'It looks good to me,' Dillon told her and tucked in.

'So now you're here Sean and dressed like an English gentleman,' Fahy turned to Angel. 'Didn't I tell you the actor this man was? They never could put a glove on him in all these years, not once.'

She nodded eagerly, smiling at Dillon and her personality had changed with the excitement. 'Are you on a job now, Mr Dillon, for the IRA, I mean?'

'It would be a cold day in hell before I put myself on the line for that bunch of old washerwomen,' Dillon said.

'But you are working on something, Sean?' Fahy said. 'I can tell. Come on, let's in on it.'

Dillon lit a cigarette. 'What if I told you I was working for the Arabs, Danny, for Saddam Hussein himself?'

'Jesus, Sean, and why not? And what is it he wants you to do?'

'He wants something now – a coup. Something big. America's too far away. That leaves the Brits.'

'What could be better?' Fahy's eyes were gleaming.

'Thatcher was in France the other day seeing Mitterrand.

I had plans for her on the way to her plane. Perfect set-up, quiet country road and then someone I trusted let me down.'

'And isn't that always the way?' Fahy said. 'So you're looking for another target? Who, Sean?'

'I was thinking of John Major.'

'The new Prime Minister?' Angel said in awe. 'You wouldn't dare.'

'Sure and why wouldn't he? Didn't the boys nearly get the whole bloody British Government at Brighton?' Danny Fahy told her. 'Go on, Sean, what's your plan?'

'I haven't got one, Danny, that's the trouble, but there would be a pay day for this like you wouldn't believe.'

'And that's as good a reason to make it work as any. So you've come to Uncle Danny looking for help?' Fahy went to a cupboard, came back with a bottle of Bushmills and two glasses and filled them. 'Have you any ideas at all?'

'Not yet, Danny. Do you still work for the movement?'

'Stay in deep cover, that was the order from Belfast so many years ago I've forgotten. Since then not a word and me bored out of my socks, so I moved down here. It suits me. I like the countryside here, I like the people. They keep to themselves. I've built up a fair business repairing agricultural machinery and I run a few sheep. We're happy here, Angel and me.'

'And still bored out of your socks. Do you remember Martin Brosnan, by the way?'

'I do so. You were bad friends with that one.'

'I had a run-in with him in Paris recently. He'll probably turn up in London looking for me. He'll be working for Brit intelligence.'

164

'The bastard.' Fahy frowned as he refilled his pipe. 'Didn't I hear some fanciful talk of how Brosnan got into Ten Downing Street as a waiter years ago and didn't do anything about it?'

'I heard that story too. A flight of fancy and no one would get in these days as a waiter or anything else. You know they've blocked the street off? The place is a fortress. No way in there, Danny.'

'Oh, there's always a way, Sean. I was reading in a magazine the other day how a lot of French Resistance people in the Second World War were held at some Gestapo headquarters. Their cells were on the ground floor, the Gestapo on the first floor. The RAF had a fella in a Mosquito fly in at fifty feet and drop a bomb that bounced off the street and went in through the first-floor window, killing all the bloody Gestapo so the fellas downstairs got away.'

'What in the hell are you trying to say to me?' Dillon demanded.

'That I'm a great believer in the power of the bomb and the science of ballistics. You can make a bomb go anywhere if you know what you're doing.'

'What is this?' Dillon demanded.

Angel said, 'Go on, show him, Uncle Danny.'

'Show me what?' Dillon said.

Danny Fahy got up, putting another match to his pipe. 'Come on, then,' and he turned and went to the door.

Fahy opened the door of the second barn and led the way in. It was enormous, oak beams rearing up to a steeply pitched roof. There was a loft stuffed with hay and reached by a ladder. There were various items of farm machinery including a tractor. There was also a fairly new Land Rover, an old BSA 500cc motorcycle in fine condition, up on its stand.

'This is a beauty,' Dillon said in genuine admiration.

'Bought it second-hand last year. Thought I'd renovate it to make a profit, but now I'm finished, I can't bear to let it go. It's as good as a BMW.' There was another vehicle in the shadows of the rear and Fahy switched on a light and a white Ford Transit van stood revealed.

'So?' Dillon said. 'What's so special?'

'You wait, Mr Dillon,' Angel told him. 'This is really something.'

Fahy said, 'Not what it seems.'

There was an excited look on his face, a kind of pride as he opened the sliding door. Inside there was a battery of metal pipes, three in all, bolted to the floor, pointing up to the roof at an angle.

'Mortars, Sean, just like the lads have been using in Ulster.'

Dillon said, 'You mean this thing works?'

'Hell, no, I've no explosives. It would work, that's all I can say.'

'Explain it to me.'

'I've welded a steel platform to the floor, that's to stand the recoil and I've also welded the tubing together. That's standard cast-iron stuff available anywhere. The electric timers are dead simple. Stuff you can buy at any do-it-yourself shop.'

'How would it work?'

'Once switched on it would give you a minute to get out of the van and run for it. The roof is cut out. That's just stretched polythene covering the hole. You can see

I've sprayed it the same colour. It gives the mortars a clean exit. I've even worked out an extra little device linked to the timer that will self-destruct the van after it's fired the mortars.'

'And where would they be?'

'Over here.' Fahy walked to a work bench. 'Standard oxygen cylinders.' There were several stacked together, the bottom plates removed.

'And what would you need for those, Semtex?' Dillon asked, naming the Czechoslovakian explosive so popular with terrorists everywhere.

'I'd say about twelve pounds in each would do nicely, but that's not easily come by over here.'

Dillon lit a cigarette and walked around the van, his face blank. 'You're a bad boy, Danny. The movement told you to stay in deep cover.'

'Like I told you, how many years ago was that?' Fahy demanded. 'A man would go crazy.'

'So you found yourself something to do?'

'It was easy, Sean. You know I was in the light engineering for years.'

Dillon stood looking at it. Angel said, 'What do you think?'

'I think he's done a good job.'

'As good as anything they've done in Ulster,' Fahy said.

'Maybe, but whenever they've been used, they've never been too strong on accuracy.'

'They worked like a dream in that attack on Newry Police Station six years ago. Killed nine coppers.'

'What about all the other times they couldn't hit a barn door? Someone even blew himself up with one of these things in Portadown. A bit hit and miss.'

'Not the way I'd do it. I can plot the target on a large-scale map, have a look at the area on foot beforehand, line the van up and that's it. Mind you, I've been thinking that some sort of fin welded onto the oxygen cylinders would help steady them in flight. A nice big curve and then down and the whole world blows up. All the security in the world wouldn't help. I mean, what good are gates if you go over them?'

'You're talking Downing Street now?' Dillon said.

'And why not?'

'They meet at ten o'clock every morning in the Cabinet Room. What they call the War Cabinet. You'd not only get the Prime Minister, you'd get virtually the whole Government.'

Fahy crossed himself. 'Holy Mother of God, it would be the hit of a lifetime.'

'They'd make up songs about you, Danny,' Dillon told him. 'They'd be singing about Danny Fahy in bars all over Ireland fifty years from now.'

Fahy slammed a clenched fist into his palm. 'All hot air, Sean, no meaning to it without the Semtex and like I said, that stuff's impossible to get your hands on over here.'

'Don't be too sure, Danny,' Dillon said. 'There might be a source. Now let's go and have a Bushmills and sort this out.'

Fahy had a large-scale map of London spread across the table and examined it with a magnifying glass. 'Here would be the place,' he said. 'Horseguards Avenue running up from the Victoria Embankment at the side of the Ministry of Defence.'

'Yes.' Dillon nodded.

'If we left the Ford on the corner with Whitehall then as long as I had a pre-determined sighting, to get my direction, I reckon the mortar bombs would go over those roofs in a bloody great curve and land smack on Ten Downing Street!' He put his pencil down beside the ruler. 'I'd like to have a look, mind you.'

'And so you will,' Dillon said.

'Would it work, Mr Dillon?' Angel demanded.

'Oh, yes,' he said. 'I think it really could. Ten o'clock in the morning, the whole bloody War Cabinet.' He started to laugh. 'It's beautiful, Danny, beautiful.' He grabbed the other man's arm. 'You'll come in with me on this?'

'Of course I will.'

'Good,' Dillon said. 'Big, big money, Danny. I'll set you up for your old age. Total luxury. Spain, Greece, anywhere you want to go.' Fahy rolled up the map and Dillon said, 'I'll stay overnight. We'll go up to London tomorrow and have a look.' He smiled and lit another cigarette. 'It's looking good, Danny. Really good. Now tell me about this airfield near here at Grimethorpe?'

'A real broken down sort of a place. It's only three miles from here. What would you want with Grimethorpe?'

'I told you I learned to fly in the Middle East. A good way of getting out of places fast. Now what's the situation at this Grimethorpe place?'

'It goes way back into the past. A flying club in the thirties. Then the RAF used it as a feeder station during the Battle of Britain so they built three hangars. Someone tried it as a flying club a few years ago. There's a tarmac runway. Anyway, it failed. A fella called Bill Grant turned up three years ago. He has two planes there, that's all I know. His firm is called Grant's Air Taxis. I heard recently he was in trouble. His two mechanics had left. Business was bad.' He smiled. 'There's a recession on, Sean, and it even affects the rich.'

'Does he live on the premises?'

'Yes,' Angel said. 'He did have a girlfriend, but she moved on.'

'I think I'd like to meet him,' Dillon said. 'Maybe you could show me, Angel?'

'Of course.'

'Good, but first I'd like to make a phone call.'

He rang Tania Novikova at her flat. She answered at once. 'It's me,' he said.

'Has it gone well?'

'Unbelievable. I'll tell you tomorrow. Did you pick up the money?'

'Oh, yes, no problem.'

'Good. I'll be at the hotel at noon. I'm overnighting here. See you then,' and he rang off.

Brosnan and Mary Tanner went up in the freight elevator with Charlie Salter and found Mordecai waiting for them. He pumped Brosnan's hand up and down. 'It's great to see you, Professor. I can't tell you how great. Harry's been on hot bricks.'

'This is Mary Tanner,' Brosnan said. 'You'd better be nice. She's an army captain.'

'Well, this is a pleasure, miss.' Mordecai shook her hand. 'I did my National Service in the Grenadier Guards, but lance corporal was all I managed.'

He led them into the sitting room. Harry Flood was seated at the desk going over some accounts. He glanced up and jumped to his feet. 'Martin.' He rushed round the desk and embraced Brosnan, laughing in delight.

Brosnan said, 'Mary Tanner. She's army, Harry, a real hot-shot so watch your step. I'm working for Brigadier Charles Ferguson of British intelligence and she's his aide.'

'Then I'll behave.' Flood took her hand. 'Now come over here and let's have a drink and you tell me what all this is about, Martin.'

They sat in the sofa complex in the corner and Brosnan covered everything in finest detail. Mordecai leaned against the wall listening, no expression on his face.

When Brosnan was finished, Flood said, 'So what do you want from me, Martin?'

'He always works the underworld, Harry, that's where he gets everything he needs. Not only physical help, but explosives, weaponry. He'll work the same way now, I know he will.'

'So what you want to know is who he'd go to?'

'Exactly.'

Flood looked up at Mordecai. 'What do you think?'

'I don't know, Harry. I mean there are plenty of legit arms dealers, but what you need is someone who's willing to supply the IRA.'

'Any ideas?' Flood asked.

'Not really, guv. I mean, most of your real East End villains love Maggie Thatcher and wear Union Jack underpants. They don't go for Irish geezers letting off bombs at Harrods. We could make enquiries, of course.'

'Then do that,' Flood said. 'Put the word out now, but discreetly.'

Mordecai went out and Harry Flood reached for the champagne bottle. 'You're still not drinking?' Brosnan said.

'Not me, old buddy, but no reason you shouldn't. You

can fill me in with the events of recent years and then we'll go along to the *Embassy*, one of my more respectable clubs, and have something to eat.'

At around the same time, Sean Dillon and Angel Fahy were driving along the dark country road from Cadge End to Grimethorpe. The lights of the car picked out light snow and frost on the hedgerows.

'It's beautiful, isn't it?' she said.

'I suppose so.'

'I like it here, the countryside and all that. I like Uncle Danny, too. He's been really good to me.'

'That makes sense. You were raised in the country back there in Galway.'

'It wasn't the same. It was poor land there. It was hard work to make any kind of living and it showed in the people, my mother, for instance. It was as if they'd been to war and lost and there was nothing to look forward to.'

'You've got a way with the words, girl,' he told her.

'My English teacher used to say that. She said if I worked hard and studied I could do anything.'

'Well that must have been a comfort.'

'It didn't do me any good. My stepfather just saw me as an unpaid farm labourer. That's why I left.'

The lights picked out a sign that said Grimethorpe Airfield, the paintwork peeling. Dillon turned into a narrow tarmac road that was badly potholed. A few moments later, they came to the airfield. There were three hangars, an old control tower, a couple of Nissen huts, a light at the windows of one of them. A Jeep was parked there and Dillon pulled in beside it. As they got out, the door of the Nissen hut opened and a man stood there.

'Who is it?'

'It's me, Mr Grant, Angel Fahy. I've brought someone to see you.'

Grant, like most pilots, was small and wiry. He looked to be in his mid-forties, wore jeans and an old flying jacket of the kind used by American aircrews in the Second World War. 'You'd better come in, then.'

The interior of the Nissen hut was warm, heated by a coke-burning stove, the pipe going up through the roof. Grant obviously used it as a living room. There was a table with the remains of a meal on it, an old easy chair by the stove facing a television set in the corner. Beneath the windows on the other side there was a long sloping desk with a few charts.

Angel said, 'This is a friend of my uncle's.'

'Hilton,' Dillon said, 'Peter Hilton.'

Grant put his hand out, looking wary. 'Bill Grant. I don't owe you money, do I?'

'Not to my knowledge.' Dillon was back in his public school role.

'Well that makes a nice change. What can I do for you?'

'I want a charter in the next few days. Just wanted to check if you might be able to do something before I tried anywhere else.'

'Well that depends.'

'On what? You do have a plane, I take it?'

'I've got two. The only problem is how long the bank lets me hang on to them. Do you want to have a look?'

'Why not?'

They went out, crossed the apron to the end hangar and he opened a Judas so they could step through. He reached to one side, found a switch and lights came on. There were two planes there, side by side, both twin-engines.

Dillon walked up to the nearest. 'I know this baby, a Cessna Conquest. What's the other?'

'Navajo Chieftain.'

'If things are as tricky as you say, what about fuel?'

'I always keep my planes juiced up, Mr Hilton, always full tanks. I'm too old a hand to do otherwise. You never know when a job might come up.' He smiled ruefully. 'Mind you, I'll be honest. What with the recession, there aren't too many people looking for charters these days. Where would you like me to take you?'

'Actually I was thinking of going for a spin myself one day,' Dillon said. 'I'm not sure when.'

'You're certified then?' Grant looked dubious.

'Oh, yes, fully.' Dillon took out his pilot's licence and passed it across.

Grant examined it quickly and handed it back. 'You could handle either of these two, but I'd rather come myself, just to make sure.'

'No problem,' Dillon said smoothly. 'It's the West Country I was thinking of. Cornwall. There's an airfield at Land's End.'

'I know it well. Grass runway.'

'I've got friends near there. I'd probably want to stay overnight.'

'That's fine by me.' Grant switched off the lights and they walked back to the Nissen hut. 'What line are you in, Mr Hilton?'

'Oh, finance, accountancy, that sort of thing,' Dillon said.

'Have you any idea when you might want to go? I

should point out that kind of charter's going to be expensive. Around two thousand five hundred pounds. With half a dozen passengers that's not so bad, but on your own . . .'

'That's fine,' Dillon said.

'Then there would be my overnight expenses. A hotel and so on.'

'No problem.' Dillon took ten fifty-pound notes from his wallet and put them on the table. 'There's five hundred down. It's a definite booking for sometime in the next four or five days. I'll phone you here to let you know when.'

Grant's face brightened as he picked up the bank notes. 'That's fine. Can I get you a coffee or something before you go?'

'Why not?' Dillon said.

Grant went into the kitchen at the far end of the Nissen hut. They heard him filling a kettle, Dillon put a finger to his lips, made a face at Angel and crossed to the charts on the desk. He went through them quickly, found the one for the general English Channel area and the French coast. Angel stood beside him watching as he traced his finger along the Normandy coast. He found Cherbourg and moved south. There it was, St Denis, with the landing strip clearly marked, and he pushed the charts back together. Grant in the kitchen had been watching through the half-open door. As the kettle boiled, he quickly made coffee in three mugs and took them in.

'Is this weather giving you much trouble?' Dillon said. 'The snow?'

'It will if it really starts to lay,' Grant said. 'It could make it difficult for that grass runway at Land's End.'

'We'll just have to keep our fingers crossed.' Dillon put down his mug. 'We'd better be getting back.'

Grant went to the door to see them off. They got in the Mini and drove away. He waved, closed the door and went to the desk and examined the charts. It was the third or fourth down, he was sure of that. *General English Channel area and the French coast.*

He frowned and said softly, 'And what's your game, mister, I wonder?'

As they drove back through the dark country lanes Angel said, 'Not Land's End at all, Mr Dillon, it's that St Denis place in Normandy, that's where you want to fly to.'

'Our secret,' he said and put his left hand on hers, still steering. 'Can I ask you to promise me one thing?'

'Anything, Mr Dillon.'

'Let's keep it to ourselves, just for now. I don't want Danny to know. You do drive, do you?'

'Drive? Of course I do. I take the sheep to market in the Morris van myself.'

'Tell me, how would you like a trip up to London tomorrow morning with me, you and Danny?'

'I'd like it fine.'

'Good, that's all right then.'

As they carried on through the night her eyes were shining.

9

It was a cold, crisp morning, winter on every hand, but the roads were clear as Dillon drove up to London, Angel and Danny Fahy following in the Morris van. Angel was driving and more than competently. He could see her in his rear-view mirror and she stayed right on his tail all the way into London until they came to the Bayswater Road. There was a plan already half-formed in his mind and he got out of the Mini Cooper, parked it at the kerb and opened the doors of Tania's garage.

As Angel and Danny drew up behind him he said, 'Put the Morris inside.' Angel did as she was told. When she and Danny Fahy came out, Dillon closed the doors and said, 'You'll remember the street and the garage, if you lose me, that is?'

'Don't be silly, Mr Dillon, of course I will,' Angel said.

'Good. It's important. Now get in the Mini. We're going for a little run round.'

Harry Flood was sitting at the desk in his apartment at Cable Wharf checking the casino accounts from the night before when Charlie Salter brought in coffee on a tray. The phone rang and the small man picked it up. He handed it to Flood.

'The Professor.'

'Martin, how goes it?' Flood said. 'I enjoyed last night. The Tanner lady is something special.'

'Is there any news? Have you managed to come up with anything?' Brosnan asked.

'Not yet, Martin, just a minute.' Flood put a hand over the receiver and said to Salter, 'Where's Mordecai?'

'Doing the rounds, Harry, just like you asked him, putting the word out discreetly.'

Flood returned to Brosnan. 'Sorry, old buddy, we're doing everything we can, but it's going to take time.'

'Which we don't really have,' Brosnan said. 'All right, Harry, I know you're doing your best. I'll stay in touch.'

He was standing at Mary Tanner's desk in the living room of her Lowndes Square flat. He put the phone down, walked to the window and lit a cigarette.

'Anything?' she asked and crossed the room to join him.

'I'm afraid not. As Harry has just said, it takes time. I was a fool to think anything else.'

'Just try and be patient, Martin.' She put a hand on his arm.

'But I can't,' he said. 'I've got this feeling and it's hard to explain. It's like being in a storm and waiting for that bloody great thunderclap you know is going to come. I know Dillon, Mary. He's moving fast on this. I'm certain of it.'

'So what would you like to do?'

'Will Ferguson be at Cavendish Square this morning?'

'Yes.'

'Then let's go to see him.'

Dillon parked the Mini Cooper near Covent Garden. An enquiry in a bookshop nearby led them to a shop not too far away specialising in maps and charts of every description. Dillon worked his way through the large-scale Ordnance Survey maps of Central London until he found the one covering the general area of Whitehall.

'Would you look at the detail in that thing?' Fahy whispered. 'You could measure the size of the garden at Number Ten to half an inch.'

Dillon purchased the map which the assistant rolled up tightly and inserted into a protective cardboard tube. He paid for it and they walked back to the car.

'Now what?' Danny asked.

'We'll take a run round. Have a look at the situation.'

'That suits me.'

Angel sat in the rear, her uncle beside Dillon as they drove down towards the river and turned into Horseguards Avenue. Dillon paused slightly on the corner before turning into Whitehall and moving towards Downing Street.

'Plenty of coppers around,' Danny said.

'That's to make sure people don't park.' A car had drawn in to the kerb on their left and as they pulled out to pass, they saw that the driver was consulting a map.

'Tourist, I expect,' Angel said.

'And look what's happening,' Dillon told her.

She turned and saw two policemen converging on the car. A quiet word, it started up and moved away.

Angel said, 'They don't waste time.'

'Downing Street,' Dillon announced a moment later.

'Would you look at those gates?' Danny said in wonder. 'I like the Gothic touch. Sure and they've done a good job there.'

Dillon moved with the traffic round Parliament Square and went back up Whitehall towards Trafalgar Square. 'We're going back to Bayswater,' he said. 'Notice the route I've chosen.'

He moved out of the traffic of Trafalgar Square through Admiralty Arch along the Mall, round the Queen Victoria monument past Buckingham Palace and along Constitution Hill, eventually reaching Marble Arch by way of Park Lane and turning into the Bayswater Road.

'And that's simple enough,' Danny Fahy said.

'Good,' Dillon said. 'Then let's go and get a nice cup of tea at my truly awful hotel.'

Ferguson said, 'You're getting too restless, Martin.'

'It's the waiting,' Brosnan told him. 'Flood's doing his best, I know that, but I don't think time is on our side.'

Ferguson turned from the window and sipped a little of the cup of tea he was holding. 'So what would you like to do?'

Brosnan hesitated, glanced at Mary and said, 'I'd like to go and see Liam Devlin in Kilrea. He might have some ideas.'

'Something he was never short of.' Ferguson turned to Mary. 'What do you think?'

'I think it makes sense, sir. After all, a trip to Dublin's no big deal. An hour and a quarter from Heathrow on either Aer Lingus or BA.'

'And Liam's place at Kilrea is only half an hour from the city,' Brosnan said.

'All right,' Ferguson said, 'you've made your point, both of you, but make it Gatwick and the Lear jet, just in case anything comes up and you need to get back here in a hurry.'

'Thank you, sir,' Mary said.

As they reached the door, Ferguson added, 'I'll give the old rogue a call, just to let him know you're on your way,' and he reached for the phone.

As they went downstairs Brosnan said, 'Thank God. At least I feel we're doing something.'

'And I get to meet the great Liam Devlin at long last,' Mary said and led the way out to the limousine.

In the small café at the hotel Dillon, Angel and Fahy sat at a corner table drinking tea. Fahy had the Ordnance Survey map partially open on his knee. 'It's extraordinary. The things they give away. Every detail.'

'Could it be done, Danny?'

'Oh, yes, no trouble. You remember that corner, Horseguards Avenue and Whitehall? That would be the place, slightly on an angle. I can see it in my mind's eye. I can plot the distance from that corner to Number Ten exactly from this map.'

'You're sure you'd clear the buildings in between?'

'Oh, yes. I've said before, Sean, ballistics is a matter of science.'

'But you can't stop there,' Angel said. 'We saw what happened to that man in the car. The police were on him in seconds.'

Dillon turned to Fahy. 'Danny?'

'Well, that's all you need. Everything pre-timed, Angel. Press the right switch to activate the circuit, get out of the

181

van and the mortars start firing within a minute. No policeman could act fast enough to stop it.'

'But what would happen to you?' she demanded.

It was Dillon who answered. 'Just listen to this. We drive up from Cadge End one morning early, you, Danny, in the Ford Transit and Angel and me in the Morris van. We'll have that BSA motorcycle in the back of that. Angel will park the Morris, like today, in the garage at the end of the road. We'll have a duckboard in the back so I can run the BSA out.'

'And you'll follow me, is that it?'

'I'll be right up your tail. When we reach the corner of Horse Guards Avenue and Whitehall, you set your switch, get out and jump straight on my pillion and we'll be away. The War Cabinet meets every morning at ten. With luck we could get the lot.'

'Jesus, Sean, they'd never know what hit them.'

'Straight back to Bayswater to Angel waiting in the garage with the Morris, BSA in the back and away we go. We'll be in Cadge End while they're still trying to put the fires out.'

'It's brilliant, Mr Dillon,' Angel told him.

'Except for one thing,' Fahy said. 'Without the bloody explosives, we don't have any bloody bombs.'

'You leave that to me,' Dillon said. 'I'll get your explosives for you.' He stood up. 'But I've got things to do. You two go back to Cadge End and wait. I'll be in touch.'

'And when would that be, Sean?'

'Soon – very soon,' and Dillon smiled as they went out.

Tania was knocking at his door precisely at noon. He opened it and said, 'You've got it?'

She had a briefcase in her right hand, opened it on the table to reveal the thirty thousand dollars he'd asked for.

'Good,' he said. 'I'll just need ten thousand to be going on with.'

'What will you do with the rest?'

'I'll hand it in at the desk. They can keep your briefcase in the hotel safe.'

'You've worked something out, I can tell.' She looked excited. 'What happened at this Cadge End place?'

So he told her and in detail, the entire plan. 'What do you think?' he asked when he'd finished.

'Incredible. The coup of a lifetime. But what about the explosives? You'd need Semtex.'

'That's all right. When I was operating in London in eighty-one I used to deal with a man who had access to Semtex.' He laughed. 'In fact he had access to everything.'

'And who is this man? How can you be sure he's still around?'

'A crook named Jack Harvey and he's around all right. I looked him up.'

'But I don't understand?'

'Amongst other things he has a funeral business in Whitechapel. I looked it up in Yellow Pages and it's still there. By the way, your Mini, I can still use it?'

'Of course.'

'Good. I'll park it somewhere in the street. I want that garage free.'

He picked up his coat. 'Come on, we'll go and have a bite to eat and then I'll go and see him.'

'You've read the file on Devlin, I suppose?' Brosnan asked Mary Tanner as they drove through the centre of Dublin

183

and crossed the River Liffey by St George's Quay and moved on out of the other side of the city, driven by a chauffeur in a limousine from the Embassy.

'Yes,' she said, 'but is it all true? The story about his involvement with the German attempt to get Churchill in the war?'

'Oh, yes.'

'The same man who helped you break out of that French prison in nineteen seventy-nine?'

'That's Devlin.'

'But Martin, you said he claimed to be seventy. He must be older than that.'

'A few years is a minor detail where Liam Devlin is concerned. Let's put it this way, you're about to meet the most extraordinary man you've ever met in your life. Scholar, poet and gunman for the IRA.'

'The last part is no recommendation to me,' she said.

'I know,' he told her. 'But never make the mistake of lumping Devlin in with the kind of rubbish the IRA employs these days.'

He retreated into himself, suddenly sombre, and the car continued out into the Irish countryside, leaving the city behind.

Kilrea Cottage, the place was called, on the outskirts of the village next to a convent. It was a period piece, single-storeyed with Gothic-looking gables and leaded windows on either side of the porch. They sheltered in there from the light rain while Brosnan tugged an old-fashioned bell pull. There was the sound of footsteps, the door opened.

'*Cead míle fáilte*,' Liam Devlin said in Irish. 'A hundred

thousand welcomes,' and he flung his arms around Brosnan.

The interior of the house was very Victorian. Most of the furniture was mahogany, the wallpaper was a William Morris replica, but the paintings on the walls, all Atkinson Grimshaws, were real.

Liam Devlin came in from the kitchen with tea things on a tray. 'My housekeeper comes mornings only. One of the good sisters from the convent next door. They need the money.'

Mary Tanner was totally astonished. She'd expected an old man and found herself faced with this ageless creature in black silk Italian shirt, black pullover, grey slacks in the latest fashionable cut. There was still considerable colour in hair that had once been black and the face was pale, but she sensed that had always been so. The blue eyes were extraordinary as was that perpetual ironic smile with which he seemed to laugh at himself as much as the world.

'So, you work for Ferguson, girl?' he said to Mary as he poured the tea.

'That's right.'

'That business in Derry the other year when you moved that car with the bomb. That was quite something.'

She felt herself flushing. 'No big deal, Mr Devlin, it just seemed like the right thing to do at the time.'

'Oh, we can all see that on occasions, it's the doing that counts.' He turned to Brosnan. 'Anne-Marie. A bad business, son.'

'I want him, Liam,' Brosnan said.

'For yourself or for the general cause?' Devlin shook

his head. 'Push the personal thing to one side, Martin, or you'll make mistakes and that's something you can't afford to do with Sean Dillon.'

'Yes, I know,' Brosnan said. 'I know.'

'So, he intends to take a crack at this John Major fella, the new Prime Minister?' Devlin said.

'And how do you think he's likely to do that, Mr Devlin?' Mary asked.

'Well, from what I hear about security at Ten Downing Street these days, I wouldn't rate his changes of getting in very high.' He looked at Brosnan and grinned. 'Mind you, Mary, my love, I remember a young fella of my acquaintance called Martin Brosnan who got into Number Ten posing as a waiter at a party not ten years ago. Left a rose on the Prime Minister's desk. Of course, the office was held by a woman then.'

Brosnan said, 'All in the past, Liam, what about now?'

'Oh, he'll work as he always has using contacts in the underworld.'

'Not the IRA?'

'I doubt whether the IRA has any connection with this whatsoever.'

'But they did last time he worked in London ten years ago.'

'So?'

'I was wondering. If we knew who recruited him that time, it could help.'

'I see what you mean, give you some sort of lead as to who he worked with in London?'

'All right, not much of a chance, but the only one we've got, Brosnan.'

'There's still your friend Flood, in London.'

'I know and he'll pull out all the stops, but that takes time and we don't have much to spare.'

Devlin nodded. 'Right, son, you leave it with me and I'll see what I can do.' He glanced at his watch. 'One o'clock. We'll have a sandwich and perhaps a Bushmills together and I suggest you go to your Lear jet and hare back to London. I'll be in touch, believe me, the minute I have something.'

Dillon parked round the corner from Jack Harvey's funeral business in Whitechapel and walked, the briefcase in one hand. Everything was beautifully discreet down to the bell push that summoned the day porter to open the door.

'Mr Harvey,' Dillon lied cheerfully. 'He's expecting me.'

'Down the hall past the chapels of rest and up the stairs. His office is on the first floor. What was the name, sir?'

'Hilton.' Dillon looked around at the coffins on display, the flowers. 'Not much happening.'

'Trade you mean.' The porter shrugged. 'That all comes in the back way.'

'I see.'

Dillon moved down the hall, pausing to glance into one of the chapels of rest, taking in the banked flowers, the candles. He stepped in and looked down at the body of a middle-aged man neatly dressed in a dark suit, hands folded, the face touched with make-up.

'Poor sod,' Dillon said and went out.

At the reception desk, the porter picked up a phone. 'Miss Myra? A visitor. A Mr Hilton, says he has an appointment.'

Dillon opened the door to Harvey's outer office and moved in. There were no office furnishings, just a couple of potted plants and several easy chairs. The door to the inner office opened and Myra entered. She wore skin-tight black trews, black boots and a scarlet three-quarter-length kaftan. She looked very striking.

'Mr Hilton?'

'That's right.'

'I'm Myra Harvey. You said you had an appointment with my uncle.'

'Did I?'

She looked him over in a casual way and behind him the door opened and Billy Watson came in. The whole thing was obviously pre-arranged. He leaned against the door, suitably menacing in a black suit, arms folded.

'Now what's your game?' she said.

'That's for Mr Harvey.'

'Throw him out, Billy,' she said and turned to the door.

Billy put one rough hand on Dillon's shoulder. Dillon's foot went all the way down the right leg stamping on the instep, he pivoted and struck sideways with clenched fist, the knuckles on the back of the hand connecting with Billy's temple. Billy cried out in pain and fell back into one of the chairs.

'He's not very good, is he?' Dillon said.

He opened his briefcase and took out ten one-hundred-dollar bills with a rubber band round them and threw them at Myra. She missed the catch and had to bend to pick them up. 'Would you look at that,' she said. 'And brand new.'

'Yes, new money always smells so good,' Dillon said. 'Now tell Jack an old friend would like to see him with more of the same.'

She stood there looking at him for a moment, eyes

narrowed, then she turned and opened the door to Harvey's office. Billy tried to get up and Dillon said, 'I wouldn't advise it.'

Billy subsided as the door opened and Myra appeared. 'All right, he'll see you.'

The room was surprisingly businesslike with walls panelled in oak, a green carpet in Georgian silk and a gas fire that almost looked real, burning in a steel basket on the hearth. Harvey sat behind a massive oak desk smoking a cigar.

He had the thousand dollars in front of him and looked Dillon over calmly. 'My time's limited so don't muck me about, son.' He picked up the bank notes. 'More of the same?'

'That's right.'

'I don't know you. You told Myra you were an old friend, but I've never seen you before.'

'A long time ago, Jack, ten years to be precise. I looked different then. I was over from Belfast on a job. We did business together, you and me. You did well out of it as I recall. All those lovely dollars raised by IRA sympathisers in America.'

Harvey said, 'Coogan. Michael Coogan.'

Dillon took off his glasses. 'As ever was, Jack.'

Harvey nodded slowly and said to his niece, 'Myra, an old friend, Mr Coogan from Belfast.'

'I see,' she said. 'One of those.'

Dillon lit a cigarette, sat down, the briefcase on the floor beside him and Harvey said, 'You went through London like bloody Attila the Hun last time. I should have charged you more for all that stuff.'

'You gave me a price, I paid it,' Dillon said. 'What could be fairer?'

'And what is it this time?'

'I need a little Semtex, Jack. I could manage with forty pounds, but that's the bottom line. Fifty would be better.'

'You don't want much, do you? That stuff's like gold. Very strict government controls.'

'Bollocks,' Dillon said. 'It passes from Czechoslovakia to Italy, Greece, onwards to Libya. It's everywhere, Jack, you know it and I know it so don't waste my time. Twenty thousand dollars.' He opened the briefcase on his knee and tossed the rest of the ten thousand packet by packet across the desk. 'Ten now and ten on delivery.'

The Walther with the Carswell silencer screwed on the end of the barrel lay ready in the briefcase. He waited, the lid up and then Harvey smiled. 'All right, but it'll cost you thirty.'

Dillon closed the briefcase. 'No can do, Jack. Twenty-five I can manage, but no more.'

Harvey nodded. 'All right. When do you want it?'

'Twenty-four hours.'

'I think I can manage that. Where can we reach you?'

'You've got it wrong way round, Jack, I contact you.'

Dillon stood up and Harvey said affably, 'Anything else we can do for you?'

'Actually there is,' Dillon said. 'Sign of goodwill, you might say. I could do with a spare handgun.'

'Be my guest, my old son.' Harvey pushed his chair back and opened the second drawer down on his right-hand side. 'Take your pick.'

There was a Smith & Wesson .38 revolver, a Czech Cesca and an Italian Beretta which was the one Dillon selected. He checked the clip and slipped the gun in his pocket. 'This will do nicely.'

'Lady's gun,' Harvey said, 'but that's your business. We'll be seeing you then tomorrow.'

Myra opened the door. Dillon said, 'A pleasure, Miss Harvey,' and he brushed past Billy and walked out.

Billy said, 'I'd like to break that little bastard's legs.'

Myra patted his cheek. 'Never mind, sunshine, on your two feet you're useless. It's in the horizontal position you come into your own. Now go and play with your motorbike or something,' and she went back in her uncle's office.

Dillon paused at the bottom of the stairs and slipped the Beretta inside the briefcase. The only thing better than one gun was two. It always gave you an ace in the hole and he walked back to the Mini Cooper briskly.

Myra said, 'I wouldn't trust him an inch, that one.'

'A hard little bastard,' Harvey said. 'When he was here for the IRA in nineteen eighty-one I supplied him with arms, explosives, everything. You were at college then, not in the business, so you probably don't remember.'

'Is Coogan his real name?'

'Course not.' He nodded. 'Yes, hell on wheels. I was having a lot of hassle in those days from George Montoya down in Bermondsey, the one they called Spanish George. Coogan knocked him off for me one night, him and his brother, outside a bar called the Flamenco. Did it for free.'

'Really?' Myra said. 'So where do we get him Semtex?'

He laughed, opened the top drawer and took out a bunch of keys. 'I'll show you.' He led the way out and along the corridor and unlocked a door. 'Something even you didn't know, darling.'

The room was lined with shelves of box files. He put his hand on the middle shelf of the rear wall and it swung open. He reached for a switch and turned on a light revealing a treasure house of weapons of every description.

'My God!' she said.

'Whatever you want, it's here,' he said. 'Handguns, AK assault rifles, M15s.' He chuckled. 'And Semtex.' There were three cardboard boxes on a table. 'Fifty pounds in each of those.'

'But why did you tell him it might take time?'

'Keep him dangling.' He led the way out and closed things up. 'Might screw a few more bob out of him.'

As they went back into his office she said, 'What do you think he's up to?'

'I couldn't care less. Anyway, why should you worry? You suddenly turned into a bleeding patriot or something?'

'It isn't that, I'm just curious.'

He clipped another cigar. 'Mind you, I have had a thought. Very convenient if I got the little bugger to knock off Harry Flood for me,' and he started to laugh.

It was just after six and Ferguson was just about to leave his office at the Ministry of Defence when his phone rang. It was Devlin. 'Now then, you old sod, I've news for you.'

'Get on with it then,' Ferguson said.

'Dillon's control in eighty-one in Belfast was a man called Tommy McGuire. Remember him?'

'I do indeed. Wasn't he shot a few years ago? Some sort of IRA feud?'

'That was the story, but he's still around up there using another identity.'

'And what would that be?'

'I've still to find that out. People to see in Belfast. I'm driving up there tonight. I take it, by the way, that involving myself in this way makes me an official agent of Group Four? I mean I wouldn't like to end up in prison, not at my age.'

'You'll be covered fully, you have my word on it. Now what do you want us to do?'

'I was thinking that if Brosnan and your Captain Tanner wanted to be in on the action, they could fly over in the morning in that Lear jet of yours, to Belfast, that is and wait for me at the Europa Hotel in the bar. Tell Brosnan to identify himself to the head porter. I'll be in touch probably around noon.'

'I'll see to it,' Ferguson said.

'Just one more thing. Don't you think you and I are getting just a little geriatric for this sort of game?'

'You speak for yourself,' Ferguson said and put the phone down.

He sat thinking about it, then phoned through for a secretary. He also called Mary Tanner at the Lowndes Square flat. As he was talking to her, Alice Johnson came in with her notepad and pencil. Ferguson waved her down and carried on speaking to Mary.

'So, early start in the morning. Gatwick again, I think. You'll be there in an hour in the Lear. Are you dining out tonight?'

'Harry Flood suggested the River Room at the Savoy, he likes the dance band.'

'Sounds like fun.'

'Would you like to join us, sir?'

'Actually, I would,' Ferguson said.

'We'll see you then. Eight o'clock.'

Ferguson put down the phone and turned to Alice Johnson. 'A brief note, eyes of the Prime Minister only, the special file.' He quickly dictated a report that brought everything up to date including his conversation with Devlin. 'One copy for the PM and alert a messenger. Usual copy for me and the file. Hurry it up and bring them along for my signature. I want to get away.'

She went down to the office quickly. Gordon Brown was standing at the copier as she sat behind the typewriter. 'I thought he'd gone?' he said.

'So did I, but he's just given me an extra. Another eyes of the Prime Minister only.'

'Really.'

She started to type furiously, was finished in two minutes. She stood up. 'He'll have to hang on. I need to go to the toilet.'

'I'll do the copying for you.'

'Thanks, Gordon.'

She went out and along the corridor, was opening the toilet door when she realised she'd left her handbag on the desk. She turned and hurried back to the office. The door was partially open and she could see Gordon standing at the copier reading a copy of the report. To her astonishment, he folded it, slipped it in his inside pocket and hurriedly did another.

Alice was totally thrown, had no idea what to do. She went back along the corridor to the toilet, went in and tried to pull herself together. After a while she went back.

The report and a file copy were on her desk. 'All done,' Gordon Brown said, 'and I've requested a messenger.'

She managed a light smile. 'I'll get them signed.'

'Right, I'm just going down to the canteen. I'll see you later.'

Alice went along the corridor, knocked on Ferguson's door and went in. He was at his desk writing and looked up. 'Oh, good. I'll sign those and you can get the PM's copy off to Downing Street straight away.' She was trembling now and he frowned. 'My dear Mrs Johnson, what is it?'

So she told him.

He sat there, grim-faced and as she finished, reached for the telephone. 'Special Branch, Detective Inspector Lane for Brigadier Ferguson, Group Four. Top Priority, no delay. My office now.'

He put the phone down. 'Now this is what you do. Go back to the office and behave as if nothing has happened.'

'But he isn't there, Brigadier, he went to the canteen.'

'Really?' Ferguson said. 'Now why would he do that?'

When Tania heard Gordon Brown's voice she was immediately angry. 'I've told you about this, Gordon.'

'Yes, but it's urgent.'

'Where are you?'

'In the canteen at the Ministry. I've got another report.'

'Is it important?'

'Very.'

'Read it to me.'

'No, I'll bring it round after I come off shift at ten.'

'I'll see you at your place, Gordon, I promise, but I want to know what you've got now and if you refuse, then don't bother to call again.'

'No, that's all right, I'll read it.'

Which he did and when he was finished she said, 'Good boy, Gordon, I'll see you later.'

He put the phone down and turned, folding the copy of the report. The door to the phone box was jerked open and Ferguson plucked the report from his fingers.

10

Dillon was in his room at the hotel when Tania called him. 'I've got rather hot news,' she said. 'The hunt for a lead on you is moving to Belfast.'

'Tell me,' he said.

Which she did. When she was finished, she said, 'Does any of this make any sense?'

'Yes,' he said. 'The McGuire fella was a big name with the Provos in those days.'

'And he's dead, is he, or is he still around?'

'Devlin's right about that. His death was reported, supposedly because of in-fighting in the movement, but it was just a ruse to help him drop out of sight.'

'If they found him, could it give you problems?'

'Maybe, but not if I found him first.'

'And how could you do that?'

'I know his half-brother, a fella called Macey. He would know where he is.'

'But that would mean a trip to Belfast yourself.'

'That would be no big deal. An hour and a quarter by

British Airways. I don't know what time the last plane tonight gets in, I'd have to check.'

'Just a minute, I've got a BA Worldwide Timetable here.' she said and opened her desk drawer. She found it and looked at the Belfast schedule. 'The last plane is eight-thirty. You'll never make it. It's quarter to seven now. It's murder getting out to Heathrow in the evening traffic and this weather will make it worse. Probably at least an hour or maybe an hour and a half.'

'I know,' Dillon said. 'What about the morning?'

'Same time, eight-thirty.'

'I'll just have to get up early.'

'Is it wise?'

'Is anything in this life? I'll handle it, don't worry. I'll be in touch.'

He put the phone down, thought about it for a while then called British Airways and booked a seat on the morning flight with an open return. He lit a cigarette and walked to the window. Was it wise, she'd said, and he tried to remember what Tommy McGuire had known about him in eighty-one. Nothing about Danny Fahy, that was certain because Fahy wasn't supposed to be involved that time. That had been personal. But Jack Harvey was another matter. After all, it had been McGuire who'd put him on to Harvey as an arms supplier in the first place.

He pulled on his jacket, got his trenchcoat from the wardrobe and went out. Five minutes later he was hailing a cab on the corner. He got in and told the driver to take him to Covent Garden.

* * *

Gordon Brown sat on the other side of Ferguson's desk in the half-light. He had never been so frightened in his life. 'I didn't mean any harm, Brigadier, I swear it.'

'Then why did you take a copy of the report?'

'It was just a whim. Stupid, I know, but I was so intrigued with it being for the Prime Minister.'

'You realise what you've done, Gordon, a man of your service? All those years in the army? This could mean your pension.'

Detective Inspector Lane of Special Branch was in his late thirties and in his crumpled tweed suit and glasses looked like a schoolmaster. He said, 'I'm going to ask you again, Mr Brown.' He leaned on the end of the desk. 'Have you ever taken copies like this before?'

'Absolutely not, I swear it.'

'You've never been asked by another person to do such a thing?'

Gordon managed to look suitably shocked. 'Good heavens, Inspector, that would be treason. I was a sergeant major in the Intelligence Corps.'

'Yes, Mr Brown, we know all that,' Lane said.

The internal phone went and Ferguson lifted it. It was Lane's sergeant, Mackie. 'I'm outside, Brigadier, just back from the flat in Camden. I think you and the Inspector should come out.'

'Thank you.' Ferguson put the phone down. 'Right, I think we'll give you time to think things over, Gordon. Inspector?'

He nodded to Lane, got up and moved to the door and Lane followed him. Mackie was standing in the anteroom still in trilby and raincoat, a plastic bag in one hand.

'You found something, Sergeant?' Lane asked.

'You could call it that, sir.' Mackie took a cardboard file from his plastic bag and opened it. 'A rather interesting collection.'

The copies of the reports were neatly stacked in order, the latest ones for the Prime Minister's attention on top.

Lane said, 'Christ, Brigadier, he's been at it for a while.'

'So it would seem,' Ferguson said. 'But to what purpose?'

'You mean he's working for someone, sir?'

'Without a doubt. The present operation I'm engaged on is most delicate. There was an attack on a man working for me in Paris. A woman died. We wondered how the villain of the piece knew about them, if you follow me. Now we know. Details of these reports were passed on to a third party. They must have been.'

Lane nodded. 'Then we'll have to work on him some more.'

'No, we don't have the time. Let's try another way. Let's just let him go. He's a simple man. I think he'd do the simple thing.'

'Right, sir.' Lane turned to Mackie. 'If you lose him, you'll be back pounding the pavement in Brixton, and so will I because I'm coming with you.'

They hurried out and Ferguson opened the door and went back in the office. He sat down behind the desk. 'A sad business, Gordon.'

'What's going to happen to me, Brigadier?'

'I'll have to think about it.' Ferguson picked up the copy of the report. 'Such an incredibly stupid thing to do.' He sighed. 'Go home, Gordon, go home. I'll see you in the morning.'

Gordon Brown couldn't believe his luck. He got the door open somehow and left, hurrying down the corridor to the staff cloakroom. The narrowest escape of his life. It could have meant the end of everything. Not only his career and pension, but prison. But that was it: no more and Tania would have to accept that. He went downstairs to the car park, pulling on his coat, found his car and was turning into Whitehall a few moments later, Mackie and Lane hard on his tail in the sergeant's unmarked Ford Capri.

Dillon knew that late-night shopping was the thing in the Covent Garden area. There were still plenty of people around in spite of the winter cold and he hurried along until he came to the theatrical shop, Clayton's, near Neal's Yard. The lights were on in the window, the door opened to his touch, the bell tinkling.

Clayton came through the bead curtain and smiled. 'Oh, it's you. What can I do for you?'

'Wigs,' Dillon told him.

'A nice selection over here.' He was right. There was everything, short, long, permed, blonde, red-head. Dillon selected one that was shoulder length and grey.

'I see,' Clayton said. 'The granny look?'

'Something like that. What about costume? I don't mean anything fancy. Second-hand?'

'In here.'

Clayton went through the bead curtain and Dillon followed him. There was rack upon rack of clothes and a jumbled heap in the corner. He worked very quickly, sorting through, selected a long brown skirt with an elastic waist and a shabby raincoat that almost came down to his ankles.

Clayton said, 'What are you going to play, Old Mother Riley or a bag lady?'

'You'd be surprised.' Dillon had seen a pair of jeans on top of the jumble in the corner. He picked them up and searched through a pile of shoes beside them, selecting a pair of runners that had seen better days.

'These will do,' he said. 'Oh, and this,' and he picked an old headscarf from a stand. 'Stick 'em all in a couple of plastic bags. How much?'

Clayton started to pack them. 'By rights I should thank you for taking them away, but we've all got to live. Ten quid to you.'

Dillon paid him and picked up the bags. 'Thanks a lot.'

Clayton opened the door for him. 'Have a good show, luv, give 'em hell.'

'Oh, I will,' Dillon said and he hurried down to the corner, hailed a cab and told the driver to take him back to the hotel.

When Tania Novikova went down to answer the bell and opened the door to find Gordon Brown there she knew, by instinct, that something was wrong.

'What's this, Gordon? I told you I'd come round to your place.'

'I must see you, Tania, it's essential. Something terrible has happened!'

'Calm down,' she said. 'Just take it easy. Come upstairs and tell me all about it.'

Lane and Mackie were parked at the end of the street and the Inspector was already on the car phone to Ferguson and gave him the address.

'Sergeant Mackie's done a quick check at the door, sir. The card says a Miss Tania Novikova.'

'Oh, dear,' Ferguson said.

'You know her, sir?'

'Supposedly a secretary at the Soviet Embassy, Inspector. In fact she's a captain in the KGB.'

'That means she's one of Colonel Yuri Gatov's people, sir, he runs London station.'

'I'm not so sure. Gatov is a Gorbachev man and very pro-West. On the other hand, I always understood the Novikova woman to be to the right of Genghis Khan. I'd be surprised if Gatov knew about this.'

'Are you going to notify him, sir?'

'Not yet. Let's see what she's got to say first. It's information we're after.'

'Shall we go in, sir?'

'No, wait for me. I'll be with you in twenty minutes.'

Tania peered cautiously through a chink in the curtains. She saw Mackie standing by his car at the end of the street and it was enough. She could smell policemen anywhere in the world, Moscow, Paris, London – it was always the same.

'Tell me again, Gordon, exactly what happened.'

Gordon Brown did as he was told and she sat there listening patiently. She nodded when he'd finished. 'We were lucky, Gordon, very lucky. Go and make us a cup of coffee in the kitchen. I've got a couple of phone calls to make.' She squeezed his hand. 'Afterwards we'll have a very special time together.'

'Really?' His face brightened and he went out.

She picked up the phone and called Makeev at his Paris apartment. It rang for quite a time and she was about to put it down when it was picked up at the other end.

'Josef, it's Tania.'

'I was in the shower,' he said. 'I'm dripping all over the carpet.'

'I've only got seconds, Josef. I just wanted to say goodbye. I'm blown. My mole was exposed. They'll be kicking in the door any minute.'

'My God!' he said. 'And Dillon?'

'He's safe. All systems go. What that man has planned will set the world on fire.'

'But you, Tania?'

'Don't worry, I won't let them take me. Goodbye, Josef.'

She put the phone down, lit a cigarette, then called the hotel and asked for Dillon's room. He answered at once.

'It's Tania,' she said. 'We've got trouble.'

He was quite calm. 'How bad?'

'They rumbled my mole, let him go and the poor idiot came straight here. I smell Special Branch at the end of the street.'

'I see. What are you going to do?'

'Don't worry, I won't be around to tell them anything. One thing. They'll know that Gordon gave me the contents of tonight's report. He was in the telephone booth in the Ministry canteen when Ferguson arrested him.'

'I see.'

'Promise me one thing,' she said.

'What's that?'

'Blow them away, all of them.' The doorbell rang. She said, 'I've got to go. Luck, Dillon.'

As she put down the phone, Gordon Brown came in with the coffee. 'Was that the door?'

'Yes, be an angel, Gordon, and see who it is.'

He opened the door and started downstairs. Tania took

a deep breath. Dying wasn't difficult. The cause she believed in had always been the most important thing in her life. She stubbed out her cigarette, opened a drawer in the desk, took out a Makarov pistol and shot herself through the right temple.

Gordon Brown, halfway down the stairs, turned and bounded up, bursting into the room. At the sight of her lying there beside the desk, the pistol still in her right hand, he let out a terrible cry and fell on his knees.

'Tania, my darling,' he moaned.

And then he knew what he must do as he heard something heavy crash against the door below. He prised the Makarov from her hand and as he raised it, his own hand was trembling. He took a deep breath to steady himself and pulled the trigger in the same moment that the front door burst open and Lane and Mackie started upstairs, Ferguson behind them.

There was a small crowd at the end of the street exhibiting the usual public curiosity. Dillon joined in, his collar up, hands in pockets. It started to snow slightly as they opened the rear doors of the ambulance. He watched as the two blanket-covered stretchers were loaded. The ambulance drove away. Ferguson stood on the pavement for a few moments talking to Lane and Mackie. Dillon recognised the Brigadier straight away, had been shown his photo many years previously. Lane and Mackie were obviously policemen.

After a while, Ferguson got in his car and was driven away, Mackie went into the flat and Lane also drove away. The stratagem was obvious. For Mackie to wait just in case someone turned up. One thing was certain. Tania

Novikova was dead and so was the boyfriend and Dillon knew that thanks to her sacrifice, he was safe.

He went back to the hotel and phoned Makeev at his flat in Paris. 'I've got bad news, Josef.'

'Tania?'

'How did you know?'

'She phoned. What's happened?'

'She was blown or rather her mole was. She killed herself, Josef, rather than get taken. A dedicated lady.'

'And the mole? The boyfriend?'

'Did the same. I've just seen the bodies carted out to an ambulance. Ferguson was there.'

'How will this affect you?'

'In no way. I'm off to Belfast in the morning to cut off the only chance of a lead they might have.'

'And then?'

'I'll amaze you, Josef, and your Arab friend. How does the entire British War Cabinet sound to you?'

'Dear God, you can't be serious?'

'Oh, but I am. I'll be in touch very soon now.'

He replaced the phone, put on his jacket and went down to the bar, whistling.

Ferguson was sitting in a booth in the lounge bar of the pub opposite Kensington Park Gardens and the Soviet Embassy, waiting for Colonel Yuri Gatov. The Russian, when he appeared, looked agitated, a tall, white-haired man in a camel overcoat. He saw Ferguson and hurried over.

'Charles, I can't believe it. Tania Novikova dead. Why?'

'Yuri, you and I have known each other for better than twenty-five years, often as adversaries, but I'll take a chance on you now, a chance that you really do want to see change in our time and an end to East–West conflict.'

'But I do, you know that.'

'Unfortunately, not everyone in the KGB would agree with you, and Tania Novikova was one.'

'She was a hardliner, true, but what are you saying, Charles?'

So Ferguson told him, Dillon, the attempt on Mrs Thatcher, Gordon Brown, Brosnan, everything.

Gatov said, 'This IRA wild card intends to attempt the life of the Prime Minister, that's what you're telling me, and Tania was involved?'

'Oh, very directly.'

'But Charles, I knew nothing, I swear.'

'And I believe you, old chap, but she must have had a link with someone. I mean she managed to convey vital information to Dillon in Paris. That's how he knew about Brosnan and so on.'

'Paris,' Gatov said. 'That's a thought. Did you know she was in Paris for three years before transferring to London and you know who's head of Paris station for the KGB?'

'Of course, Josef Makeev,' Ferguson said.

'Anything but a Gorbachev man. Very much of the old guard.'

'It would explain a great deal,' Ferguson said. 'But we'll never prove it.'

'True,' Gatov nodded. 'But I'll give him a call anyway, just to worry him.'

Makeev had not strayed far from the phone and picked it up the moment it rang.

'Makeev here.'

'Josef? Yuri Gatov. I'm phoning from London.'

'Yuri. What a surprise,' Makeev said, immediately wary.

'I've got some distressing news, Josef. Tania, Tania Novikova.'

'What about her?'

'She committed suicide earlier this evening along with some boyfriend of hers, a clerk at the Ministry of Defence.'

'Good heavens.' Makeev tried to sound convincing.

'He was feeding her classified information. I've just had a session with Charles Ferguson of Group Four. You know Charles?'

'Of course.'

'I was quite shocked. I must tell you I had no knowledge of Tania's activities. She worked for you for three years, Josef, so you know her as well as anyone. Have you any thoughts on the matter?'

'None, I'm afraid.'

'Ah, well, if you can think of anything, let me know.'

Makeev poured himself a Scotch and went and looked out into the frostbound Paris street. For a wild moment he'd had an impulse to phone Michael Aroun, but what would be the point? And Tania had sounded so certain. Set the world on fire, that had been her phrase.

He raised his glass. 'To you, Dillon,' he said softly. 'Let's see if you can do it.'

It was almost eleven in the River Room at the Savoy, the band still playing and Harry Flood, Brosnan and Mary were thinking of breaking up the party when Ferguson appeared at last.

'If ever I've needed a drink I need one now. A Scotch and a very large one.'

Flood called a waiter and gave the order and Mary said, 'What on earth's happened?'

Ferguson gave them a quick résumé of the night's events. When he was finished, Brosnan said, 'It explains a great deal, but the infuriating thing is it gets us no closer to Dillon.'

'One point I must make,' Ferguson said. 'When I arrested Brown in the canteen at the Ministry he was on the phone and he had the report in his hand. I believe it likely he was speaking to the Novikova woman then.'

'I see what you're getting at,' Mary said. 'You think she, in her turn, may have transmitted the information to Dillon?'

'Possibly,' Ferguson said.

'So what are you suggesting?' Brosnan asked. 'That Dillon would go to Belfast too?'

'Perhaps,' Ferguson said. 'If it was important enough.'

'We'll just have to take our chances then.' Brosnan turned to Mary. 'Early start tomorrow. We'd better get moving.'

As they walked through the lounge to the entrance, Brosnan and Ferguson went ahead and stood talking. Mary said to Flood, 'You think a lot of him, don't you?'

'Martin?' He nodded. 'The Viet Cong had me in a pit for weeks. When the rains came, it used to fill up with water and I'd have to stand all night so I didn't drown. Leeches, worms, you name it, and then one day, when it was as bad as it could be, a hand reached down and pulled me out and it was Martin in a headband, hair to his shoulders and his face painted like an Apache Indian. He's special people.'

Mary looked across at Brosnan. 'Yes,' she said. 'I suppose that just about sums him up.'

Dillon ordered a taxi to pick him up at six o'clock from the hotel. He was waiting for it on the steps, his case in one hand when it arrived, a briefcase in the other. He was wearing his trenchcoat, suit, striped tie and glasses to fit the Peter Hilton persona, carried the Jersey driving licence and the flying licence as proof of identity. In the case was a toilet bag and the items he had obtained from Clayton at Covent Garden, all neatly folded. He'd included a towel from the hotel, socks and underpants. It all looked terribly normal and the wig could be easily explained.

The run to Heathrow was fast at that time in the morning. He went and picked up his ticket at the booking desk, then put his case through and got his seat assignment. He wasn't carrying a gun. No possible way he could do that, not with the kind of maximum security that operated on the Belfast planes.

He got a selection of newspapers, went up to the gallery restaurant and ordered a full English breakfast, then he started to work his way through the papers, checking on how the war in the Gulf was doing.

At Gatwick, there was a light powdering of snow at the side of the runway as the Lear jet lifted off. As they levelled off, Mary said, 'How do you feel?'

'I'm not sure,' Brosnan said. 'It's been a long time since I was in Belfast. Liam Devlin, Anne-Marie. So long ago.'

'And Sean Dillon?'

'Don't worry, I wasn't forgetting him, I could never do that.'

He turned and stared far out into the distance as the Lear jet lifted up out of the clouds and turned north-west.

Although Dillon wasn't aware of it, Brosnan and Mary had already landed and were on their way to the Europa Hotel when his flight touched down at Aldergrove Airport outside Belfast. There was a half-hour wait for the baggage and when he got his case, he made for the green line and followed a stream of people through. Customs officers stopped some, but he wasn't one of them and within five minutes he was outside and into a taxi.

'English, are you?' the driver asked.

Dillon slipped straight into his Belfast accent. 'And what makes you think that?'

'Jesus, I'm sorry,' the driver said. 'Anywhere special?'

'I'd like a hotel in the Falls Road,' Dillon said. 'Somewhere near Craig Street.'

'You won't get much round there.'

'Scenes of my youth,' Dillon told him. 'I've been working in London for years. Just in town for business overnight. Thought I'd like to see the old haunts.'

'Suit yourself. There's the Deepdene, but it's not much, I'm telling you.'

A Saracen armoured car passed then and as they turned into a main road, they saw an army patrol. 'Nothing changes,' Dillon said.

'Sure and most of those lads weren't even born when the whole thing started,' the driver told him. 'I mean, what are we in for? Another hundred years war?'

'God knows,' Dillon said piously and opened his paper.

*　　*　　*

The driver was right. The Deepdene wasn't much. A tall Victorian building in a mean side street off the Falls Road. He paid off the driver, went in and found himself in a shabby hall with a worn carpet. When he tapped the bell on the desk a stout, motherly woman emerged.

'Can I help you, dear?'

'A room,' he said. 'Just the one night.'

'That's fine.' She pushed a register at him and took a key down. 'Number nine on the first floor.'

'Shall I pay now?'

'Sure and there's no need for that. Don't I know a gentleman when I see one?'

He went up the stairs, found the door and unlocked it. The room was as shabby as he'd expected, a single brass bedstead, a wardrobe. He put his case on the table and went out again, locking the door, then went the other way along the corridor and found the backstairs. He opened the door at the bottom into an untidy backyard. The lane beyond backed on to incredibly derelict houses, but it didn't depress him in the slightest. This was an area he knew like the back of his hand, a place where he'd led the British Army one hell of a dance in his day. He moved along the alley, a smile on his face, remembering, and turned into the Falls Road.

11

'I remember them opening this place in seventy-one,' Brosnan said to Mary. He was standing at the window of the sixth-floor room of the Europa Hotel in Great Victoria Street next to the railway station. 'For a while it was a prime target for IRA bombers, the kind who'd rather blow up anything rather than nothing.'

'Not you, of course.'

There was a slight, sarcastic edge which he ignored. 'Certainly not. Devlin and I appreciated the bar too much. We came in all the time.'

She laughed in astonishment. 'What nonsense. Are you seriously asking me to believe that with the British Army chasing you all over Belfast you and Devlin sat in the Europa's bar?'

'Also the restaurant on occasion. Come on, I'll show you. Better take our coats, just in case we get a message while we're down there.'

As they were descending in the lift, she said, 'You're not armed, are you?'

'No.'

'Good, I'd rather keep it that way.'

'How about you?'

'Yes,' she said calmly. 'But that's different. I'm a serving officer of Crown forces in an active service zone.'

'What are you carrying?'

She opened her handbag and gave him a brief glimpse of the weapon. It was not much larger than the inside of her hand, a small automatic.

'What is it?' he asked.

'Rather rare. An old Colt .25. I picked it up in Africa.'

'Hardly an elephant gun.'

'No, but it does the job.' She smiled bleakly. 'As long as you can shoot, that is.'

The lift doors parted and they went across the lounge.

Dillon walked briskly along the Falls Road. Nothing had changed, nothing at all. It was just like the old days. He twice saw RUC patrols backed up by soldiers and once, two armoured troop carriers went by, but no one paid any attention. He finally found what he wanted in Craig Street about a mile from the hotel. It was a small, double-fronted shop with steel shutters on the windows. The three brass balls of a pawnbroker hung over the entrance with the sign 'Patrick Macey'.

Dillon opened the door and walked into musty silence. The dimly lit shop was crammed with a variety of items. Television sets, video recorders, clocks. There was even a gas cooker and a stuffed bear in one corner.

There was a mesh screen running along the counter and the man who sat on a stool behind it was working on a watch, a jeweller's magnifying glass in one eye. He glanced up, a wasted-looking individual in his sixties, his face grey and pallid.

'And what can I do for you?'

Dillon said, 'Nothing ever changes, Patrick. This place still smells exactly the same.'

Macey took the magnifying glass from his eye and frowned. 'Do I know you?'

'And why wouldn't you, Patrick? Remember that hot night in June of seventy-two when we set fire to that Orangeman Stewart's warehouse and shot him and his two nephews as they ran out. Let me see, there were the three of us.' Dillon put a cigarette in his mouth and lit it carefully. 'There was you and your half-brother, Tommy McGuire, and me.'

'Holy Mother of God, Sean Dillon, is that you?' Macey said.

'As ever was, Patrick.'

'Jesus, Sean, I never thought to see you in Belfast City again. I thought you were . . .'

He paused and Dillon said, 'Thought I was where, Patrick?'

'London,' Patrick Macey said. 'Somewhere like that,' he added lamely.

'And where would you have got that idea from?' Dillon went to the door, locking it and pulled down the blind.

'What are you doing?' Macey demanded in alarm.

'I just want a nice private talk, Patrick, me old son.'

'No, Sean, none of that. I'm not involved with the IRA, not any more.'

'You know what they say, Patrick, once in never out. How is Tommy these days, by the way?'

'Ah, Sean, I'd have thought you'd know. Poor Tommy's

been dead these five years. Shot by one of his own. A stupid row between the Provos and one of the splinter groups. INLA were suspected.'

'Is that a fact?' Dillon nodded. 'Do you see any of the other old hands these days? Liam Devlin for instance?'

And he had him there for Macey was unable to keep the look of alarm from his face. 'Liam? I haven't seen him since the seventies.'

'Really?' Dillon lifted the flap at the end of the counter and walked round. 'It's a terrible liar you are.' He slapped him across the face. 'Now get in there,' and pushed him through the curtain that led to the office at the rear.

Macey was terrified. 'I don't know a thing.'

'About what? I haven't asked you anything yet, but I'm going to tell you a few things. Tommy McGuire isn't dead. He's living somewhere else in this fair city under another name and you're going to tell me where. Secondly, Liam Devlin has been to see you. Now I'm right on both counts, aren't I?' Macey was frozen with fear, terrified and Dillon slapped him again. 'Aren't I?'

The other man broke then. 'Please, Sean, please. It's my heart. I could have an attack.'

'You will if you don't speak up, I promise you.'

'All right. Devlin was here a little earlier this morning enquiring about Tommy.'

'And shall I tell you what he said?'

'Please, Sean.' Macey was shaking. 'I'm ill.'

'He said that bad old Sean Dillon was on the loose in London Town and that he wanted to help run him down and who could be a better source of information than Dillon's old chum, Tommy McGuire. Am I right?'

Macey nodded. 'Yes.'

'Good, now we're getting somewhere.' Dillon lit another cigarette and nodded at the large old-fashioned safe in the corner. 'Is that where the guns are?'

'What guns, Sean?'

'Come on, don't muck me about. You're been dealing in handguns for years. Get it open.'

Macey took a key from his desk drawer, went and opened the safe. Dillon pulled him to one side. There were several weapons in there. An old Webley, a couple of Smith & Wesson revolvers. The one that really caught his eyes was an American Army Colt .45 automatic. He hefted it in his hand and checked the magazine.

'Wonderful, Patrick. I knew I could depend on you.' He put the gun on the desk and sat down opposite Macey. 'So what happened?'

Macey's face was very strange in colour now. 'I don't feel well.'

'You'll feel better when you've told me. Get on with it.'

'Tommy lives on his own about half a mile from here in Canal Street. He's done up the old warehouse at the end. Calls himself Kelly, George Kelly.'

'I know that area well, every stick and stone.'

'Devlin asked for Tommy's phone number and called him there and then. He said it was essential to see him. That it was to do with Sean Dillon. Tommy agreed to see him at two o'clock.'

'Fine,' Dillon said. 'See how easy it was? Now I can call on him myself before Devlin does and discuss old times only I won't bother to phone. I think I'll surprise him. Much more fun.'

'You'll never get in to see him,' Macey said. 'You can only get in at the front, all the other doors are welded.

He's been paranoid for years. Terrified someone's going to knock him off. You'd never get in the front door. It's all TV security cameras and that kind of stuff.'

'There's always a way,' Dillon said.

'There always was for you.' Macey tore at his shirt collar, choking. 'Pills,' he moaned and got the drawer in front of him open. The bottle he took fell from his hands.

He lay back on the chair and Dillon got up and went round and picked up the bottle. 'Trouble is, Patrick, the moment I go out of the door you'll be on the phone to Tommy and that wouldn't do, would it?'

He walked across to the fireplace and dropped the pill bottle into the gleaming coals. There was a crash behind him and he turned to find Macey had tumbled from the chair to the floor. Dillon stood over him for a moment. Macey's face was very suffused with purple now and his legs were jerking. Suddenly, he gave a great gasp like air escaping, his head turned to one side and he went completely still.

Dillon put the Colt in his pocket, went through the shop and opened the door, locking it with the Yale, leaving the blind down. A moment later he turned the corner into the Falls Road and walked back towards the hotel as fast as he could.

He laid the contents of the case on the bed in the shabby hotel room, then he undressed. First of all he put on the jeans, the old runners and a heavy jumper. Then came the wig. He sat in front of the mirror at the small dressing-table, combing the grey hair until it looked wild and unkempt. He tied the headscarf over it and studied himself. Then he pulled on the skirt that reached his ankles. The old raincoat that was far too large completed the outfit.

He stood in front of the wardrobe examining himself in the mirror. He closed his eyes, thinking the role and when he opened them again it wasn't Dillon any more, it was a decrepit, broken, bag lady.

He hardly needed any make-up, just a foundation to give him the sallow look and the slash of scarlet lipstick for the mouth. All wrong, of course, but totally right for the character. He took a half-bottle of whiskey from a pouch in the briefcase and poured some into his cupped hands, slapping it over his face, then he splashed some more over the front of the raincoat. He put the Colt, a couple of newspapers and the whiskey bottle into a plastic bag and was ready to leave.

He glanced in the mirror at that strange, nightmarish old woman. 'Showtime,' he whispered and let himself out.

All was quiet as he went down the backstairs and went out into the yard. He closed the door behind him carefully and crossed to the door which led to the alley. As he reached it, the hotel door opened behind him.

A voice called, 'Here, what do you think you're doing?'

Dillon turned and saw a kitchen porter in a soiled white apron putting a cardboard box in the dustbin.

'Go fuck yourself,' Dillon croaked.

'Go on, get out of it, you old bag!' the porter shouted.

Dillon closed the door behind him. 'Ten out of ten, Sean,' he said softly and went up the alley.

He turned into the Falls Road and started to shuffle along the pavement, acting so strangely that people stepped out of the way to avoid him.

*   *   *

219

It was almost one and Brosnan and Mary Tanner at the bar of the Europa were thinking about lunch when a young porter approached. 'Mr Brosnan?'

'That's right.'

'Your taxi is here, sir.'

'Taxi?' Mary said. 'But we didn't order one.'

'Yes we did,' Brosnan said.

He helped her on with her coat and they followed the young porter through the foyer, down the steps at the front entrance to the black cab waiting at the kerb. Brosnan gave the porter a pound and they got in. The driver on the other side of the glass wore a tweed cap and an old reefer coat. Mary Tanner pulled the sliding glass partition to one side.

'I presume you know where we're going?' she said.

'Oh, I certainly do, my love.' Liam Devlin smiled at her over his shoulder, moved into gear and drove away.

It was just after one-thirty when Devlin turned the taxi into Canal Street. 'That's the place at the end,' he said. 'We'll park in the yard at the side.' They got out and moved back into the street and approached the entrance. 'Be on your best behaviour, we're on television,' he said and reached to a bell push beside the massive ironbound door.

'Not very homelike,' Mary commented.

'Yes, well with Tommy McGuire's background he needs a fortress rather than a cosy semi-detached on some desirable estate.' Devlin turned to Brosnan. 'Are you carrying, son?'

'No,' Brosnan said. 'But she is. You are, I suppose?'

'Call it my innate caution or perhaps the wicked habits of a lifetime.'

A voice sounded through the box beside the door. 'Is that you, Devlin?'

'And who else, you stupid bugger. I've got Martin Brosnan with me and a lady-friend of his and we're freezing in this damn cold so get the door open.'

'You're early. You said two o'clock.'

They could hear steps on the other side and then the door opened to reveal a tall, cadaverous man in his mid-sixties. He wore a heavy Aran pullover and baggy jeans and carried a Sterling sub-machine gun.

Devlin brushed past him, leading the way in. 'What do you intend to do with that thing, start another war?'

McGuire closed the door and barred it. 'Only if I have to.' He looked them over suspiciously. 'Martin?' He held out a hand. 'It's been a long time. As for you, you old sod,' he said to Devlin, 'whatever's keeping you out of your grave you should bottle it. We'd make a fortune.' He looked Mary over. 'And who might you be?'

'A friend,' Devlin told him. 'So let's get on with it.'

'All right, this way.'

The interior of the warehouse was totally bare except for a van parked to one side. A steel staircase led to a landing high above with what had once been glass-fronted offices. McGuire went first and turned into the first office on the landing. There was a desk and a bank of television equipment, one screen showing the street, another the entrance. He put the Sterling on the desk.

Devlin said, 'You live here?'

'Upstairs. I've turned what used to be the storage loft into a flat. Now let's get on with it, Devlin. What is it you want? You mentioned Sean Dillon.'

'He's on the loose again,' Brosnan said.

'I thought he must have come to a bad end. I mean, it's been so long.' McGuire lit a cigarette. 'Anyway, what's it to do with me?'

'He tried to knock off Martin here in Paris. Killed his girlfriend instead.'

'Jesus!' McGuire said.

'Now he's on the loose in London and I want him,' Brosnan told him.

McGuire looked at Mary again. 'And where does she fit in?'

'I'm a captain in the British Army,' she said crisply. 'Tanner's the name.'

'For God's sake, Devlin, what is this?' McGuire demanded.

'It's all right,' Devlin told him. 'She hasn't come to arrest you although we all know that if Tommy McGuire was still in the land of the living he'd draw about twenty-five years.'

'You bastard!' McGuire said.

'Be sensible,' Devlin told him. 'Just answer a few questions and you can go back to being George Kelly again.'

McGuire put a hand up defensively. 'All right, I get the point. What do you want to know?'

'Nineteen eighty-one, the London bombing campaign,' Brosnan said. 'You were Dillon's control.'

McGuire glanced at Mary. 'That's right.'

'We know Dillon would have experienced the usual problems as regards weapons and explosives, Mr McGuire,' Mary said. 'And I've been given to understand he always favours underworld contacts in that sort of situation. Is that so?'

'Yes, he usually worked in that way,' McGuire said reluctantly and sat down.

'Have you any idea who he used in London in nineteen eighty-one?' Mary persisted.

McGuire looked hunted. 'How would I know? It could have been anybody.'

Devlin said, 'You lying bastard, you know something, I can tell you do.' His right hand came out of the pocket of the reefer holding an old Luger pistol and he touched McGuire between the eyes. 'Quick now, tell us or I'll . . .'

McGuire pushed the gun to one side. 'All right, Devlin, you win.' He lit another cigarette. 'He dealt with a man in London called Jack Harvey, a big operator, a real gangster.'

'There, that wasn't so hard, was it?' Devlin said.

There was a thunderous knocking on the door below and they all looked at the television screen to see an old bag lady on the front step. Her voice came clearly through the speaker. 'The lovely man you are, Mr Kelly. Could you spare a poor soul a quid?'

McGuire said into the microphone, 'Piss off, you old bag.'

'Oh Jesus, Mr Kelly, I'll die here on your step in this terrible cold so I will for the whole world to see.'

McGuire got up. 'I'll go and get rid of her. I'll only be a minute.'

He hurried down the stairs and extracted a five-pound note from an old wallet as he approached the door. He got it open and held it out. 'Take this and clear off.'

Dillon's hand came up out of the plastic shopping bag holding the Colt. 'A fiver, Tommy boy. You're getting generous in your old age. Inside.'

He pushed him through and closed the door. McGuire was terrified. 'Look, what is this?'

'Nemesis,' Dillon said. 'You pay for your sins in this life, Tommy, we all do. Remember that night in seventy-two, you, me and Patrick when we shot the Stewarts as they ran out of the fire?'

'Dillon?' McGuire whispered. 'It's you?' He started to turn and raised his voice. 'Devlin!' he called.

Dillon shot him twice in the back breaking his spine, driving him on his face. As he got the door open behind him, Devlin appeared on the landing, the Luger in his hand, already firing. Dillon fired three times rapidly, shattering the office window, then was outside, slamming the door behind him.

As he started up the street, two stripped-down Land Rovers, four soldiers in each, turned out of the main road, attracted by the sound of the firing and came towards him. The worst kind of luck, but Dillon didn't hesitate. As he came to a drain in the gutter, he pretended to slip and dropped the Colt through the bars.

As he got up someone called, 'Stay where you are.'

They were paratroopers in camouflage uniforms, flak jackets and red berets, each man with his rifle ready and Dillon gave them the performance of his life. He staggered forward, moaning and crying and clutching at the young lieutenant in charge.

'Jesus, sir, there's terrible things going on back there in that warehouse. There's me sheltering from the cold and these fellas come on and start shooting each other.'

The young officer smelt the whiskey and pushed him away. 'Check what's in the carrier, Sergeant.'

The sergeant riffled through. 'Bottle of hooch and some newspapers, sir.'

'Right, go and wait over there.' The officer pushed

Dillon along the pavement behind the patrol and got a loud-hailer from one of the Land Rovers. 'You inside,' he called. 'Throw your weapons out through the door then follow them with your hands up. Two minutes or we'll come in to get you.'

All members of the patrol were in a readiness posture, intent only on the entrance. Dillon eased back into the courtyard, turned and hurried past Devlin's taxi, finding what he was seeking in seconds, a manhole cover. He got it up and went down a steel ladder, pulling the cover behind him. It had been a way in which he had evaded the British Army on many occasions in the old days and he knew the system in the Falls Road area perfectly.

The tunnel was small and very dark. He crawled along it, aware of the sound of rushing water and came out on the sloping side of a larger tunnel, the main sewer. There were outlets to the canal that ran down to Belfast Lough, he knew that. He pulled off the skirt, the wig and threw them in the water using the headscarf to wipe his lips and face vigorously, then he hurried along the side until he came to another steel ladder. He started up towards the rays of light beaming in through the holes in the cast iron, waited a moment, then eased it up. He was on a cobbled pathway beside the canal, the backs of decaying, boarded-up houses on the other side. He put the manhole cover back in place and made for the Falls Road as fast as possible.

In the warehouse, the young officer stood beside McGuire's body and examined Mary Tanner's ID card. 'It's perfectly genuine,' she said. 'You can check.'

'And these two?'

'They're with me. Look, Lieutenant, you'll get a full explanation from my boss. That's Brigadier Charles Ferguson at the Ministry of Defence.'

'All right, Captain,' he said defensively. 'I'm only doing my job. It's not like the old days here, you know. We have the RUC on our backs. Every death has to be investigated fully otherwise there's the Devil to pay.'

The sergeant came in. 'The colonel's on the wire, boss.'

'Fine,' the young lieutenant said and went out.

Brosnan said to Devlin, 'Do you think it was Dillon?'

'A hell of a coincidence if it wasn't. A bag lady?' Devlin shook his head. 'Who'd have thought it?'

'Only Dillon would be capable.'

'Are you trying to say he came over from London specially?' Mary demanded.

'He knew what we were about thanks to Gordon Brown and how long is the scheduled flight from London to Belfast?' Brosnan asked. 'An hour and a quarter?'

'Which means he's got to go back,' she said.

'Perhaps,' Liam Devlin nodded. 'But nothing's absolute in this life, girl, you'll learn that and you're dealing with a man who's kept out of police hands for twenty years or more, all over Europe.'

'Well, it's time we got the bastard.' She looked down at McGuire. 'Not too nice, is it?'

'The violence, the killing. Drink with the Devil and this is what it comes down to,' Devlin told her.

Dillon went in through the back door of the hotel at exactly two-fifteen and hurried up to his room. He stripped off the jeans and jumper, put them in the case and shoved them up into a cupboard above the wardrobe. He washed his face quickly, then dressed in white shirt and tie, dark suit and blue Burberry. He was out of the room and descending the backstairs, briefcase in hand, within five minutes of having entered. He went up the alley, turned into the Falls Road and started to walk briskly. Within five minutes he managed to hail a taxi and told the driver to take him to the airport.

The officer in charge of Army Intelligence for the Belfast city area was a Colonel McLeod and he was not best pleased with the situation with which he was confronted.

'It really isn't good enough, Captain Tanner,' he said. 'We can't have you people coming in here like cowboys and acting on your own initiative.' He turned to look at Devlin and Brosnan. 'And with people of very dubious background into the bargain. There is a delicate situation here these days and we do have the Royal Ulster Constabulary to placate. They see this as their turf.'

'Yes, well, that's as may be,' Mary told him. 'But your sergeant outside was kind enough to check on flights to London for me. There's one at four-thirty and another at six-thirty. Don't you think it would be a good idea to check out the passengers rather thoroughly?'

'We're not entirely stupid, Captain. I've already put that in hand, but I'm sure I don't need to remind you that we are not an army of occupation. There is no such thing as martial law here. It's impossible for me to close down the airport, I don't have the authority. All I can do is notify the police and airport security in the usual way and as you've been at pains to explain, where this man Dillon is concerned, we don't have much to tell them.' His phone went. He picked it up and said, 'Brigadier Ferguson? Sorry

227

to bother you, sir. Colonel McLeod, Belfast HQ. We appear to have a problem.'

But Dillon, at the airport, had no intention of returning on the London flight. Perhaps he could get away with it, but madness to try when there were other alternatives. It was just after three as he searched the departure board. He'd just missed the Manchester flight, but there was a flight to Glasgow due out at three-fifteen and it was delayed.

He crossed to the booking desk. 'I was hoping to catch the Glasgow flight,' he told the young woman booking clerk, 'but got here too late. Now I see it's delayed.'

She punched details up on her screen. 'Yes, half-hour delay, sir, and there's plenty of space. Would you like to try for it?'

'I certainly would,' he said gratefully and got the money from his wallet as she made out the ticket.

There was no trouble with security and the contents of his briefcase were innocuous enough. Passengers had already been called and he boarded the plane and sat in a seat at the rear. Very satisfactory. Only one thing had gone wrong. Devlin, Brosnan and the woman had got to McGuire first. A pity, that, because it raised the question of what he'd told them. Harvey, for example. He'd have to move fast there, just in case.

He smiled charmingly when the stewardess asked him if he'd like a drink. 'A cup of tea would be just fine,' he said and took a newspaper from his briefcase.

McLeod had Brosnan, Mary and Devlin taken up to the airport and they arrived just before the passengers were called for the four-thirty London flight. An RUC police inspector took them through to the departure lounge.

'Only thirty passengers as you can see and we've checked them all thoroughly.'

'I've an idea we're on a wild goose chase,' McLeod said.

The passengers were called and Brosnan and Devlin stood by the door and looked each person over as they went through. When they'd passed, Devlin said, 'The old nun, Martin, you didn't think of doing a strip search?'

McLeod said impatiently, 'Oh, for God's sake, let's get moving.'

'An angry man,' Devlin said as the colonel went ahead. 'They must have laid the cane on something fierce at his public school. It's back to London for you two then?'

'Yes, we'd better get on with it,' Brosnan said.

'And you, Mr Devlin?' Mary asked. 'Will you be all right?'

'Ah, Ferguson, to be fair, secured me a clean bill of health years ago for services rendered to Brit intelligence. I'll be fine.' He kissed her on the cheek. 'A real pleasure, my love.'

'And for me.'

'Watch out for the boy here. Dillon's the original tricky one.'

They had reached the concourse. He smiled and suddenly was gone, disappeared into the crowd.

Brosnan took a deep breath. 'Right, then, London. Let's get moving,' and he took her arm and moved through the throng.

The flight to Glasgow was only forty-five minutes. Dillon landed at four-thirty. There was a shuttle service plane to

London at five-fifteen. He got a ticket at the desk, hurried through to the departure lounge where the first thing he did was phone Danny Fahy at Cadge End. It was Angel who answered.

'Put your Uncle Danny on, it's Dillon,' he told her.

Danny said, 'Is that you, Sean?'

'As ever was. I'm in Glasgow waiting for a plane. I'll be arriving at Heathrow Terminal One at six-thirty. Can you come and meet me? You'll just have time.'

'No problem, Sean. I'll bring Angel for the company.'

'That's fine and, Danny, be prepared to work through the night. Tomorrow could be the big one.'

'Jesus, Sean,' but Dillon put the phone down before Fahy could say anything more.

Next, he phoned Harvey's office at the undertakers in Whitechapel. It was Myra who answered.

'This is Peter Hilton here, we met yesterday. I'd like a word with your uncle.'

'He isn't here. He's gone up to Manchester for a function. Won't be back until tomorrow morning.'

'That's no good to me,' Dillon said. 'He promised me my stuff in twenty-four hours.'

'Oh, it's here,' Myra said. 'But I'd expect cash on delivery.'

'You've got it.' He looked at his watch and allowed for the time it would take to drive from Heathrow to Bayswater to get the money. 'I'll be there about seven forty-five.'

'I'll be waiting.'

As Dillon put the phone down, the flight was called and he joined the crowd of passengers hurrying through.

* * *

Myra, standing by the fire in her uncle's office, came to a decision. She got the key of the secret room from his desk drawer and then went out to the head of the stairs.

'Billy, are you down there?'

He came up a moment later. 'Here I am.'

'Been in the coffin room again, have you? Come on, I need you.' She went along the corridor to the end door, opened it and pulled back the false wall. She indicated one of the boxes of Semtex. 'Take that to the office.'

When she rejoined him, he'd put the box on the desk. 'A right bloody weight. What is it?'

'It's money, Billy, that's all that concerns you. Now listen and listen good. That small guy, the one who roughed you up yesterday.'

'What about him?'

'He's turning up here at seven forty-five to pay me a lot of money for what's in that box.'

'So?'

'I want you waiting outside from seven-thirty in those nice black leathers of yours with your BMW handy. When he leaves, you follow him, Billy, to bloody Cardiff if necessary.' She patted his face, 'And if you lose him, sunshine, don't bother coming back.'

It was snowing lightly at Heathrow as Dillon came through at Terminal One. Angel was waiting for him and waved excitedly.

'Glasgow,' she said. 'What were you doing there?'

'Finding out what Scotsmen wear under their kilts.'

She laughed and hung on to his arm. 'Terrible, you are.'

They went out through the snow and joined Fahy in the Morris van. 'Good to see you, Sean. Where to?'

'My hotel in Bayswater,' Dillon said. 'I want to book out.'

'You're moving in with us?' Angel asked.

'Yes,' Dillon nodded, 'but I've a present to pick up for Danny first at an undertakers in Whitechapel.'

'And what would that be, Sean?' Fahy demanded.

'Oh, about fifty pounds of Semtex.'

The van swerved and skidded slightly, Fahy fighting to control it. 'Holy Mother of God!' he said.

At the undertakers, the night porter admitted Dillon at the front entrance.

'Mr Hilton, is it? Miss Myra's expecting you, sir.'

'I know where to go.'

Dillon went up the stairs, along the corridor and opened the door of the outer office. Myra was waiting for him. 'Come in,' she said.

She was wearing a black trouser suit and smoking a cigarette. She went and sat behind the desk and tapped the carton with one hand. 'There it is. Where's the money?'

Dillon put the briefcase on top of the carton and opened it. He took out fifteen thousand, packet by packet, and dropped it in front of her. That left five thousand dollars in the briefcase, the Walther with the Carswell silencer and the Beretta. He closed the case and smiled.

'Nice to do business with you.'

He placed the briefcase on top of the carton and picked it up and she went to open the door for him.

'What are you going to do with that, blow up the Houses of Parliament?'

'That was Guy Fawkes,' he said and moved along the passage and went downstairs.

The pavement was frosty as he walked along the street and turned the corner to the van. Billy, waiting anxiously in the shadows, manhandled his BMW up the street past the parked cars until he could see Dillon stop at the Morris van. Angel got the back door open and Dillon put the carton inside. She closed it and they went round and got in beside Fahy.

'Is that it, Sean?'

'That's it, Danny, a fifty-pound box of Semtex with the factory stamp on it all the way from Prague. Now let's get out of here, we've got a long night ahead of us.'

Fahy drove through a couple of side streets and turned onto the main road and as he joined the traffic stream, Billy went after him on the BMW.

12

For technical reasons the Lear jet had not been able to get a flight slot out of Aldergrove Airport until five-thirty. It was a quarter to seven when Brosnan and Mary landed at Gatwick and a Ministry limousine was waiting. Mary checked on the car phone and found Ferguson at the Cavendish Square flat. He was standing by the fire warming himself when Kim showed them in.

'Beastly weather and a lot more snow on the way, I fear.' He sipped some of his tea. 'Well, at least you're in one piece, my dear, it must have been an enlivening experience.'

'That's one way of describing it.'

'You're absolutely certain it was Dillon?'

'Well let's put it this way,' Brosnan said, 'if it wasn't it was one hell of a coincidence that someone decided to choose that moment to shoot Tommy McGuire. And then there's the bag lady act. Typical Dillon.'

'Yes, quite remarkable.'

'Admittedly he wasn't on the London plane, sir, coming back,' Mary said.

'You mean you *think* he wasn't on the plane,' Ferguson corrected her. 'For all I know the damned man might have passed himself off as the pilot. He seems capable of anything.'

'There is another plane due out to London at eight-thirty, sir. Colonel McLeod said he'd have it thoroughly checked.'

'A waste of time.' Ferguson turned to Brosnan. 'I suspect you agree, Martin?'

'I'm afraid so.'

'Now let's go over the whole thing again. Tell me everything that happened.'

When Mary was finished, Ferguson said, 'I checked the flight schedules out of Aldergrove a little while ago. There were planes available to Manchester, Birmingham, Glasgow. There was even a flight to Paris at six-thirty. No big deal to fly back to London from there. He'd be here tomorrow.'

'And there's always the sea trip,' Brosnan reminded him. 'The ferry from Larne to Stranraer in Scotland and a fast train from there to London.'

'Plus the fact that he could have crossed the Irish border, gone to Dublin and proceeded from there in a dozen different ways,' Mary said, 'which doesn't get us anywhere.'

'The interesting thing is the reason behind his trip,' Ferguson said. 'He didn't know of your intention to seek out McGuire until last night when Brown revealed the contents of that report to Novikova and yet he went rushing off to Belfast at the earliest opportunity. Now why would that be?'

'To shut McGuire's mouth,' Mary said. 'It's an interesting point that our meeting with McGuire was arranged for two o'clock, but we were nearly half an hour early. If we hadn't been, Dillon would have got to him first.'

'Even so he still can't be certain what McGuire told you, if anything.'

'But the point was, sir, that Dillon *knew* McGuire had something on him, that's why he went to such trouble to get to him and it was obviously the information that this man Jack Harvey was his arms supplier in the London campaign of eighty-one.'

'Yes, well when you spoke to me at Aldergrove before you left I ran a check. Detective Inspector Lane of Special Branch tells me that Harvey is a known gangster and on a big scale. Drugs, prostitution, the usual things. The police have been after him for years with little success. Unfortunately, he is now also a very established businessman. Property, clubs, betting shops and so forth.'

'What are you trying to say, sir?' Mary asked.

'That it isn't as easy as you might think. We can't just pull Harvey in for questioning because a dead man accused him of something that happened ten years ago. Be sensible, my dear. He'd sit still, keep his mouth shut and a team of the best lawyers in London would have him out on the pavement in record time.'

'In other words it would be laughed out of court?' Brosnan said.

'Exactly.' Ferguson sighed. 'I've always had a great deal of sympathy for the idea that where the criminal classes are concerned, the only way we're going to get any justice is to take all the lawyers out into the nearest square and shoot them.'

Brosnan peered out of the window at the lightly falling snow. 'There is another way.'

'I presume you're referring to your friend Flood?' Ferguson smiled tightly. 'Nothing at all to stop you seeking his advice, but I'm sure you'll stay within the bounds of legality.'

'Oh, we will, Brigadier, I promise you.' Brosnan picked up his coat. 'Come on, Mary, let's go and see Harry.'

Following the Morris wasn't too much of a problem for Billy on his BMW. The snow was only lying on the sides of the road and the tarmac was wet. There was plenty of traffic all the way out of London and through Dorking. There wasn't quite as much on the Horsham road but still enough to give him cover.

He was lucky when the Morris turned at the Grimethorpe sign because it had stopped snowing and the sky had cleared exposing a half-moon. Billy switched off his headlamp and followed the lights of the Morris at a distance, anonymous in the darkness. When it turned at the Doxley sign, he followed cautiously, pausing on the brow of the hill, watching the lights move in through the farm gate.

He switched off his engine and coasted down the hill, pulling in by the gate and the wooden sign that said Cadge End Farm. He walked along the track through the trees and could see into the lighted interior of the barn across the yard. Dillon, Fahy and Angel were standing beside the Morris. Dillon turned, came out and crossed the yard.

Billy beat a hasty retreat, got back on the BMW and rolled on down the hill, only switching on again when he was some distance from the farm. Five minutes later he was on the main road and returning to London.

*   *   *

In the sitting room Dillon called Makeev at the Paris apartment. 'It's me,' he said.

'I've been worried,' Makeev told him, 'what with Tania . . .'

'Tania took her own way out,' Dillon said, 'I told you. It was her way of making sure they didn't get anything out of her.'

'And this business you mentioned, the Belfast trip?'

'Taken care of. It's all systems go, Josef.'

'When?'

'The War Cabinet meets at ten o'clock in the morning at Downing Street. That's when we'll hit.'

'But how?'

'You can read about it in the papers. The important thing now is for you to tell Michael Aroun to fly down to his St Denis place in the morning. I hope to be flying in sometime in the afternoon.'

'As quickly as that?'

'Well I won't be hanging about, will I? What about you, Josef?'

'I should think I might well make the flight from Paris to St Denis with Aroun and Rashid myself.'

'Good. Till our next merry meeting, then, and remind Aroun about that second million.'

Dillon put the phone down, lit a cigarette, then picked up the phone again and called Grimethorpe Airfield. After a while he got an answer.

'Bill Grant here.' He sounded slightly drunk.

'Peter Hilton, Mr Grant.'

'Oh, yes,' Grant said, 'and what can I do for you?'

'That trip I wanted to make to Land's End, tomorrow, I think.'

'What time?'

'If you could be ready from noon onwards. Is that all right?'

'As long as the snow holds off. Much more and we could be in trouble.'

Grant put the phone down slowly, reached for the bottle of Scotch whisky at his hand and poured a generous measure, then he opened the table drawer. There was an old Webley service revolver in there and a box of .38 cartridges. He loaded the weapon then put it back in the drawer.

'Right, Mr Hilton, we'll just have to see what you're about, won't we?' and he swallowed the whisky down.

'Do I know Jack Harvey?' Harry Flood started to laugh, sitting there behind his desk and looked up at Mordecai Fletcher. 'Do I know, Mordecai?'

The big man smiled at Brosnan and Mary who were standing there, still with their coats on. 'Yes, I think you could say we know Mr Harvey rather well.'

'Sit down, for God's sake, and tell me what happened in Belfast,' Flood said.

Which they did, Mary giving him a rapid account of the entire affair. When she was finished she said, 'Do you think it's possible that Harvey was Dillon's weapons supplier in eighty-one?'

'Nothing would surprise me about Jack Harvey. He and his niece, Myra, run a tight little empire that includes every kind of criminal activity. Women, drugs, protection, big-scale armed robbery, you name it, but arms for the IRA?' He looked up at Mordecai. 'What do you think?'

'He'd dig up his granny's corpse and sell it if he thought there was a profit in it,' the big man said.

'Very apt.' Flood turned to Mary. 'There's your answer.'

'Fine,' Brosnan said, 'and if Dillon used Harvey in eighty-one, the chances are he's using him again.'

Flood said, 'The police would never get anywhere with Harvey on the basis of your story, you must know that. He'd walk.'

'I should imagine the Professor was thinking of a more subtle approach like beating it out of the bastard,' Mordecai said and slammed a fist into his palm.

Mary turned to Brosnan who shrugged. 'What else would you suggest? Nobody's going to get anywhere with a man like Harvey by being nice.'

'I have an idea,' Harry Flood said. 'Harvey's been putting a lot of pressure on me lately to form a partnership. What if I tell him I'd like to have a meeting to discuss things?'

'Fine,' Brosnan said, 'but as soon as possible. We can't hang around on this, Harry.'

Myra was sitting at her uncle's desk going through club accounts when Flood called her.

'Harry,' she said, 'what a nice surprise.'

'I was hoping for a word with Jack.'

'Not possible, Harry, he's in Manchester at some sporting club function at the Midland.'

'When is he due back?'

'First thing. He's got some business later in the morning so he's getting up early and catching the seven-thirty breakfast shuttle from Manchester.'

'So he should be with you about nine?'

'More like nine-thirty with the morning traffic into London. Look, what is this, Harry?'

'I've been thinking, Myra, maybe I've been stupid. About a partnership, I mean. Jack might have a point. There's a lot we could do if we got together.'

'Well I'm sure he'll be pleased to hear that,' Myra said.

'I'll see you then, nine-thirty sharp in the morning with my accountant,' Flood told her and rang off.

Myra sat there looking at the phone for a while, then she picked it up, rang the Midland in Manchester and asked for her uncle. Jack Harvey, champagne and more than one brandy inside him, was in excellent humour when he picked up the phone at the hotel's front desk.

'Myra, my love, what's up? A fire or something or a sudden rush of bodies?'

'Even more interesting. Harry Flood's been on the phone.'

She told him what had happened and Harvey sobered up instantly. 'So he wants to meet at nine-thirty?'

'That's right. What do you think?'

'I think it's a load of cobblers. Why should he suddenly change his mind just like that? No, I don't like it.'

'Shall I phone him back and cancel?'

'No, not at all, I'll meet him. We'll just take precautions, that's all.'

'Listen,' she said, 'Hilton or whatever his bloody name is called and told me he wanted his stuff. He came round, paid cash and went on his way. Is that all right?'

'Good girl. Now as regards Flood, all I'm saying is be

ready to give him the proper reception, just in case. Know what I mean?'

'I think so, Jack,' she said, 'I think so.'

Harry Flood said, 'We'll meet outside the Harvey Funeral Emporium just before half-nine in the morning then. I'll bring Mordecai and you can play my accountant,' he told Brosnan.

'What about me?' Mary demanded.

'We'll see.'

Brosnan got up and went and stood at the French windows looking at the river. 'I wish I knew what the bastard was doing right now,' he said.

'Tomorrow, Martin,' Flood told him. 'All things come to he who waits.'

It was around midnight when Billy parked the BMW in the yard at the rear of the Whitechapel premises and went in. He climbed the stairs wearily to Myra's apartment. She heard him coming, got her door open and stood there, light flowing through her short nightdress.

'Hello, sunshine, you made it,' she said to Billy.

'I'm bloody frozen,' Billy told her.

She got him inside, sat him down and started to unzip his leathers. 'Where did he go?'

He reached for a bottle of brandy, poured a large one and got it down. 'Only an hour out of London, Myra, but the back of bloody beyond.'

He told her everything, Dorking, the Horsham road, Grimethorpe, Doxley and Cadge End Farm.

'Brilliant, sunshine. What you need is a nice hot bath.'

She went into the bathroom and turned on the taps. When she went back into the living room Billy was asleep on the couch, legs sprawled. 'Oh, dear,' she said, got a blanket to cover him, then went to bed.

When Makeev knocked on the door at the Avenue Victor Hugo it was opened by Rashid. 'You've news for us?' the young Iraqi asked.

Makeev nodded. 'Where's Michael?'

'He's waiting for you.'

Rashid took him through to the drawing room where Aroun was standing beside the fire. He was wearing a black dinner jacket for he had been to the opera.

'What is it?' he demanded. 'Has something happened?'

'I've had Dillon on the phone from England. He wants you to fly down to St Denis in the morning. He intends to fly in himself sometime in the afternoon.'

Aroun was pale with excitement. 'What is it? What does he intend?'

He poured the Russian a cognac and Rashid passed it to him. 'He told me he intends some sort of attack on the British War Cabinet at Downing Street.'

There was total silence, only astonishment on Aroun's face. It was Rashid who spoke. 'The War Cabinet? All of them? That's impossible. How could he even attempt such a thing?'

'I've no idea,' Makeev said. 'I'm simply telling you what he told me, that the War Cabinet meets at ten in the morning and that is when he makes his move.'

'God is great,' Michael Aroun said. 'If he can do this thing, now, in the middle of the war, before the land offensive starts, the effect on the whole Arab world would be incredible.'

'I should imagine so.'

Aroun took a step forward and fastened his right hand in Makeev's lapel. 'Can he, Josef, can he do it?'

'He seems certain.' Makeev disengaged himself. 'I only tell you what he has told me.'

Aroun turned and stood looking down at the fire, then said to Rashid, 'We'll leave at nine from Charles de Gaulle in the Citation. We'll be there in not much more than an hour.'

'At your orders,' Rashid said.

'You can phone old Alphonse at the Château now. I want him out of there at breakfast time. He can take a few days off. I don't want him around.'

Rashid nodded and went out to the study. Makeev said, 'Alphonse?'

'The caretaker. At this time of the year he's on his own unless I tell him to bring the servants in from the local village. They're all on retainers.'

Makeev said, 'I'd like to come with you if that's all right.'

'Of course, Josef.' Aroun poured two more glasses of cognac. 'God forgive me, I know I drink when I should not, but on this occasion.' He raised his glass. 'To Dillon and may all go as he intends.'

It was one o'clock in the morning and Fahy was working on one of the oxygen cylinders on the bench when Dillon entered the barn.

'How's it going?'

'Fine,' Fahy said. 'Nearly finished. This one and one to go. How's the weather?'

Dillon walked to the open door. 'It's stopped snowing, but more's expected. I checked on the teletext on your television.'

Fahy carried the cylinder to the Ford Transit, got inside and fitted it into one of the tubes with great care while Dillon watched. Angel came in with a jug and two mugs in one hand. 'Coffee?' she asked.

'Lovely.' Her uncle held a mug while she filled it and then did the same for Dillon.

Dillon said, 'I've been thinking. The garage where I wanted you to wait with the van, Angel, I'm not sure that's such a good idea now.'

Fahy paused, a spanner in his hand and looked up. 'Why not?'

'It was where the Russian woman, my contact, kept her car. The police will probably know that. If they're keeping an eye on her flat they may well be checking the garage too.'

'So what do you suggest?'

'Remember where I was staying, the hotel on the Bayswater Road? There's a supermarket next door with a big parking area at the rear. We'll use that. It won't make much of a difference,' he said to Angel. 'I'll show you when we get there.'

'Anything you say, Mr Dillon.' She stayed watching as Fahy finished the fitting of his improvised mortar bomb and moved back to the bench. 'I was thinking, Mr Dillon, this place in France, this St Denis?'

'What about it?'

'You'll be flying straight off there afterwards?'

'That's right.'

She said carefully, 'Where does that leave us?'

Fahy paused to wipe his hands. 'She's got a point, Sean.'

'You'll be fine, the both of you,' Dillon said. 'This is

a clean one, Danny, the cleanest I ever pulled. Not a link with you or this place. If it works tomorrow, and it will, we'll be back here by eleven-thirty at the outside and that will be the end of it.'

'If you say so,' Fahy said.

'But I do, Danny, and if it's the money you're worried about, don't. You'll get your share. The man I'm working for can arrange financial payments anywhere. You can have it here if you want or Europe if that's better.'

'Sure and the money was never the big thing, Sean,' Fahy said, 'you know that. It's just that if there's a chance of something going wrong, any kind of chance.' He shrugged. 'It's Angel I'm thinking about.'

'No need. If there was any risk I'd be the first to say come with me, but there won't be.' Dillon put his arm about the girl. 'You're excited, aren't you?'

'Me stomach's turning over something dreadful, Mr Dillon.'

'Go to bed.' He pushed her towards the door. 'We'll be leaving at eight.'

'I won't sleep a wink.'

Try. Now go on, that's an order.'

She went out reluctantly. Dillon lit another cigarette and turned back to Fahy. 'Is there anything I can do?'

'Not a thing, another half-hour should do it. Go and put your head down yourself, Sean. As for me, I'm as bad as Angel. I don't think I could. I've found some old biker's leathers for you, by the way,' Fahy added. 'They're over there by the BSA.'

There was a jacket and leather trousers and boots. They'd all seen considerable service and Dillon smiled. 'Takes me back to my youth. I'll go and try them on.'

Fahy paused and ran a hand over his eyes as if tired. 'Look, Sean, does it have to be tomorrow?'

'Is there a problem?'

'I told you I wanted to weld some fins onto the oxygen cylinders to give more stability in flight. I haven't time to do that now.' He threw his spanner down on the bench. 'It's all too rushed, Sean.'

'Blame Martin Brosnan and his friends, not me, Danny,' Dillon told him. 'They're breathing down my neck. Nearly had me in Belfast. God knows when they might turn up again. No, Danny, it's now or never.'

He turned and went out and Fahy picked up his spanner reluctantly and went back to work.

The leathers weren't bad at all and Dillon stood in front of the wardrobe mirror as he zipped up the jacket. 'Would you look at that?' he said softly. 'Eighteen years old again when the world was young and anything seemed possible.'

He unzipped the jacket again, took it off then opened his briefcase and unfolded the bulletproof waistcoat Tania had given him at their first meeting. He pulled it snugly into place, fastened the Velcro tabs, then put his jacket on again. He sat on the edge of the bed, took the Walther out of the briefcase, examined it and screwed the Carswell silencer in place. Next he checked the Beretta and put it on the bedside locker close to hand. He put the briefcase in the wardrobe then switched off the light and lay on the bed, looking up at the ceiling through the darkness.

He never felt emotional, not about anything, and it was exactly the same now, on the eve of the greatest coup of his life. 'You're making history with this one, Sean,' he said softly. 'History.'

He closed his eyes and after a while, slept.

It snowed again during the night and just after seven, Fahy walked along the track to check the road. He walked back and found Dillon standing at the farmhouse door eating a bacon sandwich, a mug of tea in his hand.

'I don't know how you can,' Fahy told him. 'I couldn't eat a thing. I'd bring it straight up.'

'Are you scared, Danny?'

'To death.'

'That's good. It sharpens you up, gives you that edge that can make all the difference.'

They crossed to the barn and stood beside the Ford Transit. 'Well, she's as ready as she ever will be,' Fahy said.

Dillon put a hand on his shoulder. 'You've done wonders, Danny, wonders.'

Angel appeared behind them. She was dressed ready to go in her old trousers and boots, anorak and sweater and the tam-o'-shanter. 'Are we moving?'

'Soon,' Dillon said. 'We'll get the BSA into the Morris now.'

They opened the rear doors of the Morris, put the duckboard on the incline and ran the bike up inside. Dillon lifted it up on its stand and Fahy shoved the duckboard in. He passed a crash helmet through. 'That's for you. I'll have one for myself in the Ford.' He hesitated. 'Are you carrying, Sean?'

Dillon took the Beretta from inside his black leather jacket. 'What about you?'

'Jesus, Sean, I always hated guns, you know that.'

Dillon slipped the Beretta back in place and zipped up

his jacket. He closed the van doors and turned. 'Everybody happy?'

'Are we ready for off then?' Angel asked.

Dillon checked his watch. 'Not yet. I said we'd leave at eight. We don't want to be too early. Time for another cup of tea.'

They went across to the farmhouse and Angel put the kettle on in the kitchen. Dillon lit a cigarette and leaned against the sink watching. 'Don't you have any nerves at all?' she asked him. 'I can feel my heart thumping.'

Fahy called, 'Come and see this, Sean.'

Dillon went in the living room. The television was on in the corner and the morning show was dealing with the snow which had fallen over London overnight. Trees in the city squares, statues, monuments, were all covered, and many of the pavements.

'Not good,' Fahy said.

'Stop worrying, the roads themselves are clear,' Dillon said as Angel came in with a tray. 'A nice cup of tea, Danny, with plenty of sugar for energy and we'll be on our way.'

At the Lowndes Square flat Brosnan was boiling eggs in the kitchen and watching the toast when the phone went. He heard Mary answer it. After a while she looked in. 'Harry's on the phone, he'd like a word.'

Brosnan took the phone. 'How goes it?'

'Okay, old buddy, just checking you were leaving soon.'

'How are we going to handle things?'

'We'll just have to play it by ear, but I also think we'll have to play rough.'

'I agree,' Brosnan said.

'I'm right in assuming that would give Mary a problem?'

'I'm afraid so.'

'Then she definitely can't go in. Leave it to me. I'll handle it when we get there. See you soon.'

Brosnan put the phone down and went back to the kitchen where Mary had put out the eggs and toast and was pouring tea. 'What did he have to say?' she asked.

'Nothing special. He was just wondering what the best approach would be.'

'And I suppose you think that would be to batter Harvey over the head with a very large club?'

'Something like that.'

'Why not thumbscrews, Martin?'

'Why not indeed?' He reached for the toast. 'If that's what it takes.'

The early morning traffic on the Horsham road to Dorking and onwards to London was slower than usual because of the weather. Angel and Dillon led the way in the Morris, Fahy close behind in the Ford Transit. The girl was obviously tense, her knuckles white as she gripped the wheel too tightly, but she drove extremely well. Epsom then Kingston and on towards the river, crossing the Thames at Putney Bridge. It was already nine-fifteen as they moved along the Bayswater Road towards the hotel.

'Over there,' Dillon said. 'There's the supermarket. The entrance to the car park is down the side.' She turned in, changing to the lowest gear, crawling along as she went into the car park which was already quite full. 'There at the far end,' Dillon said. 'Just the spot.'

There was a huge trailer parked there, protected by a plastic sheet that was itself covered by snow. She parked on the other side of it and Fahy stopped nearby. Dillon jumped out, pulling on his crash helmet, went round and opened the doors. He put the duckboard in the right position, got inside and eased the BSA out, Angel helping. As he threw a leg over the seat she shoved the duckboard back inside the van and closed the doors. Dillon switched on and the BSA responded sweetly, roaring into life. He glanced at his watch. It was nine-twenty. He pulled the machine up on its stand and went over to Fahy in the Ford.

'Remember, the timing is crucial and we can't go round and round in circles at Whitehall, somebody might get suspicious. If we're too early try and delay things on the Victoria Embankment. Pretend you've broken down and I'll stop as if I'm assisting, but from the Embankment up Horseguards Avenue to the corner with Whitehall will only take a minute, remember that.'

'Jesus, Sean.' Fahy looked terrified.

'Easy, Danny, easy,' Dillon said. 'It'll be fine, you'll see. Now get moving.'

He swung a leg over the BSA again and Angel said, 'I prayed for you last night, Mr Dillon.'

'Well that's all right then. See you soon,' and he rode away and joined up behind the Ford.

13

Harry Flood and Mordecai were waiting in the Mercedes, Salter at the wheel, when a taxi drew up outside the undertakers in Whitechapel and Brosnan and Mary got out. They picked their way carefully through the snow on the pavement and Flood opened the door for them to get in.

He glanced at his watch. 'Just coming up to nine-thirty. We might as well go straight in.'

He took a Walther from his breast pocket and checked the slider. 'You want something, Martin?' he asked.

Brosnan nodded. 'It's a thought.'

Mordecai opened the glove compartment, took out a Browning and passed it over the seat. 'That suit you, Professor?'

Mary said, 'For God's sake, anybody would think you were trying to start the Third World War.'

'Or prevent it starting,' Brosnan said. 'Have you ever thought of that?'

'Let's move,' Flood said. Brosnan followed him out and Mordecai emerged from the other side. As Mary tried to follow, Flood said, 'Not this time, lover. I told Myra I'd be bringing my accountant which takes care of Martin, and Mordecai goes everywhere with me. That's all they're expecting.'

'Now look here,' she said, 'I'm the case officer on this, the official representative of the Ministry.'

'Well bully for you. Take care of her, Charlie,' Flood told Salter and he turned to the entrance where Mordecai was already ringing the bell.

The porter who admitted them smiled obsequiously. 'Morning, Mr Flood, Mr Harvey presents his compliments and wonders whether you'd mind stepping into the waiting room for a few moments. He's only just arrived from Heathrow.'

'That's fine,' Flood said and followed him through.

The waiting room was suitably subdued with dark leather chairs, rust-coloured walls and carpet. The lighting was mainly provided by fake candles and music suitable to the establishment played softly over a speaker system.

'What do you think?' Brosnan asked.

'I think he's just in from Heathrow,' Flood said. 'Don't worry.'

Mordecai peered out through the entrance and across to one of the chapels of rest. 'Flowers, that's what I find funny about these places. I always associate death with flowers.'

'I'll remember that when your turn comes to go,' Flood said. 'No flowers by request.'

It was approximately nine-forty as the Ford Transit pulled into a lay-by on the Victoria Embankment and Fahy's hands were sweating. In the rear-view mirror, he saw Dillon pull the BSA up on its stand and walk towards him. He leaned in the window.

'Are you okay?'

'Fine, Sean.'

'We'll stay here for as long as we can get away with it. Fifteen minutes would be ideal. If a traffic warden comes, just pull away and I'll follow you. We'll drive along the Embankment for half a mile, turn and come back.'

'Right, Sean.' Fahy's teeth were chattering.

Dillon took out a packet of cigarettes, put two in his mouth, lit them and passed one to Fahy. 'Just to show you what a romantic fool I am,' and he started to laugh.

When Harry Flood, Brosnan and Mordecai went into the outer office, Myra was waiting for them. She was wearing the black trouser suit and boots and carried a sheaf of documents in one hand.

'You look very businesslike, Myra,' Flood told her.

'So I should, Harry, the amount of work I do around here.' She kissed him on the cheek and nodded to Mordecai. 'Hello, muscles.' Then she looked Brosnan over. 'And this is?'

'My new accountant, Mr Smith.'

'Really?' She nodded. 'Jack's waiting.' She opened the door and led the way into the office.

The fire burned brightly in the grate, it was warm and comfortable. Harvey sat behind the desk smoking his usual cigar. Billy was over to the left sitting on the arm of the sofa, his raincoat casually draped across his knee.

'Jack,' Harry Flood said. 'Nice to see you.'

'Is that so?' Harvey looked Brosnan over. 'Who's this?'

'Harry's new accountant, Uncle Jack.' Myra moved round the desk and stood beside him. 'This is Mr Smith.'

Harvey shook his head. 'I've never seen an accountant that looked like Mr Smith, have you, Myra?' He turned back to Flood. 'My time's valuable, Harry, what do you want?'

'Dillon,' Harry Flood said. 'Sean Dillon.'

'Dillon?' Harvey looked totally mystified. 'And who the Christ is Dillon?'

'Small man,' Brosnan said, 'Irish, although he can pass as anything he wants. You sold him guns and explosives in nineteen eighty-one.'

'Very naughty of you that, Jack,' Harry Flood said. 'He blew up large parts of London and now we think he's at it again.'

'And where else would he go for his equipment except his old chum, Jack Harvey?' Brosnan said. 'I mean, that's logical, isn't it?'

Myra's grip tightened on her uncle's shoulder and Harvey, his face flushed said, 'Billy!'

Flood put up a hand. 'I'd just like to say that if that's a sawn-off he's got under the coat I hope it's cocked.'

Billy fired instantly through the raincoat, catching Mordecai in the left thigh as the big man drew his pistol. Flood's Walther came out of his pocket in one smooth motion and he hit Billy in the chest, sending him back over the sofa, the other barrel discharging, some of the shot catching Flood in the left arm.

Jack Harvey had the desk drawer open, his hand came up clutching a Smith & Wesson and Brosnan shot him very deliberately through the shoulder. There was chaos for a moment, the room full of smoke and the stench of cordite.

Myra leaned over her uncle who sank back into the

255

chair, moaning. Her face was set and angry. 'You bastards!' she said.

Flood turned to Mordecai. 'You okay?'

'I will be when Dr Aziz has finished with me, Harry. The little bastard was quick.'

Flood, still holding the Walther, clutched his left arm, blood seeping between his fingers. He glanced at Brosnan. 'Okay, let's finish this.'

He took two paces to the desk and raised the Walther directly at Harvey. 'I'll give it to you right between the eyes if you don't tell us what we want to know. What about Sean Dillon?'

'Screw you!' Jack Harvey said.

Flood lowered the Walther for a moment and then took deliberate aim and Myra screamed, 'No, for God's sake, leave him alone. The man you want calls himself Peter Hilton. He was the one Uncle Jack dealt with in eighty-one. He used another name then. Michael Coogan.'

'And more recently?'

'He bought fifty pounds of Semtex. Picked it up last night and paid cash. I had Billy follow him home on his BMW.'

'And where would that be?'

'Here.' She picked a sheet of paper up from the desk. 'I'd written it all down for Jack.'

Flood looked it over and passed it to Brosnan, managing a smile in spite of the pain. 'Cadge End Farm, Martin, sounds promising. Let's get out of here.'

He walked to the door and Mordecai limped out ahead of him, dripping blood. Myra had crossed to Billy who started to groan loudly. She turned and said harshly, 'I'll get you for this, the lot of you.'

'No you won't, Myra,' Harry Flood told her. 'If you're sensible you'll put it all down to experience and give your personal doctor a call,' and he turned and went out followed by Brosnan.

It was just before ten as they got into the Mercedes. Charlie Salter said, 'Jesus, Harry, we're getting blood all over the carpets.'

'Just drive, Charlie, you know where to go.'

Mary looked grim. 'What happened in there?'

'This happened.' Brosnan held up the sheet of paper with the directions to Cadge End Farm.

'My God,' Mary said as she read it. 'I'd better call the Brigadier.'

'No you don't,' Flood said. 'I figure this is our baby considering the trouble we've gone to and the wear and tear, wouldn't you agree, Martin?'

'Definitely.'

'So, the first thing we do is call at the quiet little nursing home in Wapping run by my good friend Dr Aziz so he can take care of Mordecai and see to my arm. After that, Cadge End.'

As Fahy turned out of the traffic on the Victoria Embankment into Horseguards Avenue past the Ministry of Defence building, he was sweating in spite of the cold. The road itself was clear and wet from the constant traffic, but there was snow on the pavements and the trees and the buildings on either hand. He could see Dillon in his rear-view mirror, a sinister figure in his black leathers on the BSA and then it was the moment of truth and everything seemed to happen at once.

He pulled in at the junction of Horseguards Avenue and Whitehall on the angle he'd worked out. On the other side of the road at Horse Guards Parade there were two troopers of the Household Cavalry, mounted as usual, with drawn sabres.

Some distance away, a policeman turned and saw the van. Fahy turned off the engine, switched on the timers and pulled on his crash helmet. As he got out and locked the door the policeman called to him and hurried forward. Dillon swerved in on the BSA, Fahy swung a leg over the pillion seat and they were away, sliding past the astonished policeman in a half-circle and moving fast up towards Trafalgar Square. As Dillon joined the traffic around the square, the first explosion sounded. There was another, perhaps two, and then it all seemed to become one with the greater explosion of the Ford Transit self-destructing.

Dillon kept on going, not too fast, through Admiralty Arch and along the Mall. He was at Marble Arch and turning along the Bayswater Road within ten minutes and rode into the car park of the supermarket soon after. As soon as she saw them, Angel was out of the van. She got the doors open and put the duckboard in place. Dillon and Fahy shoved the bike inside and slammed the doors.

'Did it work?' Angel demanded. 'Did everything go all right?'

'Just leave it for now. Get in and drive,' Dillon told her. She did as she was told and he and Fahy got in beside her. A minute later and they were turning into the Bayswater Road. 'Just go back the way we came and not too fast,' Dillon said.

Fahy switched on the radio, fiddling his way through

the various BBC stations. 'Nothing,' he said. 'Bloody music and chat.'

'Leave it on,' Dillon told him, 'and just be patient. You'll hear all about it soon enough.'

He lit a cigarette and sat back, whistling softly.

In the small theatre at the nursing home just off Wapping High Street, Mordecai Fletcher lay on the operating table while Dr Aziz, a grey-haired Indian in round steel spectacles, examined his thigh.

'Harry, my friend, I thought you'd given this kind of thing up?' he said. 'But here we are again like a bad Saturday night in Bombay.'

Flood was sitting in a chair, jacket off, while a young Indian nurse attended to his arm. She had cut the shirt sleeve off and was swabbing the wound. Brosnan and Mary stood watching.

Flood said to Aziz, 'How is he?'

'He'll have to stay in for two or three days. I can only get some of this shot out under anaesthetic and an artery is severed. Now let's look at you.'

He held Flood's arm and probed gently with a pair of small pincers. The nurse held an enamel bowl. Aziz dropped one piece of shot in it then two. Flood winced with pain. The Indian found another. 'That could be it, Harry, but we'll need an X-ray.'

'Just bandage it up for now and give me a sling,' Flood said. 'I'll be back later.'

'If that's what you want.'

He bandaged the arm skilfully, assisted by the nurse, then opened a cupboard and found a pack of morphine ampoules. He jabbed one in Flood's arm.

'Just like Vietnam, Harry,' Brosnan said.

'It will help with the pain,' Aziz told Flood as the nurse eased him into his jacket. 'I'd advise you to be back no later than this evening though.'

The nurse fastened a sling behind Flood's neck. As she put his overcoat across his shoulders, the door burst open and Charlie Salter came in. 'All hell's broken loose, just heard it on the radio. Mortar attack on Ten Downing Street.'

'Oh, my God!' Mary Tanner said.

Flood showed her through the door and she turned to Brosnan. 'Come on, Martin, at least we know where the bastard's gone.'

The War Cabinet had been larger than usual that morning, fifteen including the Prime Minister. It had just begun its meeting in the Cabinet Room at the back of Number Ten Downing Street when the first mortar, curving in a great arc of some two hundred yards from the Ford Transit van at the corner of Horseguards Avenue and Whitehall, landed. There was a huge explosion, so loud that it was clearly audible in the office of Brigadier Charles Ferguson at the Ministry of Defence overlooking Horseguards Avenue.

'Christ!' Ferguson said and like most people in the Ministry, rushed to the nearest window.

At Downing Street in the Cabinet Room the specially strengthened windows cracked but most of the blast was absorbed by the special blast-proof net curtains. The first bomb left a crater in the garden, uprooting a cherry tree. The other two landed further off target in Mountbatten Green where some outside broadcast vehicles were parked. Only one of those exploded, but at the same moment, the van blew up as Fahy's self-destruct device went into action. There was surprisingly little panic in the Cabinet Room. Everyone crouched, some seeking the protection of the table. There was a draught of cold air from shattered windows, voices in the distance.

The Prime Minister stood up and actually managed a smile. With incredible calm he said, 'Gentlemen, I think we had better start again somewhere else,' and he led the way out of the room.

Mary and Brosnan were in the back of the Mercedes, Harry Flood in the passenger seat beside Charlie Salter who was making the best time he could through heavy traffic.

Mary said, 'Look, I need to speak to Brigadier Ferguson. It's essential.'

They were crossing Putney Bridge. Flood turned and looked at Brosnan who nodded. 'Okay,' Flood said. 'Do what you like.'

She used her car phone, ringing the Ministry of Defence, but Ferguson wasn't there. There was some confusion as to his whereabouts. She left the car phone number with the control room and put the phone down.

'He'll be running round half-demented like everyone else,' Brosnan said and lit a cigarette.

Flood said to Salter, 'Okay, Charlie, Epsom, then Dorking and the Horsham road beyond that and step on it.'

The BBC newsflash which came over the radio in the Morris van was delivered in the usual calm and unemotional way. There had been a bomb attack on Number Ten Downing

Street at approximately 10.00 a.m. The building had sustained some damage, but the Prime Minister and members of the War Cabinet meeting together at that time were all safe.

The van swerved as Angel sobbed. 'Oh, God, no!'

Dillon put a hand on the wheel. 'Steady girl,' he said calmly. 'Just stick to your driving.'

Fahy looked as if he was going to be sick. 'If I'd had time to put those fins on the cylinders it would have made all the difference. You were in too much of a hurry, Sean. You let Brosnan rattle you and that was fatal.'

'Maybe it was,' Dillon said, 'but at the end of the day all that matters is we missed.'

He took out a cigarette, lit it and suddenly started to laugh helplessly.

Aroun had left Paris at nine-thirty, flying the Citation jet himself, Rashid having the rating qualifying him as the second pilot necessary under flight regulations. Makeev, in the cabin behind them, was reading the morning paper when Aroun called in to the control tower at Maupertus Airport at Cherbourg to clear for his landing on the private strip at St Denis.

The controller gave him his clearance and then said, 'We've just had a newsflash. Bomb attack on the British Cabinet at Downing Street in London.'

'What happened?' Aroun demanded.

'That's all they're saying at the moment.'

Aroun smiled excitedly at Rashid who'd also heard the message. 'Take over and handle the landing.' He scrambled back to the cabin and sat opposite Makeev. 'Newsflash just in. Bomb attack on Ten Downing Street.'

Makeev threw down his paper. 'What happened?'

'That's all for the moment.' Aroun looked up to heaven, spreading his hands. 'Praise be to God.'

Ferguson was standing beside the outside broadcast vans at Mountbatten Green with Detective Inspector Lane and Sergeant Mackie. It was snowing slightly and a police forensic team were making a careful inspection of Fahy's third mortar bomb, the one which hadn't exploded.

'A bad business, sir,' Lane said. 'To use an old-fashioned phrase, right at the heart of Empire. I mean, how can they get away with this kind of thing?'

'Because we're a democracy, Inspector, because people have to get on with their lives and that means we can't turn London into some Eastern-European-style armed fortress.'

A young constable came across with a mobile phone and whispered to Mackie. The sergeant said, 'Excuse me, Brigadier, it's urgent. Your office has been trying to contact you. Captain Tanner's been on the line.'

'Give it to me.' Ferguson took the phone. 'Ferguson here. I see. Give me the number.' He gestured to Mackie who took out pad and pencil and wrote it down as Ferguson dictated it.

The Mercedes was passing through Dorking when the phone went. Mary picked it up at once. 'Brigadier?'

'What's going on?' he demanded.

'The mortar attack on Number Ten. It has to be Dillon. We found out he picked up fifty pounds of Semtex in London last night, supplied by Jack Harvey.'

'Where are you now?'

'Just leaving Dorking, sir, taking the Horsham road, Martin and me and Harry Flood. We've got an address for Dillon.'

'Give it to me.' He nodded to Mackie again and repeated it aloud so the sergeant could write it down.

Mary said, 'The road's not good, sir, with the snow, but we should be at this Cadge End place in half an hour.'

'Fine. Nothing rash, Mary, my love, but don't let the bastard get away. We'll get back-up to you as soon as possible. I'll be in my car, so you've got the phone number.'

'All right, sir.'

She put the phone down and Flood turned. 'Okay?'

'Back-up on the way, but we're not to let him get away.'

Brosnan took the Browning from his pocket and checked it. 'He won't,' he said grimly. 'Not this time.'

Ferguson quietly filled in Lane on what had happened. 'What do you think Harvey will be up to, Inspector?'

'Receiving treatment from some bent doctor in a nice little private nursing home somewhere, sir.'

'Right, have that checked out and if it's as you say, don't interfere. Just have them watched, but this Cadge End place is where we go and fast. Now go and organise the cars.'

Lane and Mackie hurried away and as Ferguson made to follow them the Prime Minister appeared round the corner of the building. He was wearing a dark overcoat, the Home Secretary and several aides with him. He saw Ferguson and came over.

'Dillon's work, Brigadier?'

'I believe so, Prime Minister.'

'Rather close.' He smiled. 'Too close for comfort. A remarkable man, this Dillon.'

264

'Not for much longer, Prime Minister. I've just had an address for him at last.'

'Then don't let me detain you, Brigadier. Carry on, by all means.'

Ferguson turned and hurried away.

The track through the trees at Cadge End was covered with more snow since they had left. Angel bumped along it to the farmyard and turned into the barn. She switched off and it seemed terribly quiet.

Fahy said, 'Now what?'

'A nice cup of tea, I think.' Dillon got out, went round and opened the van doors and pulled out the duckboard. 'Help me, Danny.' They got the BSA out and he lifted it up on its stand. 'Performed brilliantly. You did a good job there, Danny.'

Angel had gone ahead and as they followed her, Fahy said, 'You haven't a nerve in your body, have you, Sean?'

'I could never see the point.'

'Well I have, Sean, and what I need isn't bloody tea, it's whiskey.'

He went in the living room and Dillon went up to his bedroom. He found an old holdall and packed it quickly with his suit, trenchcoat, shirts, shoes and general bits and pieces. He checked his wallet. About four hundred pounds left in there. He opened his briefcase which held the five thousand dollars remaining from his expense money and the Walther with the Carswell silencer on the end. He cocked the gun, leaving it ready for action, put it back in the briefcase together with the Jersey driving licence and the pilot's licence. He unzipped his jacket, took out the Beretta and checked it, then he slipped it into the waistband of his leather trousers at the rear, tucking the butt under the jacket.

When he went downstairs carrying the holdall and brief-case Fahy was standing looking at the television set. There were shots of Whitehall in the snow, Downing Street and Mountbatten Green.

'They just had the Prime Minister on inspecting the damage. Looked as if he didn't have a worry in the world.'

'Yes, his luck is good,' Dillon said.

Angel came in and handed him a cup of tea. 'What happens now, Mr Dillon?'

'You know very well what happens, Angel, I fly off into the wild blue yonder.'

'To that St Denis place?'

'That's right.'

'Okay for you, Sean, and us left here to carry the can,' Fahy said.

'And what can would that be?'

'You know what I mean.'

'Nobody has any kind of a line on you, Danny. You're safe till domesday. I'm the one the buggers are after. Brosnan and his girlfriend, and Brigadier Ferguson, I'm the one they'll put this down to.'

Fahy turned away and Angel said, 'Can't we go with you, Mr Dillon?'

He put down his cup and put his hands on her shoulders. 'There's no need, Angel. I'm the one running, not you or Danny. They don't even know you exist.'

He went across to the phone, picked it up and rang Grimethorpe Airfield. Grant answered straight away. 'Yes, who is it?'

'Peter Hilton, old boy.' Dillon reverted to his public school persona. 'Okay for my flight? Not too much snow?'

'It's clear down at the other end in the West Country,' Grant said. 'Might be tricky taking off here though. When were you thinking of going?'

'I'll be round in half an hour. That all right?' Dillon asked.

'I'll expect you.'

As Dillon put the phone down, Angel cried, 'No, Uncle Danny.'

Dillon turned and found Fahy standing in the doorway with a shotgun in both hands. 'But it's not all right with me, Sean,' and he thumbed back the hammers.

'Danny boy,' Dillon spread his hands. 'Don't do this.'

'We're going with you, Sean and that's an end to it.'

'Is it your money you're worried about, Danny? Didn't I tell you the man I'm working for can arrange payments anywhere?'

Fahy was trembling now, the shotgun shaking in his hand. 'No, it's not the money.' He broke a little then. 'I'm frightened, Sean. Jesus, when I saw that on the television. If I'm caught, I'll spend the rest of my life in gaol. I'm too old, Sean.'

'Then why did you come in with me in the first place?'

'I wish I knew. Sitting here, all these years, bored out of my mind. The van, the mortars, it was just something to do, a fantasy and then you turned up and made it real.'

'I see,' Dillon said.

Fahy raised the shotgun. 'So that's it, Sean. If we don't go, you don't go.'

Dillon's hand at his back found the butt of the Beretta, his arm swung and he shot Fahy twice in the heart sending him staggering out into the hall. He hit the wall on the other side and slid down.

Angel screamed, ran out and knelt beside him. She stood up slowly, staring at Dillon. 'You've killed him.'

'He didn't give me any choice.'

She turned, grabbed at the front door, and Dillon went after her. She dashed across the yard into one of the barns and disappeared. Dillon moved inside the entrance and stood there listening. There was a rustling somewhere in the loft and straw dust floated down.

'Angel, listen to me. I'll take you with me.'

'No you won't. You'll kill me like me Uncle Danny. You're a bloody murderer.' Her voice was muffled.

For a moment, he extended his left arm pointing the Beretta up to the loft. 'And what did you expect? What did you think it was all about?'

There was silence. He turned, hurried across to the house, stepped over Fahy's body. He put the Beretta back in his waistband at the rear, picked up his briefcase and the holdall containing his clothes, went back to the barn and put them on the passenger seat of the Morris.

He tried once more. 'Come with me, Angel. I'd never harm you, I swear it.' There was no reply. 'To hell with you then,' he said, got behind the wheel and drove away along the track.

It was some time later, when everything was very quiet, that Angel came down the ladder and crossed to the house. She sat beside her uncle's body, back against the wall, a vacant look on her face and didn't move, not even when she heard the sound of a car driving into the courtyard outside.

14

The runway at Grimethorpe was completely covered with snow. The hangar doors were closed and there was no sign of either of the planes. Smoke was drifting up from the iron stove pipe, the only sign of life as Dillon drove up to the huts and the old tower and braked to a halt. He got out with his holdall and briefcase and walked to the door. When he went in, Bill Grant was standing by the stove drinking coffee.

'Ah, there you are, old man. Place looked deserted,' Dillon said. 'I was beginning to worry.'

'No need.' Grant, who was wearing old black flying overalls and leather flying jacket reached for a bottle of Scotch and poured some into his mug of coffee.

Dillon put down his holdall, but still carried the briefcase in his right hand. 'I say, is that wise, old chap?' he asked in his most public school voice.

'I never was particularly wise, old chap.' Grant seemed to be mocking him now. 'That's how I ended up in a dump like this.'

He crossed to his desk and sat down behind it. Dillon

saw that there was a chart on the desk, the English Channel area, the Normandy coast, the Cherbourg approaches, the chart Dillon had checked out with Angel that first night.

'Look, I'd really like to get going, old chap,' he said. 'If it's the rest of the fee you're worried about I can pay cash.' He held up the briefcase. 'I'm sure you've no objection to American dollars.'

'No, but I do have an objection to being taken for a fool.' Grant indicated the chart. 'Land's End my arse. I saw you checking this out the other night with the girl. English Channel and French coast. What I'd like to know is what you're trying to get me into?'

'You're really being very silly,' Dillon said.

Grant pulled open a drawer in the desk and took out his old Webley revolver. 'We'll see, shall we? Now just put the briefcase on the desk and stand back while I see what we've got.'

'Certainly, old chap, no need for violence.' Dillon stepped close and put the briefcase on the desk. At the same moment he pulled the Beretta from his waistband at the rear, reached across the table and shot Grant at point-blank range.

Grant went backwards over the chair. Dillon put the Beretta back in place, folded the chart, put it under his arm, picked up his holdall and briefcase and went out, trudging through the snow to the hangar. He went in through the Judas, unbolted the great sliding door inside so that the two aircraft stood revealed. He chose the Cessna Conquest for no better reason than that it was the nearest. The stairs to the door were down. He threw the holdall and the briefcase inside, went up, pulling the door behind him.

He settled in the left-hand pilot's seat and sat there studying the chart. Approximately a hundred and forty miles to the airstrip at St Denis. Unless he encountered problems with headwinds, in a plane like this he should do it in forty-five minutes. No flight plan filed, of course, so he would be a bogey on somebody's radar screen but that didn't matter. If he went straight out to sea over Brighton, he would be lost in mid-Channel before anyone knew what was going on. There was a question of the approach to St Denis, but if he hit the coast at six hundred feet, with any luck he would be below the radar screen operated at Maupertus Airport at Cherbourg.

He put the chart on the other seat where he could see it and switched on, firing first the port engine then the starboard. He took the Conquest out of the hangar and paused to make a thorough cockpit check. As Grant had boasted, the fuel tanks were full. Dillon strapped himself in and taxied across the apron and down to the end of the runway.

He turned into the wind and started forward. He was immediately aware of the drag from the snow, boosted power and gave it everything he could, easing back the column. The Conquest lifted and started to climb. He banked to turn towards his heading for Brighton and saw a black limousine down below moving out of the trees towards the hangars.

'Well, I don't know who the hell you are,' he said softly, 'but if it's me you're after you're too late,' and he turned the Conquest in a great curve and started for the coast.

Angel sat at the kitchen table, holding the mug of coffee Mary had given her. Brosnan and Harry Flood, his arm in the sling, stood listening and Charlie Salter leaned on the door.

'It was Dillon and your uncle at Downing Street, is that what you're saying?' Mary asked.

Angel nodded. 'I drove the Morris with Mr Dillon's motorbike in it. He followed Uncle Danny, he was in the Ford Transit.' She looked dazed. 'I drove them back from Bayswater and Uncle Danny was afraid, afraid of what might happen.'

'And Dillon?' Mary asked.

'He was flying away from the airfield up the road, Grimethorpe. He made arrangements with Mr Grant who runs the place. Said he wanted to go to Land's End, but he didn't.'

She sat clutching the mug, staring into space. Brosnan said gently, 'Where did he want to go, Angel, do you know?'

'He showed me on the chart. It was in France. It was down along the coast from Cherbourg. There was a landing strip marked. A place called St Denis.'

'You're sure?' Brosnan said.

'Oh, yes. Uncle Danny asked him to take us too, but he wouldn't, then Uncle Danny got upset. He came in with the shotgun and then . . .' She started to sob.

Mary put her arms around her. 'It's all right now, it's all right.'

Brosnan said, 'Was there anything else?'

'I don't think so.' Angel still looked dazed. 'He offered Uncle Danny money. He said the man he was working for could arrange payments anywhere in the world.'

'Did he say who the man was?' Brosnan asked.

'No, he never did.' She brightened. 'He did say something about working for the Arabs the first time he came.'

Mary glanced at Brosnan. 'Iraq?'

'I always did think that was a possibility.'

'Right, let's get going,' Flood said. 'Check out this Grimethorpe place. You stay here with the kid, Charlie,' he said to Salter, 'until the cavalry arrives. We'll take the Mercedes,' and he turned and led the way out.

In the Great Hall at St Denis, Rashid, Aroun and Makeev stood drinking champagne waiting for the television news.

'A day for rejoicing in Baghdad,' Aroun said. 'The people will know now how strong their President is.'

The screen filled with the announcer who spoke briefly, then the pictures followed. Whitehall in the snow, the Household Cavalry guards, the rear of Ten Downing Street, curtain hanging from smashed windows, Mountbatten Green and the Prime Minister inspecting the damage. The three men stood in shocked silence.

It was Aroun who spoke first. 'He has failed,' he whispered. 'All for nothing. A few broken windows, a hole in the garden.'

'The attempt was made,' Makeev protested. 'The most sensational attack on the British Government ever mounted and at the seat of power.'

'Who gives a damn?' Aroun tossed his champagne glass into the fireplace. 'We needed a result and he hasn't given us one. He failed with the Thatcher woman and he failed with the British Prime Minister. In spite of all your big talk, Josef, nothing but failure.'

He sat down in one of the high-backed chairs at the dining table and Rashid said, 'A good job we didn't pay him his million pounds.'

'True,' Aroun said. 'But the money is the least of it.

It's my personal position with the President which is at stake.'

'So what are we going to do?' Makeev demanded.

'Do?' Aroun looked up at Rashid. 'We're going to give our friend Dillon a very warm reception on a cold day, isn't that so, Ali?'

'At your orders, Mr Aroun,' Rashid said.

'And you, Josef, you're with us in this?' Aroun demanded.

'Of course,' Makeev said because there was little else he could say. 'Of course.' When he poured another glass of champagne, his hands were shaking.

As the Mercedes came out of the trees at Grimethorpe, the Conquest banked and flew away. Brosnan was driving, Mary beside him, Harry Flood in the back.

Mary leaned out of the window. 'Do you think that's him?'

'Could be,' Brosnan said. 'We'll soon find out.'

They drove past the open hangar with the Navajo Chieftain inside and stopped at the huts. It was Brosnan, first through the door, who found Grant. 'Over here,' he said.

Mary and Flood joined him. 'So it *was* Dillon in that plane,' she commented.

'Obviously,' Brosnan said grimly.

'Which means the bastard's slipped the lot of us,' Flood said.

'Don't be too sure,' Mary told him. 'There was another plane in the hangar,' and she turned and ran out.

'What goes on?' Flood demanded as he followed Brosnan out.

'Amongst other things, the lady happens to be an Army Air Corps pilot,' Brosnan said.

When they reached the hangar, the Airstair door of the Navajo was open and Mary was inside in the cockpit. She got up and came out. 'Full tanks.'

'You want to follow him?' Brosnan demanded.

'Why not? With any luck we'll be right up his tail.' She looked fierce and determined, opened her handbag and took out her Cellnet phone. 'I'm not having this man get away with what he's done. He needs putting down once and for all.'

She moved outside, pulled up the aerial on her phone and dialled the number of Ferguson's car.

The limousine, leading a convoy of six unmarked Special Branch cars, was just entering Dorking when Ferguson received her call. Detective Inspector Lane was sitting beside him, Sergeant Mackie in front beside the driver.

Ferguson listened to what Mary had to say and made his decision. 'I totally agree. You must follow Dillon at your soonest to this St Denis place. What do you require from me?'

'Speak to Colonel Hernu at Service Five. Ask him to discover who owns the airstrip at St Denis so we know what we're getting into. He'll want to come himself obviously, but that will take time. Ask him to deal with the authorities at Maupertus Airport at Cherbourg. They can act as a link for us when I get close to the French coast.'

'I'll see to that at once and you take down this radio frequency.' He gave her the details quickly. 'That will link you directly to me at the Ministry of Defence. If I'm not back in London they'll patch you through.'

'Right, sir.'

'And Mary, my love,' he said, 'take care. Do take care.'

'I'll do my best, sir.' She closed her Cellnet phone, put it in her handbag and went back into the hangar.

'Are we on our way then?' Brosnan asked.

'He's going to talk to Max Hernu in Paris. He'll arrange a link for us with Maupertus Airport at Cherbourg to let us know what we're getting into.' She smiled tightly. 'So let's get going. It would be a shame to get there and find he'd moved on.'

She climbed up into the Navajo and moved into the cockpit. Harry Flood went next and settled himself into one of the cabin seats. Brosnan followed, pulled up the Airstair door, then went and settled in the co-pilot's seat beside her. Mary switched on first one engine then the other, completed her cockpit check then took the Navajo outside. It had started to snow, a slight wind whipping it across the runway in a curtain as she taxied to the far end and turned.

'Ready?' she asked.

Brosnan nodded. She boosted power, the Navajo roared along the runway and lifted up into the grey sky as she pulled back the control column.

Max Hernu was sitting at his desk in his office at DGSE headquarters going through some papers with Inspector Savary when Ferguson was put through to him. 'Charles, exciting times in London this morning.'

'Don't laugh, old friend, because the whole mess could well land in your lap,' Ferguson said. 'Number one, there's a private airstrip at a place called St Denis down the coast from Cherbourg. Who owns it?'

Hernu put a hand over the phone and said to Savary, 'Check the computer. Who owns a private airstrip at St

Denis on the Normandy coast?' Savary rushed out and Hernu continued, 'Tell me what all this is about, Charles.'

Which Ferguson did. When he was finished, he said, 'We've got to get this bastard this time, Max, finish him off for good.'

'I agree, my friend.' Savary hurried in with a piece of paper and passed it to Hernu who read it and whistled. 'The airstrip in question is part of the Château St Denis estate which is owned by Michael Aroun.'

'The Iraqi billionaire?' Ferguson laughed harshly. 'All is explained. Will you arrange clearance for Mary Tanner with Cherbourg and also see that she has that information?'

'Of course, my friend. I'll also arrange a plane at once and get down there myself with a Service Five team.'

'Good hunting to all of us,' Charles Ferguson said and rang off.

There was a great deal of low cloud over the Normandy coast. Dillon, still a few miles out to sea, came out of it at about a thousand feet and went lower, approaching the coastline at about five hundred feet over a turbulent white-capped sea.

The trip had gone like a dream, no trouble at all. Navigation had always been his strong point and he came in off the sea and saw Château St Denis perched on the edge of the cliffs, the airstrip a few hundred yards beyond. There was some snow, but not as much as there had been in England. There was a small prefabricated hangar, the Citation jet parked outside. He made a single pass over the house, turned into the wind and dropped his flaps for a perfect landing.

*   *   *

Aroun and Makeev were sitting by the fire in the Great Hall when they heard the sound of a plane overhead. Rashid hurried in, went and opened the French windows. They joined him on the snow-covered terrace, Aroun holding a pair of binoculars. Three hundred yards away on the airstrip, the Cessna Conquest landed and taxied towards the hangar, turning to line itself up beside the Citation.

'So, he's here,' Aroun said.

He focused the binoculars on the plane, saw the door open and Dillon appear. He passed the binoculars to Rashid who had a look then handed them to Makeev.

'I'll go down and pick him up in the Land Rover,' Rashid said.

'No you won't.' Aroun shook his head. 'Let the bastard walk through the snow, a suitable welcome and when he gets here, we'll be waiting for him.'

Dillon left the holdall and the briefcase just inside the Conquest when he climbed down. He walked across to the Citation and lit a cigarette, looking the aircraft over. It was a plane he'd flown many times in the Middle East, a personal favourite. He finished the cigarette and lit another. It was bitterly cold and very quiet, fifteen minutes and still no sign of any transport.

'So that's the way it is,' he said softly and walked back to the Conquest.

He opened the briefcase, checked the Walther and the Carswell silencer and eased the Beretta at the small of his back, then he picked up the holdall in one hand, the briefcase in the other, crossed the runway and followed the track through the trees.

* * *

Fifty miles out to sea, Mary identified herself to the tower at Maupertus Airport. She got a reply instantly.

'We've been expecting you.'

'Am I clear to land at St Denis airstrip?' she asked.

'Things are closing in rapidly. We had a thousand feet only twenty minutes ago. It's six hundred now at the most. Advise you try here.'

Brosnan heard all this on the other headphones and turned to her in alarm. 'We can't do that, not now.'

She said to Maupertus, 'It's most urgent that I see for myself.'

'We have a message for you from Colonel Hernu.'

'Read it,' she said.

'The St Denis airstrip is part of Château St Denis and owned by Mr Michael Aroun.'

'Thank you,' she said calmly. 'Out.' She turned to Brosnan. 'You heard that? Michael Aroun.'

'One of the wealthiest men in the world,' Brosnan said, 'and Iraqi.'

'It all fits,' she said.

He unbuckled his seat belt. 'I'll go and tell Harry.'

Dillon trudged through the snow towards the terrace at the front of the house and the three men watched him come. Aroun said, 'You know what to do, Josef.'

'Of course.' Makeev took a Makarov automatic from his pocket, made sure it was ready for action and put it back.

'Go and admit him, Ali,' Aroun told Rashid.

Rashid went out. Aroun went to the sofa by the fire and picked up a newspaper. When he went to the table to sit down, he placed the newspaper in front of him, took a Smith & Wesson revolver from his pocket and slipped it under.

Rashid opened the door as Dillon came up the snow-covered steps. 'Mr Dillon,' the young captain said. 'So you made it?'

'I'd have appreciated a lift,' Dillon told him.

'Mr Aroun is waiting inside. Let me take your luggage.'

Dillon put the case down and held on to the briefcase. 'I'll keep this,' he smiled. 'What's left of the cash.'

He followed Rashid across the enormous stretch of black and white tiles and entered the Great Hall where Aroun waited at the table. 'Come in, Mr Dillon,' the Iraqi said.

'God bless all here,' Dillon told him, walked across to the table and stood there, the briefcase in his right hand.

'You didn't do too well,' Aroun said.

Dillon shrugged. 'You win some, you lose some.'

'I was promised great things. You were going to set the world on fire.'

'Another time perhaps.' Dillon put the briefcase on the table.

'Another time.' Aroun's face was suddenly contorted with rage. 'Another time? Let me tell you what you have done. You have not only failed me, you have failed Saddam Hussein, President of my country. I pledged my word to him, my word and because of your failure, my honour is in shreds.'

'What do you want me to do, say I'm sorry?'

Rashid was sitting on the edge of the table, swinging a leg. He said to Aroun, 'In the circumstances, a wise decision not to pay this man.'

Dillon said, 'What's he talking about?'

'The million in advance that you instructed me to deposit in Zurich.'

'I spoke to the manager. He confirmed it had been placed in my account,' Dillon said.

'On my instructions, you fool. I have millions on deposit at that bank. I only had to threaten to transfer it elsewhere to bring him to heel.'

'You shouldn't have done that,' Dillon said calmly. 'I always keep my word, Mr Aroun, I expect others to keep theirs. A matter of honour.'

'Honour? You talk to me of honour.' Aroun laughed out loud. 'What do you think of that, Josef?'

Makeev, who had been standing behind the door, stepped out, the Makarov in his hand. Dillon half-turned and the Russian said, 'Easy, Sean, easy.'

'Aren't I always, Josef?' Dillon said.

'Hands on head, Mr Dillon,' Rashid told him. Dillon complied. Rashid unzipped the biker's jacket, checked for a weapon and found nothing. His hands went round Dillon's waist and discovered the Beretta. 'Very tricky,' he said and put it on the table.

'Can I have a cigarette?' Dillon put a hand in his pocket and Aroun threw the newspaper aside and picked up the Smith & Wesson. Dillon produced a cigarette pack. 'All right?' He put one in his mouth and Rashid gave him a light. The Irishman stood there, the cigarette dangling from the corner of his mouth. 'What happens now? Does Josef blow me away?'

'No, I reserve that pleasure for myself,' Aroun said.

'Mr Aroun, let's be reasonable.' Dillon flicked the catches on his briefcase and started to open it. 'I'll give you back what's left of the operating money and we'll call it quits. How's that?'

'You think money can make this right?' Aroun asked.

'Not really,' Dillon said and took the Walther with the Carswell silencer from the briefcase and shot him between the eyes. Aroun went over, his chair toppling and Dillon, turning, dropped to one knee and hit Makeev twice as the Russian got off one wild shot.

Dillon was up and turning, the Walther extended and Rashid held his hands at shoulder height. 'No need for that, Mr Dillon, I could be useful.'

'You're damn right you could be,' Dillon said.

There was a sudden roaring of an aircraft passing overhead. Dillon grabbed Rashid by the shoulder and pushed him to the French windows. 'Open them,' he ordered.

'All right.' Rashid did as he was told and they went out on the terrace from where they could see the Navajo landing in spite of the mist rolling in.

'Now who might that be?' Dillon asked. 'Friends of yours?'

'We weren't expecting anyone, I swear it,' Rashid said.

Dillon shoved him back in and put the end of the Carswell silencer to the side of his neck. 'Aroun had a nice private safe hidden safely away in the apartment at the Avenue Victor Hugo in Paris. Don't tell me he didn't have the same here.'

Rashid didn't hesitate. 'It's in the study, I'll show you.'

'Of course you will,' Dillon said and shoved him towards the door.

Mary taxied the Navajo along the strip and lined it up to the Conquest and the Citation. She killed the engine. Brosnan was already into the cabin and had the door open. He went down quickly and turned to give Flood a hand. Mary followed. It was very quiet, wind lifting the snow in a flurry.

'The Citation?' Mary said. 'It can't be Hernu, there hasn't been enough time.'

'It must be Aroun's,' Brosnan told her.

Flood pointed to where Dillon's footsteps, clearly visible in the snow, led towards the track to the wood, the château standing proudly on the other side. 'That's our way,' he said and started forward, Brosnan and Mary following.

15

The study was surprisingly small and panelled in bleached oak, the usual oil paintings of past aristocrats on the walls. There was an antique desk with a chair, an empty fireplace, a television with a fax machine and shelves lined with books on one wall.

'Hurry it up,' Dillon said and he sat on the end of the desk and lit a cigarette.

Rashid went to the fireplace and put his hand to the panelling on the right-hand side. There was obviously a hidden spring. A panel opened outwards revealing a small safe. Rashid twirled the dial in the centre backwards and forwards, then tried the handle. The safe refused to open.

Dillon said, 'You'll have to do better.'

'Just give me time.' Rashid was sweating. 'I must have got the combination wrong. Let me try again.'

He tried, pausing only to wipe sweat from his eyes with his left hand and then there was a click that even Dillon heard.

'That's it,' Rashid said.

'Good,' Dillon told him. 'Let's get on with it.' He extended his left arm, the Walther pointing at Rashid's back.

Rashid opened the safe, reached inside and turned, a Browning in his hand. Dillon shot him in the shoulder spinning him around and shot him again in the back. The young Iraqi bounced off the wall, fell to the floor and rolled on his face.

Dillon stood over him for a moment. 'You never learn, you people,' he said softly.

He looked inside the safe. There were neat stacks of hundred-dollar bills, French francs, English fifty-pound notes. He went back to the Great Hall and got his brief-case. When he came back he opened it on the desk and filled it with as much money as he could from the safe, whistling softly to himself. When the briefcase could hold no more he snapped it shut. It was at that moment he heard the front door open.

Brosnan led the way up the snow-covered steps, the Browning Mordecai had given him in his right hand. He hesitated for a moment and then tried the front door. It opened to his touch.

'Careful,' Flood said.

Brosnan peered in cautiously, taking in the vast expanse of black and white tiles, the curving stairway. 'Quiet as the grave. I'm going in.'

As he started forward, Flood said to Mary, 'Stay here for the moment,' and went after him.

The double doors to the Great Hall stood fully open and Brosnan saw Makeev's body at once. He paused, then moved inside, the Browning ready. 'He's been here, all right. I wonder who this is?'

'Another on the far side of the table,' Flood told him.

They walked round and Brosnan dropped to one knee and turned the body over. 'Well, well,' Harry Flood said. 'Even I know who that is. It's Michael Aroun.'

Mary moved into the entrance hall, closing the door behind her and watched the two men go into the Great Hall. There was a slight eerie creaking on her left and she turned and saw the open door to the study. She took the Colt .25 from her handbag and went forward.

As she approached the door, the desk came into view and she also saw Rashid's body on the floor beside it. She took a quick step inside in a kind of reflex action and Dillon moved from behind the door, tore the Colt from her hand and slipped it into a pocket.

'Well, now,' he said, 'isn't this an unexpected pleasure?' and he rammed the Walther into her side.

'But why would he kill him?' Flood asked Brosnan. 'I don't understand that.'

'Because the bastard cheated me. Because he wouldn't pay his debts.'

They turned and found Mary at the door, Dillon behind her, the Walther in his left hand, the briefcase in the other. Brosnan raised the Browning. Dillon said, 'On the floor and kick it over, Martin, or she dies. You know I mean it.'

Brosnan put the Browning down carefully then kicked it across the parquet floor.

'Good,' Dillon said. 'That's much better.' He pushed Mary towards them and sent the Browning sliding into the outer hall with the toe of his boot.

'Aroun we recognise, but as a matter of interest, who was this one?' Brosnan indicated Makeev.

'Colonel Josef Makeev, KGB, Paris station. He was the fella that got me into this. A hardliner who didn't like Gorbachev or what he's been trying to do.'

'There's another body in the study,' Mary told Brosnan.

'An Iraqi intelligence captain named Ali Rashid, Aroun's minder,' Dillon said.

'Gun for sale, is that what it's come down to, Sean?' Brosnan nodded to Aroun. 'Why did you really kill him?'

'I told you, because he wouldn't pay his debts. A matter of honour, Martin, I always keep my word, you know that. He didn't. How in the hell did you find me?'

'A lady called Myra Harvey had you followed last night. That led us to Cadge End. You're getting careless, Sean.'

'So it would seem. If it's any consolation to you, the only reason we didn't blow the entire British War Cabinet to hell was because you and your friends got too close. That pushed me into doing things in a hurry, always fatal. Danny wanted to fit stabilising fins on those oxygen cylinders that we used as mortar bombs. It would have made all the difference as regards their accuracy, but there wasn't time, thanks to you.'

'I'm delighted to hear it,' Brosnan said.

'And how did you find me here?'

'That poor, wretched young woman told us,' Mary said.

'Angel? I'm sorry about her. A nice kid.'

'And Danny Fahy and Grant at the airfield? You're sorry about them too?' Brosnan demanded.

'They shouldn't have joined.'

'Belfast and the Tommy McGuire shooting, it was you?' Mary said.

'One of my better performances.'

'And you didn't come back on the London plane,' she added. 'Am I right?'

'I flew to Glasgow, then got the shuttle to London from there.'

'So what happens now?' Brosnan asked.

'To me?' Dillon held up the briefcase. 'I've got a rather large sum in cash that was in Aroun's safe in here and a choice of airplanes. The world's my oyster. Anywhere, but Iraq.'

'And us?' Harry Flood looked ill, his face drawn with pain and he eased his left arm in the sling.

'Yes, what about us?' Mary demanded. 'You've killed everyone else, what's three more?'

'But I don't have any choice,' Dillon said patiently.

'No, but I do, you bastard.'

Harry Flood's right hand slipped inside the sling, pulled out the Walther he had been concealing in there and shot him twice in the heart. Dillon staggered back against the panelling, dropping his briefcase and slid to the floor, turning over in a kind of convulsion. Suddenly he was still and lay there, face down, the Walther with the Carswell silencer still clutched in his left hand.

Ferguson was in his car and halfway back to London when Mary called him using the phone in Aroun's study.

'We got him, sir,' she said simply when he replied.

'Tell me about it.'

So she did, Michael Aroun, Makeev, Ali Rashid, everything. When she was finished, she said, 'So that's it, sir.'

'So it would appear. I'm on my way back to London, just passed through Epsom. I left Detective Inspector Lane to clear things up at Cadge End.'

'What now, Brigadier?'

'Get back on your plane and leave at once. French territory, remember. I'll speak to Hernu now. He'll take care of it. Now go and get your plane. Contact me in mid-flight and I'll give you landing arrangements.'

The moment she was off the line he phoned Hernu's office at DGSE headquarters. It was Savary who answered. 'Ferguson here, have you got an arrival time for Colonel Hernu at St Denis?'

'The weather isn't too good down there, Brigadier. They're landing at Maupertus Airport at Cherbourg and will proceed onwards by road.'

'Well, what he's going to find there rivals the last act of *Macbeth*,' Ferguson said, 'so let me explain and you can forward the information.'

Visibility was no more than a hundred yards at the airstrip, mist drifting in from the sea as Mary Tanner taxied the Navajo to the end of the runway, Brosnan sitting beside her. Flood leaned over from his seat to peer into the cockpit.

'Are you sure we can make it?' he asked.

'It's landing in this stuff that's the problem, not taking off,' she said and took the Navajo forward into the grey wall. She pulled the column back and started to climb and gradually left the mist behind and turned out to sea, levelling at nine thousand feet. After a while she put on the automatic pilot and sat back.

'You all right?' Brosnan asked.

'Fine. Slightly drained, that's all. He was so – so elemental. I can't believe he's gone.'

'He's gone all right,' Flood said cheerfully, a half-bottle

of Scotch in one hand, a plastic cup held awkwardly in the other, for he had discovered the Navajo's bar box.

'I thought you never drank?' Brosnan said.

'Special occasion.' Flood raised his cup. 'Here's to Dillon. May he roast in hell.'

Dillon was aware of voices, the front door closing. When he surfaced it was like coming back from death to life. The pain in his chest was excruciating, but that was hardly surprising. The shock effect of being hit at such close quarters was considerable. He examined the two ragged holes in his biker's jacket and unzipped it, putting the Walther on the floor. The bullets Flood had fired at him were embedded in the titanium and nylon vest Tania had given him that first night. He unfastened the Velcro tabs, pulled the vest away and threw it down, then he picked up the Walther and stood.

He'd been genuinely unconscious for a while, but that was a common experience when shot at close quarters and wearing any kind of body armour. He went to the drinks cabinet and poured a brandy, looking round the room at the bodies, his briefcase still on the floor where he had dropped it and when he heard the roar of the Navajo's engine starting up, he saw it all. Everything was being left to the French, which was logical. It was their patch after all and that probably meant Hernu and the boys from Action Service were on their way.

Time to go, but how? He poured another brandy and thought about it. There was Michael Aroun's Citation jet, but where could he fly without leaving some sort of trail? No, the best answer, as usual, was Paris. He'd always been able to fade into the woodwork there. There was the barge and the apartment over the warehouse at rue de Helier. Everything he would ever need.

He finished the brandy, picked up the briefcase and hesitated, looking down at the titanium waistcoat with the two rounds embedded in it. He smiled and said softly, 'You can chew on that, Martin.'

He pulled the French windows wide and stood on the terrace for a moment, breathing deeply on the cold air, then he went down the steps to the lawn and walked quickly across to the trees, whistling softly.

Mary tuned her radio to the frequency Ferguson had given her. She was picked up by the radio room at the Ministry of Defence immediately, a sophisticated scrambling device was brought into operation and then she was patched through to him.

'Well out over the Channel, sir, heading for home.'

'We'll make that Gatwick,' he said. 'They'll be expecting you. Hernu has just phoned me from his car on the way to St Denis. Exactly as I thought. The French don't want this kind of mess on their patch. Aroun, Rashid and Makeev died in a car crash, Dillon goes straight into a pauper's grave. No name, just a number. Similar sort of thing at our end over that chap Grant.'

'But how, sir?'

'One of our doctors has already been alerted to certify him as having died of a heart attack. We've had our own establishment to handle this sort of thing since the Second World War. Quiet Street in North London. Has its own crematorium. Grant will be five pounds of grey ash by tomorrow. No autopsy.'

'But Jack Harvey?'

'That's slightly different. He and young Billy Watson are still with us, in bed at a private nursing home in Hampstead. Special Branch are keeping an eye on them.'

'Do I get the impression that we're not going to do anything?'

'No need. Harvey doesn't want to do twenty years in prison for working with the IRA. He and his motley crew will keep their mouths shut. So, by the way, will the KGB.'

'And Angel?'

'I thought she might come and stay with you for a while. I'm sure you can handle her, my dear. The woman's touch and all that.' There was a pause and then he said, 'Don't you see, Mary, it never happened, not any of it.'

'That's it then, sir?'

'That's it, Mary, see you soon.'

Brosnan said, 'What did the old sod have to say?'

So she told them. When she was finished, Flood laughed out loud. 'So it never happened? That's marvellous.'

Mary said, 'What now, Martin?'

'God knows.' He leaned back and closed his eyes.

She turned to Harry Flood who toasted her and emptied his cup. 'Don't ask me,' he said.

She sighed, switched off the auto pilot, took control of the plane herself and flew onwards towards the English coast.

Ferguson, writing quickly, completed his report and closed the file. He got up and walked to the window. It was snowing again as he looked out to the left towards the junction of Horseguards Avenue and Whitehall where it had all happened. He was tired, more tired than he had been in a long time, but there was still one thing to do. He turned back to his desk, was reaching for the scrambler phone when it rang.

Hernu said, 'Charles, I'm at St Denis and we've got trouble.'

'Tell me,' Ferguson said and already his stomach was hollow.

'Three bodies only. Makeev, Rashid and Michael Aroun.'

'And Dillon?'

'No sign, just a very fancy bulletproof vest on the floor with two Walther rounds embedded in it.'

'Oh, my God,' Ferguson said, 'the bastard's still out there.'

'I'm afraid so, Charles. I'll put the word out to the police, of course, and all the usual agencies, but I can't say I'm particularly hopeful.'

'Why would you be?' Ferguson asked. 'We haven't succeeded in putting a hand on Dillon in twenty years so why should it be any different now?' He took a deep breath. 'All right, Max, I'll be in touch.'

He went back to the window and stood looking out at the falling snow. No point in calling the Navajo. Mary, Brosnan and Flood would hear the bad news soon enough, but there was still one thing to be done. He turned reluctantly to his desk, picked up the scrambler, pausing for only a moment before phoning Downing Street and asking to speak to the Prime Minister.

It was towards evening, snow falling heavily as Pierre Savigny, a farmer from the village of St Just outside Bayeux drove carefully along the main road towards Caen in his old Citroën truck. He almost didn't see the man in biker's leathers who stepped into the road, an arm raised.

The Citroën skidded to a halt and Dillon opened the passenger door and smiled. 'Sorry about that,' he said in his impeccable French, 'but I've been walking for quite a while.'

'And where would you be going on a filthy evening like this?' Savigny asked as Dillon climbed into the passenger seat.

'Caen. I'm hoping to catch the night train to Paris. My motorbike broke down. I had to leave it in a garage in Bayeux.'

'Then you're in luck, my friend,' Savigny said. 'I'm on my way to Caen now. Potatoes for tomorrow's market.' He moved into gear and drove away.

'Excellent.' Dillon put a cigarette in his mouth, flicked his lighter and sat there, the briefcase on his knees.

'You're a tourist then, monsieur?' Savigny asked as he increased speed.

Sean Dillon smiled softly. 'Not really,' he said. 'Just passing through,' and he leaned back in the seat and closed his eyes.